BLOOD MOON DUET
BOOK 1
I0730174

BENEATH
THE
BLOODY MOON
H.M. COLUGO

Published by Dark Muse Books
Book cover illustration by Get Covers
First edition printed July 2025
Revised edition July 2026

Print ISBN 978-1-7355671-3-6

www.darkmusestudio.com

*To my oldest friend who stood watch on the sidelines and the
women who taught me how to be a vulnerable friend again
while I navigated my path of healing.
You know who you are. This one's for you, ladies.*

Content Warnings

Please note this book briefly touches on the topic of abortion. It also depicts scenes with blood, gore, and violence. Please read with care.

CHAPTER ONE

’ll leave your ticket at the booth. You’re still coming tonight, right, Val?”

“Of course I am, Candy. There’s no way I’m going to miss your show. Not this time, girl,” Valerie said, moving her cell phone to her other ear with a smile curling across her lips. Even though attending a loud concert wasn’t her idea of a good time, she was excited to see her best friend perform on stage with her band.

She stepped to the nearest window and pulled the curtain aside. She watched her young son run across the yard. He was yelling and screaming playfully as the full-grown golden retriever puppy chased after him. “Cyrus is going to take Taylor for the night so I don’t have to worry.”

“What about your mom?”

“She has work. And Taylor needs time with his dad anyway.” She said, her voice suddenly becoming softer, almost sad. A heavy silence passed through them for a moment, full of unspoken thoughts. There was plenty she could say about the situation with her baby daddy, but she chose not to. She didn't want to replay the memory of finding out about his new girlfriend being pregnant. The very image of it made her heart ache.

"Valerie? Did I lose you?" Candice said, pulling Valerie out of her thoughts. She pulled away from the window, tucking a strand of her dirty blonde hair behind her ear.

"Yes, I'm sorry. I was watching Taylor in the backyard with Goldie."

"Are you sure you can make it tonight? I don't want to put you in a situation you're not comfortable with."

"Yes, I'm sure. I'm—we're working on it, Candy."

"Alright. I'll let you go. I should start getting ready, anyway. Maybe I'll see you afterwards?"

"I'd like that," Valerie said, sitting on the couch and tucking her phone against her ear. Leaning forward, she was hardly paying attention as she slipped on her sandals. When the call ended, she placed the phone down and headed down the hall toward the back door. With a single glance at the glowing clock on the stove, she realized dinner was quickly approaching. She needed to gather her rambunctious four year old son and dog.

Valerie opened the back door and took a deep breath of the mountain air. The afternoon breeze kicked through the trees, causing the evergreens to dance and bow. A few clouds streaked across the clear blue sky. The weatherman mentioned that a storm was arriving later that night.

The squeak of the old, rusty hinges grabbed Taylor and Goldie's attention, and they turned to see their mom step out onto the back porch and start towards the backyard. Goldie barked excitedly, and Taylor yelled out with his own excitement.

"Mama!" Taylor yelled with a beaming bright smile on his chubby cheeks. A smile curled on her lips when he came running across the yard. She leaned down to scoop him up in her arms. "Did you see me, mama?"

"I did. It looks like you and Goldie were having fun." She said, shifting Taylor to her hip. A moment later, the golden retriever brought a bright red ball and dropped it at Valerie's feet, barking. With a laugh and a shake of her head, she picked up the ball and tossed it across the yard. Goldie easily retrieved it for another throw.

Valerie threw the ball once more, bouncing off the chain-link fence at the end of the property. Goldie brought it back once again, but when Valerie threw the ball this time, it flew over the top of the fence into the bundle of evergreens just beyond. Although she was way out of practice, she never lost that championship-winning throwing arm.

Goldie ran across the yard, finally appearing to be running out of steam when she got to the fence line. She barked and scratched at the ground, moving along the fence to find an opening, which didn't take long. Valerie frowned when she noticed Goldie had slipped out of the yard. She put Taylor down inside and went running across the yard.

"Goldie!" she yelled, but she knew once that dog had a mission, she wouldn't turn back. Instead of squeezing herself through the chain-link fence, she went around the side of the house and out the gate.

Goldie was barking at something or someone, but it was the growling that caught Valerie off guard. She took a glance over her shoulder, double checking that Taylor hadn't followed her outside. She paused and inhaled a deep breath, centering herself. Finally, she stepped into the forest, feeling the rise of goosebumps on her bare arms.

"Goldie? What's wrong, girl?" she said, taking a few more cautious steps. Even though Valerie grew up in the small mountain community of Hollow's Creek, the place still made her uneasy as an adult. Growing up, she heard many tales about the shadows and other strange occurrences beyond its borders. She didn't know that she really believed them, but stepping into the forest was always a test of her bravery.

The further she walked into the forest, the quieter it became. She didn't even hear the birds chirping. Or Goldie growling for that matter. The shadows grew taller and darker. She called out to the golden retriever, who whined somewhere nearby. "What's wrong, girl?"

A strange, eerie feeling seemed to be hovering in the air, and Valerie froze. She didn't move a muscle, except for her heart pounding in her chest. Something was out there. She could feel something watching her, but the green-gray blur of the trees was hard to see through even just this deep in the forest. She just needed to get her dog. Her son's dog.

Suddenly, Goldie came trotting towards her with that bright red ball in her mouth. With a whine, she dropped it at Valerie's feet. The tension she felt started to subside when she reached to scratch between the dog's ears, but that feeling of something watching her seemed to linger.

"Fucking dog. You scared me." She said, snatching the ball. "Come, Goldie. It's almost time for dinner."

"Tonight, we have a thirty percent chance of rain in the Hollow Mountains."

"Mama! Mama!" her son yelled from down the hall, drawing her attention from the television. With a few soap suds on his dark, shoulder-length hair, he came around the corner, still slick from the bath. She immediately rose to her feet to pick him up.

"Don't run, Tay! You could slip and fall."

"When's daddy going to be here?" He asked, settling in her arms.

"I'm not sure, but hopefully soon. We should get you dressed." She said, carrying him down the hallway to his bedroom. Leaving the door cracked, she placed him on the bed to grab the outfit she had set out earlier.

Once she finally had him dressed in a pair of shorts and a T-Rex tshirt, she sat beside him with his shoes. There was a knock on the front door, but she didn't think it was her mother. Taylor sprang to his feet and ran out of the room, yelling with excitement. She followed him down the hall, quickly catching up. She reached down and lifted Taylor, heading to answer the door. "Cyrus. You made it."

"Of course I did," he said. Valerie stepped aside to let him in. The moment Taylor saw his dad, he began to squirm in her arms. Thankfully, Cyrus took Taylor. "Why would you think I wouldn't make it?"

She glanced into those deep brown eyes for a moment, eyes that had once made her swoon. Now they only made her ache for what had once been. She still couldn't believe how easily he moved on after the years they had spent together. Her gaze narrowed, but she didn't say a word. She didn't want to give in to her anger. She turned and walked down the hallway.

Taylor was babbling to his dad about one of the new cartoons he had been watching, but Valerie's head was in a completely different place. She snatched the remote from the coffee table and turned off the television.

"It's nothing, Cyrus." She grumbled under her breath, leading him down the hallway to Taylor's room. She grabbed the red duffel bag sitting at the foot of his bed, already packed for the weekend.

"Valerie...don't," he said, shifting Taylor to his opposite hip.

"Don't what?" Valerie said, waiting for him to respond. They both remained silent as she handed him the bag with their son's things. The tension in the air was palpable. She wanted to say more to him, but she knew it wasn't worth the breath. The smell of his musky scent tickled her nose, and her heart clenched. Finally, she turned out of the bedroom.

Suddenly, the front door creaked open. Her mother called out her name, leading Cyrus down the hallway. When they made it to the front of the room, Valerie's mom carried an armful of groceries. She suddenly stopped, frowning. "Val? You're still here? I figured you'd be on your way up to see Candice... Oh. Hello, Cyrus."

"Miss Loveland." He said with the ghost of a smile curling at his lips. A new tension hung in the air. Valerie stepped over to help her mom, noticing the look in her eyes. She knew how much her mom hated being called Miss Loveland since her parents had been divorced for decades, but she knew her mother disliked Cyrus even more.

"You better get going. I need to leave soon, too."

"Where you going?"

"The Graffiti Heart. I told you." She said, crossing the kitchen to take Taylor. "Candice is performing with her band tonight. It's supposed to be her last show for a while. She'll be working up at Camp Gray for the summer." Valerie said, leading Cyrus out of the house, her mom watching them close before heading inside.

After loading Taylor into the back seat of Cyrus's SUV, Cyrus moved to embrace her, but she stepped back. Instead, she offered him a smile, tucking her hair behind her ear.

"I'll see you later."

"Yeah. Take care." He said softly. He walked around to the driver's side and slipped inside the vehicle. Cyrus glanced up into his rear-view mirror, noticing Taylor sitting quietly in the backseat before noticing Valerie pull out of her mom's driveway. He watched her drive down to the stop sign and turn before finally pulling away from the curb.

Half an hour later, Valerie cleared the top of the mountain, following the highway toward the river. She crossed the narrow bridge and continued driving toward the old stucco warehouse standing on the other side of the river.

The building had once been part of the old girls' boarding school, abandoned back in the eighties. Before long, people moved in and gave new life to the area. A few locals bulldozed the oldest part of the property and sold it. They gutted the remaining bones to build the exclusive, members-only nightclub, The Silver Dollar.

In the early 2000s, an older couple moved to the area and built the very first music club open to the public. Valerie had been to the place once or twice, but she was never part of the local music scene like Candice.

Once inside, Valerie glanced over the dimly lit walls covered in vibrant graffiti letters. She could see the old paint that had dried after bleeding. The owners claimed it was supposed to be about the aesthetic, but they didn't have a lot of security guards hanging around either. Not to mention, there were plenty of rumors about werewolves prowling the area. Some said The Silver Dollar was their meeting place.

"Hi. I'm here to see the Paper Dolls," Valerie said, stepping up to the open window of the ticket booth. "Candice Olson said she left me a ticket."

"Here you go. Follow the red light to the next door." The

attendant said, tearing the ticket in half. He slipped the other half under the window to Valerie, who examined it before slipping it into her back pocket. With a gentle smile, she nodded and followed the dim red floor lights that led to the auditorium. Once through the metal detectors, security directed her inside to another set of doors that opened into a large, dark room. Standing room only.

A sea of young adults and teenagers packed the room. Valerie squeezed through the crowd. The smell of marijuana and alcohol tickled her senses. The place would smell of body odor and vomit soon. Thankfully, she found a spot somewhere in the middle of the crowd to squeeze in among a group of rocker chicks, and just in time too. All the lights shut off, and the quiet murmurs turned into a sudden wave of cheers, exclamations, and shouts of profanity.

Blue stage lights popped on, and the curtain rose into the air, revealing the band. On the drum set was a short, lean girl with a dirty blonde pixie bob, wearing hardly more than a black tube top and a pair of ripped shorts. On the bass stood an average girl standing on skyscraper boots with two-toned black and white hair. The two of them led into a song, prompting a collective scream from the crowd.

Before long, a spotlight popped on, and a woman with auburn hair dressed in a purple skater dress and matching canvas sneakers suddenly appeared with an old, worn black guitar hanging from her shoulders. Valerie smiled from ear to ear, watching her best friend step up to the microphone. She closed her kohl-rimmed eyes and let her soul pour through the cavernous room.

The crowd went wild. Yelling. Cheering. Some even singing along when her bellowing roar turned into something much softer, floating through the sound system.

UNDER THE FULL MOON, I saw your shadow
And yet you looked so sallow
Under the glow of the moonlight

REMINISCENT OF GRUNGE AND post punk bands before them, Candice and her band went on for another twenty minutes with fast, heavy guitar riffs, pounding drums, and a fat bass line. When the last song finally ended, Candice stepped up to the microphone, nearly out of breath. The sweat pouring from her temples was visible beneath the spotlight. She scanned the crowd, and a smile curled at the corners of her lips.

"Thank you! We are the Paper Dolls! We'll see you soon! Have a good night!"

She stepped away from the microphone. She and her band exited stage left, disappearing somewhere backstage. The house lights throughout the auditorium finally came back on, nearly blinding Valerie. A small man walked out onto the stage as the curtain dropped, gripping a wireless microphone.

"Let's give it up for our opening band, the Paper Dolls!" he said over the roar of the crowd. Valerie could hardly hear him talk about who they had coming up next, but she had finally seen her best friend perform on stage. She felt exhilarated and amped, feeling the cool air on her sweaty back.

Moments later, when the road crew came out to change the setup on-stage, music started playing through the speakers in the room. Several people started to squeeze through the crowd and out of the auditorium. Now seemed to be a good time to find her way backstage and locate Candice.

Out in the hallway, a line of girls waited for the bathroom. Valerie approached, asking where she could get backstage to see her friend. One girl, holding another's hand, stepped just out of line and pointed down a dark hallway.

"If you just follow that hall, you'll find the dressing rooms."

"Thanks," Valerie said. She didn't waste another moment. She turned and disappeared down the hallway, thankful for the dim lights lining it. When she made it to the end, she noticed Candice's wavy auburn hair a few yards away.

"Candice!" Valerie called out. Candice whipped her head around and smiled wide the moment she met her best friend's gaze. She stepped over to the security guard blocking the back hallway. She whispered into the guard's ear, and he stepped aside to let Valerie pass.

"You made it! I hope you enjoyed!" Candice said, greeting her friend with a warm embrace. She let out a chuckle and lifted her hand to wipe off some of the black kohl makeup that had smudged on Valerie's cheek. She smiled with appreciation.

"I had a lot of fun! Thank you for inviting me." Valerie started. "I know I never made it to any of your other shows, girlie, and I'm sorry. It's hard with Taylor sometimes."

"Yeah, of course!" Candice said with a quick shake of her head. "You don't need to apologize, I told you. Auntie Candy didn't think it was good for Taylor to come along either."

"Thanks, Candy," Valerie smiled, tucking her long blonde locks behind her ear. She appeared flushed from being around the high energy of the crowd. Candice offered Valerie a water bottle from the dressing room, glancing back over her shoulder. Valerie accepted, following her friend toward the dressing room.

Once inside the dressing room, Candice introduced Ramona and Tommie to her best friend as she grabbed a water bottle from the nearby fridge. Valerie stood there, her hands clasped in front of her while she waited.

"I think we met before." Ramona said, a smile cracking across her darkly painted lips. She sat up in the overstuffed chair, finally taking off those skyscraper boots she wore on her feet. When she looked up from her shoes, she glanced at Candice, handing the water bottle to her friend. "If you'll excuse us, though, we have some band business to discuss."

"Yeah! Remember we need to talk about our next adventure?" Tommie said, stretching out across the beanbag chair she was lying on, looking up at Candice.

"Gotta talk about going on tour!" Ramona said. Candice turned back toward Valerie, who had suddenly frowned with disappointment. Candice frowned to herself, but she knew her bandmate was right.

"I better get going, Val. We'll talk later, ok?" Candice embraced her friend once more and walked her out of the dressing room, which closed behind her. Valerie stood there for a moment before finally turning to the security guard.

"Do you mind if I leave this way?" Valerie said, pointing in the direction of the dimly lit corridor. A line of floodlights popped on, guiding her to the back door. The security guard just nodded, and she ventured out of the building.

The moment she stepped out the door, she could smell the petrichor of a light rain. The squeal of a siren in the distance pierced the air. That strange feeling of something watching her had returned. She cautiously turned her gaze towards the line of trees, rustling in the breeze. Her breathing hitched when she noticed a pair of glowing yellow eyes.

CHAPTER TWO

Another crack of thunder. A flash of lightning flickered across the night. Suddenly, the rain went from a sprinkle to pouring, soaking the parched surface of the forest floor. A siren wailed through the night. Red and blue lights flashed through the darkness. The black and white county sheriff's department sport utility vehicle hurtled down the unpaved dirt road, little pebbles and rocks crunching beneath the tires.

The vehicle drifted around the corner of the dead-end road and skidded to a stop only a few feet from the corner. Nobody would get into or leave the area without hitting the county vehicle. The driver's side door popped open.

A woman with short dark hair and a sun-damaged face hopped down from inside. She slammed the door shut behind her and took a quick scan of her surroundings. Static spilled from her shoulder radio as she took a few steps. Her hand went instinctively to her hip, and she grabbed the butt of her gun.

She glanced up at the large, dark house standing at the top of the hill. The Gray Mansion stood proudly, overlooking the mountainous Hollow Forest and the small communities that had spread further and further up the mountain over the years. Nobody seemed to be home. There was no familiar blue glow of a television screen shining in any of the windows. Even the little black sports car she pulled over at least once a month for speeding was nowhere in sight.

Grabbing her gun, she took a quick look at her watch and carefully surveyed the area, seeing nothing immediate that would've warranted a call to the sheriff's department just after midnight. She was used to working late hours, but she let out a wide yawn and continued surveying the area.

The dark haired deputy finally raised her gun and flipped on the light, following the side of the road for any sign of foul play. With the sudden downpour, the odds that the crime scene would quickly be washed away had grown significantly. Whoever had called to report the problem had used a voice changer, according to the dispatch agent. Nor did she stay on the line long enough to provide much detail either. She kept her gun close and approached the large mansion, hoping to find something soon.

Hollow's Creek was a strange town. Strange shit happened all the time, but she never seemed to understand or make sense of the truth behind what actually happened. Most of the town had that strange energy about it that could only have been explained as supernatural, but she never believed any of those lame campfire horror stories.

On many a camping trip back in high school, she remembered the stories her friends and their boyfriends used to tell. Stories of vampires, werewolves, and demons. There had even been mention of angels in a few stories. They were the stories that the locals still referred to as "local legends", but to Maggie Jones they were bullshit.

The yard appeared muddy yet green in the beam of light

coming from the end of her gun. There were no bloody handprints on the fence that hinted at foul play. The treehouse was silent. The swings on the old play set, standing tall in the backyard, were undisturbed.

The motion lights flickered on. She blinked quickly, adjusting to the sudden brightness flooding the backyard. A bush along the fence rustled at the far end, and she shouted, her voice shaking. "Hello?"

She took a few more steps forward, and the deep growl of a large dog or wolf rumbled in the not-too-distant closeness. She froze. Her heart pounded in her chest. Her eyes darted across the area. Something rustled in the bushes nearby, and with a gulp, she took two steps forward before she finally saw the culprit.

A long, fluffy silver wolf disappeared through a loose board in the tall wooden fence just past the other end of the huge mansion. The evergreens just beyond, lining the edge of the forest, danced in the cool night breeze. She stopped at the hedge and debated climbing into the backyard, but she realized there was no reason to. There was no way she would get through those narrow holes in the fence. She had never been what she thought as lean, but years on the police force had ruined her once girlish figure.

She slipped out of the side yard and back to the main road, taking the first few cautious steps toward the forest. That's when a familiar scent finally hit her. The old coppery smell of blood blasted her in the face like a ton of bricks. Her stomach churned with fear and anxiety. She closed her eyes and swallowed back a lump in her throat. Now she knew why she had been called out to Gray Mountain.

Murders were an uncommon occurrence around Hollow's Creek, but when they did happen, they were always a little grisly. She still remembered that time she encountered her first dead body in the forest—long before she even thought about joining the force.

A scream shattered through the night. Time stood still. The low hum of the party went silent for what felt like ages before anyone moved. Screams like that weren't normal at a high school party. Even in the middle of the forest.

The smell of fear and adrenaline was palpable as it floated through the evergreens like a cold breeze. Another scream shot through the forest, and Maggie ran across the clearing to find the source.

At the edge of the forest, where the trees started to thin out and form a natural path, a puddle of blood had soaked the ground. A young man, not much older than she or anybody else around her, was sprawled across the forest floor. His throat had been ripped open. There was also a strange animal scent that seemed to linger in the air. At first, she thought it had been an animal attack because it certainly wasn't natural. She told herself it couldn't be something supernatural.

She had never been able to scrub those images out of her mind, but it led her to join the force. She vowed to devote her time and energy to protecting the citizens of the community from whatever had killed that kid in the forest that one fatal night.

When she opened her eyes again, the blood and entrails splattered across the forest floor made her stomach churn aggressively. She even caught a whiff of that strange animal smell she had caught many times before. That smell had been ingrained in her senses, sparking old memories and thoughts she didn't care to deal with.

She lifted her elbow to cover her nose, trying not to retch. She took a few more steps forward, silently praying that she didn't know the victim. However, that wasn't how things worked in a small town. She knew better than that. Luckily, when she spotted the face, she didn't recognize him. Hopefully, this man's face wouldn't haunt her the same.

She stepped away to take a breather, trying to clear her senses of the smell of death in the air. After counting to five, she grabbed her walkie and pressed the side button.

"This is Lieutenant Maggie Jones. I need backup on Gray Mountain, just alongside the forest on the Gray property. I could also use the coroner and a crime scene analyst up here. We got a dead body. We might need his dental records to identify him."

"Ten four."

Before the emergency vehicles arrived, she grabbed the crime scene tape from her vehicle and marked off the area between Gray Mansion and several yards into the forest. Thankfully, the vehicles arrived much quicker than she had hoped, allowing her to step away from the area.

Cameras flashed. People in biohazard suits rushed by. She made it to her county vehicle before finally pulling out her cell phone. She glanced around, realizing there were too many open ears around her. There were too many chances that someone would overhear what she said and report it to the sheriff.

Maggie had that feeling in her gut that something supernatural was afoot. She struggled to accept it as she stared at her screen for several moments. The presence of the silver0white wolf was confirmation enough. She didn't know who the wolf was, but she knew enough about the local werewolf community.

With a few quick movements of her fingers and thumb, she lifted the phone to her ear and waited for several rings. Unfortunately, the voicemail clicked on, and she heard his voice. She sighed and waited for the beep to leave a message.

"I'm sorry to call so late, but we've got trouble. I found a dead body here in the forest out on Gray Mountain. This is the second one we've found now. The murders might be starting up again. Please call me when you get this message. Please."

CHAPTER THREE

 *offee.*

That was Candice's first thought upon rising from bed that morning. Until a few years ago, when she started her first semester at community college, she found the hot brew bitter and hard to swallow. Now she didn't know how to function without a drop.

She padded downstairs in her bare feet, trying to keep quiet until she remembered it was Saturday morning. And it was graduation day. At the base of the stairs, she peeked out the front window. Both her parents' cars sat in the driveway. Even the old beat-up Ford truck her teen brother, Kevin, drove around was parked out front with one of the rear wheels sitting on the curb. He was horrible at parking.

The fresh, earthy scent of coffee brewing lingered in the air. A smile tugged at her lips, and she turned away from the window, heading down to the kitchen. She stepped into the old family dining room and headed into the kitchen.

Her two younger brothers, Kevin and Cody, sat at the

kitchen table with her father at the head, holding a paper up toward his face. He still wore his sheriff's deputy uniform from the night shift. She could only wonder why. He had always worked the graveyard shift, but he seemed to work more since his promotion.

Her mother stood by the stove, laying bacon on a sizzling pan. Dressed in an old flannel bathrobe, she had her bright red hair wrapped in a towel. Rex, the family mutt, barked at the neighbor dogs out in the backyard. It was familiar and cozy.

She cleared her throat, opening the cabinet to grab one of her favorite coffee mugs. She took it over to the counter, dumped a few teaspoons of sugar, and filled her mug. Her father lowered his newspaper with a grin on his face.

"Well, well. Look who has finally decided to join us this morning! Our own college graduate." He leaned forward and grabbed his cup of coffee, finishing the last few drops. The smell of sizzling bacon rose into the air. Her mother turned from the stove with a pair of stainless steel tongs in her hand.

"There's my big, beautiful-brained daughter." Her mother stepped over and kissed her cheek. "Breakfast will be ready soon, and we can get ready for the day. We have a graduation to attend! Jack! Can you go change out of your uniform? I don't want you driving the family out to Craven Hill in your uniform!"

"And why not, Kellie? Maybe it will scare some sense into those delinquents, and they won't misbehave while my daughter walks across that stage to get her diploma!" Her dad spoke with an edge to his voice. With his chest puffed out, he almost sounded annoyed.

"Dad! It's just a community college..." she muttered, finally taking her seat at the kitchen table. Lowering her eyes, she took a sip of her coffee, still steaming hot from the decanter.

"None of that, young lady! You're still graduating from college. That's more than me or your mother can say about ourselves."

"Hold your tongue, Jack. I did go to college after my little Candy was born." Kellie glanced over her shoulder, turning the last few slices still sizzling in the pan. "How else do you think I learned enough to start my own business? But today is all about our girl, Candy!"

"Candy this! Candy that! Blah blah blah." Said her brother, Kevin, only a few years younger than her. Where Candice had long, auburn hair and a light dusting of freckles, Kevin had short, light brown hair and a heavy spray of freckles. He was almost the spitting image of their father, except for the freckles.

With a quick glance at their father, who was back to reading the paper, Candice reached across the dining table and slapped Kevin on the head. She smirked when he looked over at her with a feigned look of hurt on his face. He yelled out.

"Mom, she hit me!"

"Now, now, Kevin! Don't act like that. Next year, it will be your turn to graduate."

"Yeah. From high school." He muttered under his breath, rubbing the side of his head. Putting down the paper, Jack rose from his seat with his coffee cup in hand. Kellie was fumbling around by the stove, filling a few serving dishes with scrambled eggs, bacon, and pancakes.

"What about me? What about me!" The littlest of the bunch, with his golden-blond hair sticking up in all different directions, said, bouncing in his seat. He reminded Candice of Alfalfa from the Little Rascals, except Cody's hair was messier.

"Ohhh...this looks delicious!" Jack said on his way to the coffee pot.

"Jack Olson! Go change! I just washed all your uniforms again. I don't feel like doing anymore laundry this weekend." Kellie snapped at her husband, smacking him on the hand with her spatula. With a chuckle, he left his coffee mug on the counter and disappeared down the hallway. "You still have quite a few years to go, Cody. Don't be in a rush. Everyone hungry?"

Cody cheered with excitement, steering his little red matchbox car across the table. Vroom, vroom. He whistled. Candice rose to help her mother carry the serving trays.

"I PRESENT THE CLASS of two thousand and eleven!"

The school dean, an older, bald-headed man in a tan suit, stood at the podium. He wore a grin on his face and turned toward Candice and the rest of her class. With a loud cheer and a round of applause, she and the rest of the graduates threw their dark green graduation caps into the air. The golden tassels floated on the breeze.

Candice stood and turned to see the proud smile on each of her parents' faces as they stood from their seats and cheered even louder. She felt proud of herself, too. She had finally finished school, at least for now. She had the one thing both her mother and father had drilled into her head since she was young —she had a degree. She was ready to take on the world, even if she had no idea what that looked like at the moment. Nothing would ever top this moment, she thought.

Once the graduating class was released to take pictures and mingle, Candice searched for her younger brothers and parents. The park where graduation took place wasn't that large, but the graduating class from the Craven Hill community college wasn't large either, really. Candice knew most of her graduating classmates, but there were a few she didn't. Mostly transfers from other parts of the state.

Looking for her family, she went around and hugged each of them, taking obligatory photos when parents and grandparents stopped them. Thankfully, it didn't take too much longer before she found her own family.

"We're so proud of you, Candy!" Her mother beamed, immediately taking her camera out to snap a few pictures. Candice enjoyed the attention. Normally, she hated pictures, but today she didn't care how many pictures her mother took. She even smiled widely.

"Have any of you seen Valerie? Did she make it?" Candice said when her mom finally lowered the camera. She glanced around, searching for her best friend. She and Valerie had grown up together in the small town of Hollow's Creek. Even though they took separate paths after graduation, they had remained good friends. Both her parents and brother, Kevin, shook their heads. "I don't see her, Candy."

"You're not looking hard enough then." A familiar voice said. Candice froze and turned to find the tall, skinny blonde. Valerie had a grin on her face and her wriggly son in her arms.

"Valerie!" Candice lunged forward, hugging them both. The young boy squirmed and groaned, pushing at Candice. Her graduation gown was brushing against his face. She pulled back and gently pinched the little boy's cheek, making him giggle and grin.

"Where's Cyrus? I thought he had Taylor this weekend?"

"Well. He did. He was supposed to have Taylor for the whole weekend, but I thought I'd bring Taylor with to see his auntie graduate. Cyrus is going to take him for one of my regular nights off so I can have a little alone time."

"This custody thing is starting to work out?"

"Yeah. Sometimes." A moment of sadness seemed to wash over her, but quickly dissipated when she spotted Taylor. A beam of happiness curled across her lips. She leaned in to rub her nose against his. Just watching them for a moment made her heart melt. Even though Candice wasn't sure about kids herself, it made her happy to see Valerie so happy.

Candice's mom stepped over, placing a hand on each of the girls' shoulders. Jack and the boys had already started toward the parking lot. She reached to bring both girls into a hug. "We're going to head back home, Candy. We'll see you later?"

"Ok, mom. I'll see you later."

Her mom kissed her forehead and gave Valerie another hug before turning toward the parking lot with her boys. Once she left, Candice gestured toward the nearest bench where they could sit and chat. The two girls were finally alone.

"It sure is nice out today." Valerie glanced up at the crystal clear blue sky. There were only a few fluffy clouds off in the distance. The temperature was nice for early summer.

"I'm so glad you could make it, Val."

"Are you kidding? I wasn't going to miss my best girl's graduation day!" Valerie sat down, setting the young boy down between them. She pulled out a bottle of juice from the diaper bag and handed it to him. She tucked her hair behind her ear. "How's everything else been with you, Candy? I know we haven't had the chance to talk much."

"Oh, you know. Nothing too exciting right now."

"Oh, come on! You and your band performed at the Graffiti last night! And I thought I overheard something about you all going on tour?" Valerie said, her blonde eyebrow quirked in curiosity. Candice shrugged nonchalantly.

"There's not much to talk about. I told the girls we had to hold off touring because of the new job. We need money before we can travel."

"Not even a new boyfriend you can tell me about?" Valerie leaned forward in a suggestive manner, touching her friend's thigh lightly with her French manicured nails. She gave Candice a wink before taking her hand back.

"No. I haven't really been interested in boys lately."

"Oh really? Don't tell me you're into girls now?"

"Um...no. You know I'm only into dudes. I'm just not really interested in dating anybody right now. I have too much going on." Candice shrugged. Valerie pouted playfully.

"Girl, have you even been with anybody since Zak left? It's been like four years now! You graduated from community college, Candy!"

"I haven't had the time for much." Candice lowered her eyes, playing with the zipper on her graduation gown. Valerie reached over and put a hand under her chin, gently nudging her to lift her head once more.

"It's ok, girl. I get it. The boys around here suck. Not that I don't love my little Tay, but he deserves to have a good daddy, you know? I need to leave this place myself and find a good man because I sure ain't gonna find him around Hollow's Creek. Or Craven Hill for that matter. A bunch of alcoholics and junkies."

"What about you? You don't think you and Cyrus will patch things up?"

"No. I love him, but we grew up in two different worlds. I'm the white girl his parents hate. And he's a Native. I'm sure you understand what that means. You remember how things were back in high school."

"Yeah. I remember." Candice nodded with a gentle smile, but she couldn't say that she understood. Zak was the only guy she had ever been with and, except for that one little difference in family money between her and Zak, she didn't understand what she went through. She never found herself attracted to any of the local boys, most of whom had several children by several girls in the Valley. What she did know is she didn't want to end up like most of them; a single mother raising a little one, living at home, and working crazy hours just to give a child what they needed.

Taylor threw the empty juice bottle on the grass and Valerie leaned over to pick it up. She wiped the bits of grass and dirt off before stuffing it back into her bag. She pulled out a hat and placed it over the young boy's head before lifting him up. "Enough about boys. Let's take a walk. I wanted to talk to you about something."

Taylor rested his head on his mother's shoulder and sucked on his thumb while Valerie and Candice walked across the lawn. They made their way to the edge of campus, where the wilderness started. Birds chirped. Leaves and twigs crunched beneath their feet. Even a few squirrels dashed across their path.

"What did you want to talk about, Val?"

"I know we talked about this before, but things are different now. Me and Cyrus are over. You're done with college." Valerie started, adjusting her son from one hip to the other. "I was thinking maybe we could look at getting an apartment together. What do you think? Me, you, and little Taylor."

"Oh, Val! That would be great! I've been ready to move out of my parents for a while, but are you sure? I don't plan on staying in Hollow's Creek long. I'm hoping to leave town with Ramona and Tommie before the new school year starts."

"You would need somewhere to come home to, right? I have some money saved up so you don't need to worry about that, Candy girl. I just don't think I can get a place alone. I want to be around for Taylor. I don't want to work my ass off and come home too tired to see him grow up." She laughed softly, rubbing Taylor's back. The two continued to the edge of the park where it met with the forest, Candice glanced over at her friend with a smile.

"Let's talk about it after I start my new job, is that ok?"

"Yes, of course, Candy. No pressure or anything." The two women kept walking and Valerie reached out to grab Candice's hand. She gave it a squeeze before releasing. They walked the path in silence, stopping when they noticed the large crowd nearby. "What's going on over there?"

"I don't know..." Candice spoke softly. She took a step forward when someone screamed. The small crowd started backing away. They whispered about a dead body in the forest. Candice turned towards Valerie. "Call the cops."

CHAPTER
FOUR

On her way home from a quick trip to Craven Hill, Candice pulled into the gas station and parked beside the gas pumps. Opening the driver's side door, she glanced around the parking lot before stepping out. The convenience store seemed busy for a Monday afternoon.

She locked up her little beat-up car and headed toward the front door of the building. She walked past a couple of older locals standing in front of the ice coolers, chattering about their grandchildren. The bell over the door jingled when she stepped inside.

"Hey Alex! Hey Mary!" Candice glanced over her shoulder, waving to the two older Native American women behind the counter. They hardly noticed her walk by as they were stocking cigarettes. She passed the first couple of aisles, listening to the conversation between them. They weren't exactly whispering.

"Do you think Mister Gray did it?"

"I'm sure he did. I mean, he did kill his wife, so what would stop him from killing someone else out on that property?"

Candice headed down the candy aisle to find a snack for later while she was lounging in bed in front of the television. With a quick glance over the candy rack, she picked a bag of regular and peanut M&M's. She then took a detour past the drink coolers and grabbed a couple of green cans of iced tea heading to the counter. Alex and Mary continued arguing. She had missed a chunk of the conversation, but she seemed to catch enough.

"Werewolves aren't real. Don't be stupid!" Alex, the younger of the two clerks with short dark hair and dark eyes squealed. She grabbed a carton of cigarettes and emptied the contents on to the nearby display behind them. Candice raised her brows and fought a laugh.

"One of these days, Alex, you will find out the truth. Hollow's Creek isn't just any small town." The older of the two women said with a raspy voice. She reached down for another container when she noticed Candice waiting.

"It's just a bunch of old superstition, Mary! I never believed in any of those stories."

"Your parents sheltered you then. Isn't that right, Candy?" Mary said. Candice stepped up and placed her items on the counter, frowning with confusion.

"Wh—what?"

"Mary is convinced there are such things as werewolves. And I told her it's just a bunch of superstitious mumbo jumbo." Alex leaned back against the stool behind her when the front doors flew open. Candice lowered her eyes in thought.

"I didn't grow up with all that stuff. Mom and dad aren't really story tellers."

"So, you don't believe those murders could have been done by werewolves, either?" Alex said when a soccer mom with a blonde ponytail stepped up to the counter, putting her hand out. With a frown of annoyance, Alex punched a few buttons and the cash drawer launched open, grabbing the woman's change.

Candice shrugged. She wasn't into all that supernatural

crap. That wasn't her thing and didn't believe in those kinds of stories. "You're on my side then! See, Mary! She doesn't believe in those superstitions either!"

"We'll talk again when they prove there are werewolves around here, kid!" Mary grumbled at the young woman and finished ringing up Candice, who held the handles of the plastic bag with her items.

"I'll talk to you two later." Candice laughed, grabbing her bag and the change from her twenty dollar bill. She turned and headed out the door. When the door swung closed behind her, she could still hear them bickering. She was too engrossed in their gossip, almost missing what was right in front of her.

"Whoa there! You might want to watch where you're going, young lady." The sheriff lifted his dark aviator sunglasses to the top of his fuzzy head. His graying crew cut resembled the hair from the war movies her parents watched late at night when she and her younger brothers were supposed to be asleep.

"Sorry about that, Mister Loveland." She muttered. He quirked a brow, still standing in her way with no intention of moving. She didn't know Mister Loveland well nor did she like being in his presence, but he was Valerie's father.

There was something off about him, she just wasn't sure what. She knew a lot of people didn't like him and she couldn't understand how he was sheriff for so long. It must've been related to all that political bullshit her parents talked about when watching the news.

"That's Sheriff Loveland to you, young lady." He puffed out his chest, clearing his throat when another customer stepped up, trying to squeeze by. The two men were much lankier than the sheriff, but the sheriff had a large presence. The darker of the two seemed afraid to interrupt. He turned, and with a crooked grin, stepped out of the way. "Excuse me."

Candice took the chance to step out of the way without him

noticing. She let out a breath she didn't know she was holding in and even dared a glance over her shoulder. The sheriff apologized firmly to the two men before they headed inside the building. She was almost at her car when he bellowed her name. "Candice!"

She whipped her head around, her auburn hair flipping across her face. He waddled across the parking lot with his chest puffed out into the air. She stuffed her hand into her pocket and held on to her keys. "Yes, sheriff?"

"You seen my daughter around lately?" He stepped out from under the awning, squinting into the bright sunlight. Without even thinking twice about it, she shook her head. He wasn't around much and didn't think she owed him anything. "Well, you tell her that Cyrus is coming around looking for her again. And that I don't appreciate her baby daddy disturbing the peace in my home."

"Why can't you tell her yourself? I'm not your messenger, sheriff." Candice bit her tongue the moment those words passed between her lips, but she meant them. She found his words slightly odd—they seemed like an excuse to be around when she knew he was hardly a part of her best friend's life or his grandson's for that matter. She clutched her keys tight, remembering the heavy bag of snacks and drinks in her other hand. He stepped close enough for her to smell the chewing tobacco on his breath.

"Look, young lady. You know who I am and I know where you live. If you're going to give me trouble about doing what I say, your parents are going to hear about how you treat the local law around here. Now, just do as I say. Do I make myself clear?"

"Yes 'sir'," She muttered, standing toe to toe with him. At that point, a few of the locals from inside the c-store stepped out to watch the confrontation. One of the clerks came out with the broom in hand. When she looked up, she recognized one of the men standing watch from the parking lot. His kid attended camp the past few years since she became a counselor. He wasn't a small man himself.

"Good. Now, run along. You be safe out there on them roads. Weatherman says we have a storm coming from the Gulf." The sheriff grinned with an extra wide smile and stepped away. She let out a heavy breath and glanced toward the front of the c-store building. The lights on the sign hanging over the roof flickered.

"You ok?" the clerk mouthed to her. Everyone else seemed to be watching the sheriff walk off to his vehicle. He must've known too because he spit on the black top just in front of the store. Candice nodded and slipped her bag into her car. It was the first time she noticed her heart was pounding in her chest.

She stepped around to the other end of her car with a quick glance up at the late afternoon sky. A cool breeze floated through the air. A bundle of dark, dangerous looking clouds floated over the mountain peaks just north of the c-store. She needed to get home before it came pouring down.

Turning, she headed toward her vehicle, noticing a familiar little red sports car pull in and park by one of the pumps. With a quick glance, she noticed the bobble head on the dashboard. She couldn't be entirely positive, but it looked like Zak's car, and her cheeks flushed with warmth.

She couldn't remember the last time she had seen her one time best friend—or ex-boyfriend for lack of a better word. He must've just arrived because she hadn't heard he was back from Colorado. She hoped he was only visiting family. Candice kept her eyes down, pumping gas until she knew Zak went inside. Now she had more reason to get back home quickly.

ON THE CORNER OF MAIN Street where the frontage road intersected stood an old building that was once the local malt shop. The property was owned by the grandparents of one of Candice's friends from junior high, but they closed down and retired to Florida when she and Candice graduated high school four years ago. The place had remained empty, but a few months ago, there was talk that the place had been sold.

Nobody knew who had bought the place though. Whoever bought the place completed renovations in silence. The new identity of the building wasn't revealed until a few days before Memorial Day weekend, which was the opening weekend of the new tavern with its brightly lit billboard sign: Troy's Tavern.

When Candice pulled into the large gravel parking lot, she had a difficult time finding a place to park at first. Everyone in town wanted to be part of the grand opening. Even a large semi was parked in the back. Luckily, she found a spot to park near the far edge of the lot. Stepping out of her vehicle, she took one glance over the rustic building that reminded her of her grandparents' cabin and headed towards the door.

Inside, the smell of greasy fried chicken and French fries wafted out the front door, beckoning to passersby. She stepped inside, spotting her parents and younger brothers in the middle of the dining area. Candice smiled at several familiar faces sitting at nearby tables, mostly those she had grown up with. A few of them sat with their boyfriends or girlfriends and their young children.

Music floated from the jukebox in the far corner. Billiard balls cracked over the murmur of conversation throughout the room. The hint of fresh paint tickled at her nose. The hardwood floors were nicely varnished, but old scars were still visible. The lingering scent sawdust mingled in the air.

Large printed photographs decorated the walls. Candice recognized a couple photographs that appeared to be of Denver. She had been there often enough to know the Rocky Mountains anywhere. Another picture she thought could have been New York before the twin towers had fallen. There were actually several of the New York skyline she soon realized, causing a sudden ache for travel.

Candice slipped into the booth beside her dad. Her family were still looking over their menus when she made herself comfortable, opening her copy of the menu. A sudden burst of cheers exploded through the room and Candice glanced toward the corner of the room, spotting a familiar face among the crowd of billiards tables.

"We were starting to wonder if you were going to join us or not, Candy."

"Sorry, I got held up at the c-store." She muttered, lifting her menu to hide her face. Cody laughed. Kevin looked over at her, rolling his eyes. "What's your problem? Did the boys see a microscopic zit on your face?"

Candice kicked her leg across the underside of the table. Kevin snickered, kicking her back, but the bickering didn't last long before mom intervened.

"Ok, you two! That's enough! You are both grown and should know better."

Jack glanced over at Candice with a frown, reaching over to lower the menu from her face. She caught sight of the raised brow on his face. He spoke softly. "Everything ok?"

Candice only nodded. Thankfully, an older woman with wavy blonde hair appeared a moment later, pulling out a notepad and pencil from her apron. "Is everyone ready to order? Do y'all need a few more minutes to decide?"

The rest of the table looked at Candice who only nodded. In

reality, she wasn't really sure what she wanted to eat. For such a small menu, everything sounded delicious. She glanced in her mom's direction when she recited her order. "I'll just have the street tacos. Extra pico de gallo on the side."

Her father ordered a steak with a baked potato and her brothers both ordered themselves a cheeseburger with fries, making her second guess her unspoken order. When the waitress finally glanced in her direction, she quickly realized everyone was looking at her.

"And how about you, miss?" The waitress said, smacking her gums. The blonde stood there waiting, pencil in hand. In that moment, she caught Eric's gaze, which caught her off guard. She hoped it ended there. The two of them were never close, but things change.

"Can I get an iced tea? And I'll have the street tacos too." She said, handing her menu to the waitress. She took a moment to confirm no changes to anybody's order and soon disappeared, heading to the kitchen.

A few moments later, the waitress reappeared with their drinks and a basket of fresh tortilla chips and salsa. Candice's stomach rumbled loudly, and she grabbed a chip, dipping it in the salsa. Candice had forgotten all about Eric until she suddenly heard someone call out.

"Hey, Candice!" She took a bite of her chip, noticing Eric walking over. He wore tan cargo shorts and a bright green polo, complete with a popped collar. He also wore a diamond in one ear and a strange scar branded into his neck. His light brown hair spiked with gel.

"Um, excuse me? And you are?" Her mom said, her gaze narrowed.

"Mom, this is Eric. We went to high school together." Her dad cleared his throat beside her. "And this is my dad. And those two jerks are my little brothers."

"Who're your parents? I feel like I've seen you around somewhere else before." Her father said, carefully inspecting the young man standing at the end of the table. Her father lifted his glass of water to his lips. Candice's cheeks flushed, and she contemplated covering her face, but she fought the urge. She just hoped Eric wouldn't linger long.

"My dad is Allan Gray. You might know my grandparents, too. Scott and Victoria Gray." Eric said with a nod. Candice's father just nodded, turning away from the young man to return his attention to the family. Her brothers snickered.

"You gonna be ok, Candy? Your face is turning all red!" Kevin said.

"Oh my!" her mother said. Her father just cleared his throat. She sank further in her seat, trying to focus on something other than the uncomfortable situation. Why did he have to come up to the table? she thought to herself.

"Ok. Enough, boys." Her mother said. When Candice lifted her face from the palm of her hand, she noticed a smirk on Kevin's face.

"Excuse me. Coming through." The waitress appeared, carrying a large tray over one shoulder, pushing past Eric. He waved a hand at their table. "Nice meeting y'all."

"Give your father our regards." Her dad said as Eric stepped away to rejoin his pool game. Luckily, the whole mood around the booth shifted. Food had arrived. Her father's steak was still sizzling from the kitchen grill. A wave of hungry smiles appeared around the table. "Let's grub!"

Candice couldn't help feeling eyes on her throughout dinner. She brushed off the feeling to enjoy her tacos and eventually forgot all about Eric. At the end of their meal, she took a detour to the restroom. When she came back, she was the last to leave with her dad, who left a few bills under his empty glass of iced tea.

"Candice, you don't want to get mixed up with him."

"What do you mean, dad?"

"That was Eric Gray. I've heard plenty about him and his family." He said, walking beside her on their way toward the front register. Candice stopped and glanced at her dad. "He's a bad influence, as far as I'm concerned. Doing drugs and shit since you two graduated. And I don't want my little Candy getting involved with someone like that. You don't have the time for someone like him.

"Go on and head outside with your mother. I'll be out in a minute."

He held his wallet and stepped over to the register. Candice waited near the front door and glanced over her shoulder, taking another quick scan of the room. There was no sign of Eric anywhere. Unsure if she was relieved or disappointed, she headed outside, contemplating her father's words. Maybe he was wrong.

She didn't know Eric well, but she knew who he was. Not only did they attend the same school system for over a decade, he was one of Zak's friends. At least so she thought. The two of them had been in basketball and track together, but Candice wasn't part of that scene. She didn't know how things worked in sports. She always thought Eric was kind of cute with those sparkling hazel eyes.

CHAPTER FIVE

nother local citizen was found dead on the edge of the forest yesterday afternoon. Law enforcement states this is the second death within several hundred yards of the Gray Mansion in a matter of days. Officials have reported that both deaths are not the cause of foul play, but rather an animal attack."

What a way to start off the day, she thought, diverting her attention from the television. For a moment, she thought it odd that both murders were reported to have happened near the Gray property. She found herself wondering what happened to the body found near the forest out in Craven Hill. After her dad arrived to start initial investigations, still dressed casually for her graduation, she had forgotten about it.

Even though the small town loved gossip—including murder—she had long since learned to keep her nose out of it because of her dad's involvement. With a glance at the grandfather clock in the corner of the room, she shut off the television and went upstairs to finish her coffee. She didn't have a lot of time to waste before work.

After a nice warm shower, Candice dressed and checked that

she had all the necessary supplies in her tote bag. Sunscreen, baseball cap, energy bars, and her refillable water bottle, the ice clinking inside. She even packed a light windbreaker just in case. Even though she doubted it was necessary in early June, her mother insisted when she was packing the night before. Finally, she grabbed her keys and headed out.

She headed up the highway to Camp Gray in her dad's SUV. She could've used her own little beat-up car, but she needed something more rugged further up the mountains. He had a better sound system too. Avril Lavigne's The Best Damn Thing popped up on the stereo. She sang at the top of her lungs, grooving to the beat and drumming her fingers against the steering wheel. Suddenly, sirens cut through her music.

When she glanced up into her rear-view mirror, a set of red and blue emergency lights flashed behind her. She drove until she found a safe spot to pull over and let the vehicle pass, waiting for the fire truck to fly up the mountain. She watched the bright red truck disappear and wondered what was going on. Was there another animal attack? She had never seen this much activity around town. The sirens whined and wailed until they faded off in the distance.

Luckily, she wasn't far from the turn off leading towards the campgrounds and drove along the side of the road. She passed the old familiar road sign and followed the dirt road leading from the highway. She could reach the campgrounds with her eyes closed though.

Every summer since she was a young girl, she attended camp and soon after moving on to high school, she applied to work as a camp counselor. She did so well that the camp's hiring managers called for her to return every summer that followed.

This year, she was the oldest camp counselor. Even among

the senior counselors. Since the position was funded by a local state grant, the managers only hired high school and college aged kids, making this her final year. She didn't mind because she was ready to move on. Although she had no idea what direction her life was going, she was ready to find her place in the world.

When the dirt path, flanked by evergreens, finally cleared to reveal the campgrounds, she spotted several other cars parked in the front of the old log cabin that was the admin building. She didn't see anybody standing outside, though. Everyone must've been inside, getting themselves oriented for the summer. Grabbing her bag from the backseat, she hopped down from the old Jeep and headed up the stairs. When she opened the door, everyone turned in her direction.

"Well, very nice of you to join us, Candice."

"Sorry, Susan." Candice muttered under her breath, shutting the door behind her. She slipped in near the back of the group. She directed her attention to Susan, the older short haired woman at the front of the room. She cleared her throat and spoke, stepping through the crowd to hand Candice a packet.

"As I was saying before we were interrupted, we have a full week of activities in preparation for camp to open on Friday. Of course, the first thing on our agenda is the bundle of paperwork for each of you. Then our senior counselors will be conducting a tour of the campgrounds for those who are new or less seasoned. We'll break for lunch and afterwards we'll start counselor boot camp where you will learn first aid and how to handle many issues that may come up over the summer. I hope you're ready to learn."

BETWEEN FIRST AID, OUTDOOR safety, and various activity classes—including a few art classes—the rest of the week flew by. Before they knew it, Friday morning finally arrived and the kids would be walking through the doors of the recreation building.

With Candice's wavy auburn hair pulled into a ponytail and dressed in a pair of long jean shorts and one of the approved uniform polo shirts with the camp logo printed on the left breast, she waited in the lobby of the recreation cabin for the front door to open. She leaned back, resting one of her sneakers against the wall, and watched several cars pull into the gravel parking lot.

"Are you ready for this, Candy?" Said another girl with short strawberry blonde hair standing nearby. A smile appeared across her bright pink glossy lips. Except for her khaki shorts, everything she wore had an accent of pink. From her sneakers to her polo shirt. Even her earrings were dangling pink butterflies. Candice glanced at her name tag before addressing her.

"Oh, yeah! Bring it on!" Candice laughed. "Are you ready, Maya?"

"Yep. I love kids!" Maya crossed the lobby to the front door where Susan stood by to direct the group. Candice wanted to roll her eyes. She hardly knew the girl except for her love of pink and that she was new to the Valley. She still couldn't understand why someone not much younger than herself would want to move to a small town.

"Are you ready, girls?" Susan glanced at Candice, who stepped away from the wall and glanced at the clock. She could feel her heart race with anticipation, which had never seemed to go away no matter how many times she opened camp for the season. Susan grabbed her keys from her pocket and unlocked the front door, letting the children inside.

The children waved to their parents over their shoulders, but a few of the younger children didn't seem too thrilled. One little girl with her corn husk golden hair tied up in messy pigtails appeared to be on the verge of tears the moment she stepped inside. She and her older brother were the last ones through the door.

"Come on, Hayley." Her brother was a few years older, but patient. He took her hand and led her across the lobby with plenty of reluctance and high-pitched whining from her. When the two siblings approached, Candice crouched down between them with a gentle smile on her face, hoping to help set the young girl at ease.

"Everything ok?" Candice glanced between them. The older brother grabbed the backpack falling from his shoulder and glanced down at her with a nod.

"Yes, Hayley's not used to being away from dad."

"Hayley? It's ok. Your daddy will be back soon. We—"

"I want mama!" Hayley let out a wailing cry and Candice glanced up at the older brother still holding on to his little sister's hand. He frowned and spoke softly to the little girl.

"You know that can't happen, Hayley."

"Jordan, I want mama and daddy!" She let out another wailing cry and the older brother dropped his backpack, giving her a hug. Candice stood up and watched them, biting her thumb. Hayley was finally starting to calm down while Jordan walked her down the hall toward the bathrooms.

"You heard about her mother, right?" Susan stepped up and whispered in her ear. Candice turned and shook her head with a frown. She waited for Susan to speak, glancing up the hallway for the two children. "Really? You didn't hear the story about Mister and Missus Gray?" Susan started, but before Candice could answer, she continued. "Hayley and Jordan's mother passed away from suspicious circumstances. Hayley, Jordan, and their parents moved into the Gray Mansion late last year, when Allan's mother came down with a flu that left her too weak to care for the house herself. She passed right before the new year and Victoria, his wife, passed away only a few weeks later."

"That's not the story! You got it all wrong!" Maya came up behind them, lowering her voice so the children wouldn't hear them. "Allan's mother passed away last year, but they moved in after the reading of the will. Missus Gray was the one who got really sick and passed away. They say it's because the place is haunted by some bad spirits."

"Oh pssshh! The haunted mansion story is a bunch of baloney, Maya! Stories that Allan's parents made up to keep the town away from the house. They don't want to associate with us poor peasant people."

"What do you mean it's all baloney? You know there are supernatural beings up there! Shifters and werewolves, they say!" Said another girl. "Some people say the Grays are a family of werewolves!"

"That's enough gossip! We have children to watch after and teach about the wilderness today! Let's get this show on the road!" Susan said, turning away in hopes to discourage the gossip.

"Yeah. Let's hop to it then." Maya smiled and patted Candice on the shoulder before disappearing down the hallway. Candice stood there and watched her co-worker, contemplating everything she heard. She heard plenty about what happened at the Gray Mansion. From the evening news reports to newspaper articles and even the usual gossip that floated around.

The only consistent piece of what she heard from any of the reports was that Victoria Gray was dead and people believed Allan had killed her. From what she knew, Allan's oldest son, Eric, took care of his younger siblings before his father was bailed out of prison a few months ago. Whatever was going on with the Gray family was their business. She never would've considered herself to be one of Eric's best friends, but she knew enough about him and his family not to participate. Besides, the rest of Hollow's Creek gossiped enough for her.

Luckily, Hayley had calmed down enough to enjoy a day filled with stories, coloring, plenty of snacks, and even recess time, while her older brother spent more of his time outside learning about the wilderness with Maya, Candice, and the others. There weren't many children at camp, but there were enough to keep everyone busy.

When three pm rolled around, Candice was exhausted. Not only had the children zapped every ounce of her energy, but the grueling summer heat had finally arrived. She felt the violent glare of the sunshine every time she stepped outside.

She shielded the sun's rays from her eyes when she stepped out the front door with Maya and Susan. Beads of sweat appeared on her forehead, waiting for the children to come out the front door. "Summer is going to be brutal this year! I hope you own a few hats, Maya!"

Maya glanced over, her whole mood drooping from the heat. Candice stifled a laugh, trying not to do more than smile, but her co-worker looked miserable. Susan, on the other hand, stepped out after the last few children, looking fresh as a daisy in her jean shorts and ball cap.

"I don't think any of us saw this heat coming. It's almost strange. This summer feels a little strange already." Susan said as she shut the front door. Candice remained silent, keeping her thoughts to herself, but she had that strange feeling too. Maybe it was all the recent activity around town—including the murders and talk about missing people in the forest. She didn't really pay much attention though.

A few children saw their parents right away and took off running toward their cars, jumping into what she hoped were air-conditioned backseats. Susan went inside when most of the children had gone home for the evening. Even Maya had taken off, but Candice said she would stay until everyone had gone home.

She leaned against the side of the building and glanced over at Hayley and Jordan sitting on the bench. Luckily, several evergreens provided shade and protection from the blistering rays of the sun. Hayley was leaning against her brother, watching him play his video game.

"Where's your dad?" Candice said.

"He's not coming. Eric said he would be late." Jordan responded without taking his eyes from the screen, which left her surprised. She didn't expect to hear that Eric would be picking them up. She didn't know how she felt about that. She just watched over the two children. Hayley swung her feet, drinking from her water bottle, her short little legs unable to reach the sandy ground.

"Do you know how late?" She asked, but Jordan shrugged his shoulders, mumbling something that sounded like he had to work. Luckily, though, the three of them weren't outside waiting long when an old black American sports car pulled into the parking lot. She knew it was Eric before he even parked. Not many people drove around Hollow's Creek with an old sleek Charger.

"Sorry, I'm late. My co-worker didn't fucking show up until five minutes ago." Eric said, popping out of his car. leaving it running. Jordan and Hayley both glanced up at their older brother with a frown.

"Daddy doesn't like those words, Eric!" Hayley perked up and yelled aloud, sliding off the bench. Jordan turned off his game and shoved it in his bag. He kept his head down as he headed over to his brother's car.

"Yeah, yeah. Sorry." Eric glanced up, and a smile appeared on his face when he met Candice's eyes. "Hey! If it isn't my old pal, Ace! I didn't expect to see you here."

"Please don't call me that, Eric." Candice said, stepping away from the side of the building to help his siblings into the car. After getting them into the backseat, he glanced toward Candice with a crooked grin on his face.

"Oh right. Only your boyfriend, Zak, can call you that."

He stepped to the rear end of the car, pulling a cigarette out of his pocket. Candice frowned, looking into his tired, bloodshot hazel eyes, making him look older than twenty-three or twenty-four. This time she didn't find the sparkles she admired. He lit up his cigarette and took a drag, staring at Candice.

"Fuck you, Eric." She muttered. Another smirk appeared across his lips. Smoke twisted up into the air. With a suggestive look on his face, he chuckled under his breath and stepped away. He paused for a moment and turned toward her, that crooked grin on his face never fading.

"What are you doing tonight? I'm having a summer party up at the mansion. I'd love it if you joined me up on the mountain like old times. What do you say, Candy girl?"

"Um..." Candice hesitated for a moment, lowering her gaze. She debated whether she should go out to a mountain top party or not. She didn't need those sparkling eyes staring straight into her soul, trying to influence her decision. She wasn't much of a partier anymore, but she needed a good time. When she lifted her head again, meeting those gorgeous eyes again, she finally returned the smile.

"Sure. Why the hell not?"

"Great. I'll see you tonight then."

CHAPTER SIX

Valerie said hi. She didn't chat long though. It looked like they were pretty busy tonight." Candice's dad said when he placed the pizza boxes on the dining room table. She wasn't surprised though. She knew many people who loved a pizza from Papi's Pizza Diner on Friday nights, including them.

Friday night almost always meant pizza. One pepperoni, mushroom, and sausage with extra cheese and another with just pepperoni and extra cheese for the picky eaters that were Candice's brothers. Kevin tried the pepperoni, mushroom, and sausage a few months ago, but ended up picking off the mushrooms when he bit into one.

Candice found she wasn't too hungry though, even after a long day handling a group of rowdy children that ranged in ages from five to thirteen. Despite her dad's warnings about his drug and alcohol use, she was looking forward to Eric's party. Maybe he had changed and her dad just didn't know it because he didn't seem to like any of the boys around the Valley.

"Where are you going, Candy?" Her mother asked, wiping the grease from her fingers with the overused paper towel beside her plate. Candice spun on her heel and with a smile on her face, contemplated her answer. It wasn't often that her parents asked about her social life, but something seemed to have changed since she graduated.

"I'm heading out tonight. An old friend invited me to a party up on Gray Mountain."

"Gray Mountain, huh?" Her father said, not lifting his eyes. The cheese stretched when he grabbed a slice. She already knew why the interest from her dad. Everyone knew about the parties on Gray Mountain, but with her dad being in the local sheriff's department, he knew Gray Mountain very well. He spent many quiet Friday and Saturday nights patrolling the area, breaking up parties long before Candice was even in high school. After all, he had grown up in the Hollow Valley.

"Yeah, dad. I'll be fine. I'm a big girl."

"Oh, we don't worry about you. We worry about those boys around here. We don't want to see you getting trapped with some dumb boy who has no life's ambition." Her father said between bites of pizza. Her mom glanced over him briefly with an unamused look on her face.

"What your father is trying to say is that we know you're a responsible adult, but accidents happen. And we don't want you ending up...stuck in something that leaves you sacrificing your dreams, Candy. You've worked so hard over the last few years."

"I'm not going to end up like that, mom. I know you worry I'm going to end up like Valerie with a kid and shit, but I'm not stupid. Why would you even think that?"

"Well...we've heard rumors that a certain boy is back in town and I just want you to be careful. I don't want you making rash decisions...in the heat of the moment." Her mother said, clearing her throat and lowering her eyes briefly. Candice knew what she was thinking, but neither of them drew attention to it.

Her mom spent most of her life taking care of Candice and her two younger brothers. It wasn't until Cody was in pre-school that she enrolled in community college courses and finished her degree. It was heartbreaking, but also motivating.

"Mom, I know. I've... I saw his car at the c-store, but you don't need to worry. I have no desire to see Zak. I don't want to see him after what he did, mom."

"Good. Well, I just wanted to make sure, you know. It's a small town and you know people like to talk. I love you, sugar."

"I love you too, mom." She said, giving her mom a gentle smile. Candice stepped over and kissed her mother's cheek. With a smile, she headed out of the room. When she reached the door, her mom yelled out. "Just be careful, Candice. Please."

"I promise." Candice yelled back before slipping down the hallway. She headed upstairs to her bedroom, thankful to have survived that uncomfortable conversation with her parents. She wasn't a fan of talking about her love life, especially in front of her brothers, but thankfully, they were occupied with food.

Shutting the bedroom door behind her, she sat on the edge of her bed, leaning down to open the bottom drawer of the side table. She pulled out an old journal that she hadn't touched in nearly five years. At least not since Zak left town and wasn't sure what was still between those pages.

When she opened the journal, a small stack of pictures hidden somewhere between the pages slipped out. She picked them up and set them aside, coming across a loose-leaf paper tucked inside. She unfolded it, reading the words she had once written in pen—an unfinished letter with a few tear stains on the corner.

Zak,
I miss the hell outta you.

And I wish you had never gone, but I know I'll see you again soon. I still don't understand why you had to leave.

With the ghost of a smile on her face, she set the journal down and picked up the pictures. She stared at the top picture for a few moments. She lifted a hand to her chest, feeling that sharp ache in her chest. Tears burned in her eyes as she remembered the day those pictures were taken. It was the last time she remembered being so in love and oblivious.

Overlooking the surface of the small fishing lake, she and Zak stood on the old bridge with their backs to Valerie. The sky was painted with pinks and oranges with a golden light coming from the setting sun. When Valerie suddenly called out their names, they turned towards the camera with a smile on their faces. Zak wrapped his arm around Candice and leaned in to kiss her cheek, inspiring the grin on her face to widen. His dark, messy hair tickled above her face and she giggled.

Candice slipped the picture behind another, which had been taken only moments later. Candice had turned, her eyes squinted. She was leaning in to kiss Zak. When she flipped the picture over in her hand, she found Soulmates - 2005 written across the back in what appeared to be Valerie's fancy handwriting, but so much changed after those pictures changed in only a matter of days.

Her junior year of high school had finally come to an end. Zak's graduation came and went and he packed his things into the back of the old sky-blue van he bought for his eighteenth birthday. The heat of summer had barely arrived when Zak left Hollow's Creek with another girl who happened to be his girlfriend. It broke her heart into a million pieces and she found herself still healing.

Valerie had been right. It was time for her to move on from

the past and with the rest of her life. Candice was about to turn twenty-two and she had a world of new experiences ahead. She stuffed the pictures into the journal and dumped it back into the drawer, slipping it closed without a doubt in her mind about how she would spend the rest of her night.

It was time for her to have fun and forget about Zak.

CANDICE DROVE DOWN THE hill and stopped just before the bridge where the river cut through the valley. Although the evening was still young, the shadows of the mountains grew longer and darker over the small town. She waited several long moments before driving over the bridge to the crossroads where turning the wrong direction could be bad.

Named for the founding family, Gray Mountain overlooks the Hollow mountain valley stretching from the town of Juniper and Hollow's Creek through the mountain pass of Craven Hill. Depending on who ask, some residents might also mention the Hollow Forest, where the evergreens outnumber people five to one and most locals avoid without question. A place many people refer to as the depths, where it is rumored that a hidden population of supernatural creatures live.

Some of the older citizens around town even believe there is a whole subculture that is controlled by some demon mafia and a coven of powerful witches that worship them. Many people believed those who have wondered away from the main road and into the depths never found their way back to civilization. Those who did, were no longer human.

The light standing at the crossroads flickered off. She glanced down the dark abyss where the highway disappeared into the thick evergreen forest that dominated the mountains.

The crickets hardly chirped, but the number of dogs howling at the waxing full moon grew.

"Stop being a big baby," she muttered. She finally moved her foot and drove through the crossroads, following the road leading up toward the mountain. Her heart thrummed in her heaving chest, keeping her eyes locked on the dark road. She followed the curving road up and around the mountains surrounding Hollow's Forest.

Candice heard the music bumping long before she reached the peak of the mountain. When she spotted the end of a line of cars, parked on either side of the dirt road, she quickly pulled over and parked. Shutting off the engine, she pocketed her keys and grabbed a few other items including a tube of bright pink lip gloss, her cell phone, and a couple of condoms, just in case, stuffing them into her pocket.

Stepping down from her old car, she followed the music toward the party. The earthy scent of smoke filled her nostrils, leading her toward a large bonfire. The heat beckoned to her, but she continued towards the large open gate at the end of the property. Laughter floated toward her and before long, that familiar large, red barn rose off in the distance.

"Hey, you made it!" A familiar voice came up behind her. She turned to find Eric approaching with a red plastic cup in one hand and a smile curled over his lips. His dirty blond hair was messy and disheveled and his eyes seemed to sparkle in the dim light of the approaching night. The dark bags beneath his eyes spoke of not one but many late nights of partying, which made her a little sad.

"Eric! You're here too!"

"Well, yeah!" He laughed, taking another drink. "Of course, I'm here! We're on Gray Mountain, baby! This is my hood! I'm glad you made it out here though. It's been too long since you came out and partied with us. Little miss ambitious Candy."

"Isn't the saying work hard, party harder?" Candice laughed.

"You know...I think it probably is." He smiled. Candice could see the alcohol's influence on his face, but she didn't care. Tonight, she was going to have plenty of fun and alcohol and forget about the worries that had recently started to plague her mind. "Come with me. Let's get you a drink."

He offered her his hand and with only a moment's hesitation, she took his hand, following him away from the crowd surrounding the bonfire. He led her towards the old barn where a keg and a punch bowl were situated. Even when she was younger, she never understood why the barn was still standing since the Gray family hadn't been farmers for decades, if not centuries. But every family had its heirlooms.

Candice grabbed a red plastic cup and filled it from the punch bowl while a group of others surrounded one of Eric's friends doing a keg stand. He hardly seemed phased by it though as he chatted with a few others in the barn. When Candice lifted the cup to her lips, smelling the pungent alcohol before taking a drink, she met Eric's eyes again. His interest seemed to be locked on her and only her. Butterflies fluttered in her stomach when he approached.

"Let's get out of here," he whispered near her ear. She lifted her gaze and smiled. Without another word, he took her hand and led her out of the barn and toward the forest just beyond the property. The evergreens surrounded them. The darkness enveloped them and the noise from the party faded into the night. She glanced around, hardly able to see more than Eric's silhouette in the shadows. He held on tight to her hand, guiding her further into the forest before the pale glow of the moonlight finally cut in through the canopy.

"It's beautiful out here." He said. She lifted her gaze to the darkening sky. Stars were starting to peek through, sparkling and twinkling in the night. She let his hand go, feeling the warmth of his body move away from her. She quickly realized she should've brought her windbreaker along.

"And quiet..." Candice observed as wind whistled through the trees, but he remained silent. When she glanced back at him, he had taken off his jacket and laid it across the fallen pine needles of the forest floor. He had lowered himself to the ground and smiled up at her. His eyes seemed to glow differently when it was just the two of them beneath the moonlight.

Without any hesitation, Candice joined him on the ground, curling her legs underneath her. Eric scooted in closer and leaned back, slipping his arm around her. He pulled her in close and rested her head against his shoulder. Closing her eyes, she inhaled a deep breath of the fresh mountain air. She also caught a whiff of the smoke in his hair and the expensive cologne at his neck, making her heart race.

"It's nothing like the city. Smoggy and loud with a crowd of people everywhere you turn. You can hear everything up here. Here you can hear yourself think and just unplug. And the stars! Look at the night sky!"

Candice opened her eyes again and glanced up at him as his gaze lifted. Several clouds floated across the sky and blocked the light of the nearly full moon. The longer she stared, the more she could've sworn that a red ring glowed around it, much like a fuzzy halo. Wolves howled off in the distance. She could feel the little hairs on the back of her neck rise.

He scooted closer to her and slipped his hand to her waist. He leaned in closer, speaking softly against her ear. "I'm so glad you made it tonight. I was hoping to see you. Spend some time with you. I don't know if you know this or not, but... I still remember the first time we met. I couldn't take my eyes off you."

Candice turned and put a finger to his lips, slipping back slightly from Eric. Looking into his dark hazel eyes, she noticed a fire in his eyes that she had never seen before. Not even in Zak's eyes. His warm breath tickled her skin, sending a shiver down her spine. She leaned in closer, her body responding to the warm closeness of his. Their breathing grew heavier and their lips met in a slow, sensuous kiss.

The kiss lingered for a good long moment before Candice pulled away, frowning deep. She lifted a hand to her lips, still able to feel him there, but it wasn't like her to just kiss a guy so quickly. She had a hard time letting herself fall under a man's seduction. Even Eric for that matter, but she silently reminded herself that she was the one who stuffed condoms in her back pocket. It might've just been a kiss, but things rarely ever ended there.

"What's wrong, Candice?" He said, visibly confused as he reached to tuck a hand beneath her chin. She felt just as confused as he looked though, but when she met his eyes, she pulled away from him. She hadn't dated anybody since Zak and somehow, he had invaded her thoughts.

"I—I don't really know." She finally admitted. "I've never been with someone...other than Zak. I don't know what you're trying to do to me, but it's not going to work. Wanting me to fall in love with you is not going to work! You can't just bring me out here in the middle of the forest and try to seduce me!"

"I would've thought it was working, Candice! You seemed to want that kiss just as much as I did!" He said, frowning hard. Even though he had plenty to drink, he seemed to know exactly what he was doing with her. He knew what he wanted from her even if she was reluctant.

"I—I don't really know what I want right now, Eric. I'm sorry. I shouldn't have come here." The words rushed out of her mouth before she could stop herself. Rising to her feet, she turned and ran out of the forest. He called out her name, but she never looked back.

CHAPTER SEVEN

Candice couldn't sleep that night. She truly felt conflicted and needed to clear her mind after what had happened between her and Eric on Gray Mountain. Maybe a night run would help. It would help her keep in shape to keep up with the kids at camp.

Stepping out on to the porch, Candice lifted her gaze toward the evening sky. Although the night was partly cloudy, there were no signs of an incoming storm. Even a few of the brightest stars sparkled, peeking through the clouds. The world was cooling down, but there was a lingering heat in the air. Although she wasn't really sure if it was the air or the passion in her veins that had been stirred by Eric.

Popping a single earbud into place, she turned on her mp3 player and jogged up the gravel driveway. When she reached the highway, she watched and waited for the handful of passing cars to disappear before running to the other side of the highway. Once on the other side, she popped in her other earbud and headed down the mountain.

Even for a small mountain community hidden in the forests of north central New Mexico, the mayor and the forest service had made sure to keep up with maintaining the different trails available. Not only for hikers, but for the joggers, walkers, and bike riders too. Of course, there were plenty of mountains to climb and explore, but not everyone was adventurous enough to climb the tall mountain peaks of the forest. Candice included.

She jogged along the path that followed the side of the highway at a slow, steady pace. Soon she was breathing heavy. Emo rock music pumped through her earbuds and with her eyes focused on her path, she was still able to hear the occasional car coming up the highway. She jogged the few miles down the mountain until she made it to the village.

In the village, there was still some activity with the lingering warmth of the summer, but it was a late Friday night. Many of the vehicles parked in the village earlier in the day were gone home. Then again, she realized there were probably more vehicles parked even further down the highway at Troy's Tavern. She wasn't planning to go that far.

The Tavern was at least another mile down the highway path and she had already turned down the short road marked with a sign that read Village Square. She was only a stone's throw from the small park hidden by a few large trees, but she could see the silhouettes of the playground equipment just before the local library.

The usual kids at the skate park were already gone for the night, leaving the park in silence. A light breeze slipped through the warm summer evening. The steel merry-go-round moved gently. One of the swings rocked slowly on its chains. The quiet sounds of the nearby babbling brook were peaceful.

Candice sat on the park bench on the edge of the generous green lawn. She laid back along the length of the bench and stared up at the sky, trying to catch her breath. For a moment, she closed her eyes listening to the music pumping through her ears, hoping to block out the thoughts threatening to take her mind on a spin. Yet, as her racing heart settled down, her mind grew restless once more.

Between her job up at Camp Gray, Zak's sudden arrival back from Denver, and the party up on Gray Mountain, she couldn't remember the last time she had to just sit alone with her thoughts. Distractions were easy to come by, but sometimes she needed a minute to sit and sort through her own thoughts.

Candice still had a lot on her mind especially when it came to Eric. She always had a sneaking suspicion that Eric had a thing for her, but she never would've thought he still had feelings after five years. Eric and his family were in a whole different social class than she and her family. In fact, Candice was sure Eric was in a higher social class than most of the community. How many guys or people their age could claim to be the heir to a local empire even one like the Hollow Valley?

But Hollow's Creek was a small town and there really weren't many new people around. At least nobody new to the area chose to live year round. On the other hand, Eric's family had money. He had the opportunity to leave many times and didn't. He could've left the big city like Zak had.

She didn't want to admit it, but maybe her dad was right about Eric being deep into drugs and alcohol. What other reason would explain why he chose to stay behind unless there was something she didn't know about. After all, what did she know about being heir to a wealthy family legacy?

She found herself wondering about him though. Maybe it was that kiss that scrambled her brain. Such a strong kiss that made her feel weak in the knees. And maybe his admitting to still being attracted to her helped. What harm would it do in going out on a few dates to get to know him better?

Zak's face popped into her head again. A sudden ache

pierced her heart because there were times she found herself missing him. She never went long without thinking about him over the years even after how he broke her heart with such reckless abandon. Nor had she forgiven him either. Playing with her band always helped. Playing the guitar gave her mind something to focus on, but she needed to get over Zak. Maybe Eric was the key.

She opened her eyes when a strong breeze whipped through the air. A muted crack of thunder rumbled in the distance. Rising from the park bench, she glanced toward the sudden emergence of dark clouds in the distance. The wind had picked up, and the clouds seemed to float away as the bloody moon rose over the horizon. With a shiver creeping through her, she headed back up the mountain.

The wind grew stronger with each few steps. Music floated through her ears, but she became more alert of her surroundings once she passed the northern most part of the village. By then the forest grew thicker while the density of houses and cabins thinned out, leaving fewer streetlights along the highway.

Another faint rumble of thunder trembled in the distance. Candice could still see that same bundle of rain clouds hovering off in the distance. The breeze whipping through the evergreens became stronger. The dark clouds floating in the sky blocked the brightness of the full moon. Wolves howled off in the distance. Chills rolled down her spine.

She jogged further up the mountain and soon passed the old church where her and her family celebrated holidays and Sunday mornings. A few drops of rain whipped her in the face and stung her cheek. The breeze turned into wind and whistled in her ears. The trees started to sway. Short hairs flew loose from her ponytail and flipped at the corner of her eyes.

Each step up the mountain became a little more difficult.

Her heart pounded harder against her ribs. Her breathing became heavier. The warmth of sweat broke against her hair line and her lower back. When the cool air blasted against her face and back, goosebumps rose on every inch of her body. She kept climbing up the mountain.

Wolves continued to howl somewhere in the mountains. The leaves were shaking and dancing in the trees. She glanced up at the sky. The clouds were closer than she originally thought down at the park. Soon the rain would come pouring down, she thought. She only hoped she'd make it home before then. Her clothing was hardly more than a thin tee shirt and a pair of neon purple running shorts.

She took shorter strides, watching her steps over the large rocks. Candice passed around a large boulder standing in the middle of her path. The cool wind whipping through the air started to feel wet. She took the path that broke off and led the forest bordering the dip of a mountain.

The shadows quickly grew around her. The towering evergreens were giants in the darkness and the feeling of the air surrounding her seemed to change. The air almost felt electric. She slowed down and glanced through the darkness, but she could see nothing more than the trees. Something still didn't feel right though.

Her heart pounded harder in her chest. Something made her feel like she shouldn't be there. The sway of the trees told her to leave. The whistle of the evergreens told her to beware. Candice felt something staring right at her. And then she heard the growling.

Her eyes widened with fear. She froze momentarily, too afraid to move, but when she realized she was relatively safe, she kept moving steadily through the forest. Maybe the different sounds of the wilderness had made her believe she was hearing that growling somewhere just ahead. She popped her earbud out and listened to the abyss of the forest.

The growling came back.

And then a twig snapped.

Only a few feet away, that growl turned into a warning bark. The world went flashing before her very eyes as a large dark brown wolf leaped from the forest floor. This wolf was much larger than any she had expected. This animal appeared to be larger than her. Could it have been...a werewolf?

The wolf landed on top of her and gnashed its jaws, lunging toward her neck. Candice drew in a deep breath and screamed. She was cursed to live in the mountains. She was about to be shred to pieces by a large wolf attack just like all those other people. Why the hell did her parents decide to raise her in this stupid town in the first place? She was going to fucking die in this stupid town.

She threw her arms up in defense and knocked against the wolf's lower jaw, hoping to deter them, but it was already too late. She screamed when she felt the warmth of the wolf's breath and its teeth sink into her neck. Warm blood dripped down her skin. She kicked her knees and legs against the beast's stomach as hard as she possibly could, trying to knock the large animal down.

There was more screaming. She couldn't focus. All she heard was the wolf growling. Suddenly, a bellowing bark rang through her ears and all went dark.

CANDICE WOKE LAYING ACROSS a gurney. She was surrounded by bright white lights and a handful of people dressed in green medical scrubs with different colored tops.

They had gloves on their hands as they pushed her through the brightness.

Her head was spinning. Her ears were ringing. And she suddenly noticed the blood soaking into the white sheet covering her. Flashes of dark, loud images shot through her mind. Loud barks and growls bounced through her mind. The male and a couple female nurses spoke to each other in loud, hurried voices, but Candice hardly followed.

"She was attacked in the forest." A woman with dark hair pulled back into a low ponytail said..

"Was it like the other attacks?" A man across her yelled back. They turned the gurney around a corner and rushed down another hallway.

"That's what they are saying, but I'm not understanding how this one has made it this far from the attack. And still alive!"

The gurney turned again and came to a slow stop where Candice found herself surrounded by foreign, but clean shining objects. The dark haired nurse that helped escort her down the hallways returned with what looked like an oxygen mask. She snapped the mask over Candice's face and she said, "You're losing a lot of blood. This is going to help."

Candice didn't say a word. She wasn't sure she actually could after the night she had. Soon her eyes were fluttering, fighting to stay awake with each breath.

"The couple who found her are saying another wolf appeared out of nowhere and attacked the one that attacked her. They rolled down the side of the hill when they got out of the car. They are lucky to be alive themselves. Two fighting wolves could have attacked them too."

"That doesn't make sense. Why would a wolf attack another so close to a human?"

"Territory, maybe?" The male nurse shrugged his shoulders,

and that's when Candice floated out of reality and into the darkness once again.

When Candice woke again, she found herself in another white room with a dim light over her head. She winced when she felt the brightness stab her in the temple. She turned to look around the room, but stopped when a sudden burning pain throbbed on the right side of her neck. The burning was replaced by a dull throbbing. She let her head fall back and closed her eyes.

"I'm still alive." She told the room in a whisper and smiled.

"Yes, you are, my Candy."

"Mom? How did you find me here?" Candice said, barely lifting her head. The throbbing pain in her head and neck made it difficult to keep her head up long.

"Your father heard about what happened on the police radio tonight. He dropped everything and escorted the ambulance to the hospital." Her mom sniffled, fighting back the tears that trickled down her face. She reached out for Candice's hand and took her cold fingers.

"Mom. I'll be fine. I'm still alive."

"You could have died out there tonight, Candy! What were you thinking, anyway? Why were you out jogging so late?" She squeezed her hand tight and Candice groaned aloud. She tried to turn her head toward her mother, but decided otherwise because of the excruciating pain.

"Kellie, leave Candice be. Let her rest." Her father had stepped into the room. She had seen his dark brown uniform for a brief moment when her eyes slipped closed. "She's not going to give you what you want right now. Let her be!"

Candice hardly noticed when her father carried her mother out into the hallway. Before long, she was falling back to sleep with the faint sound of her mother screaming her name from somewhere down the hall.

CHAPTER EIGHT

Candice shuffled into the hallway bathroom, her neck still feeling stiff and sore. Turning on the light, she stared at herself in the bathroom mirror for several long moments. She kept her eyes focused on the heavy gauze taped to her skin. Since being released from the hospital, she had yet to change her dressings, but she couldn't put it off much longer.

She carefully peeled the tape from the side of her neck, careful of the stitches beneath. She folded the bandage, not wishing to see any evidence of the wound on the cotton, and tossed it in the trash can. Washing her hands once more, she pulled out a fresh gauze and tape, but before she could finish, she caught sight of the wound on her neck.

The doctor told her to keep the stitches covered and be careful not to turn her neck too much to allow the wound to heal. He said it would take a few weeks to heal properly, but the wound she saw didn't make sense. Leaning closer to the mirror, the bite on her neck appeared to be nearly healed. There was no redness or swelling and the stitches were already gone, but she could see the indents where they once were, leaving her confused. Why had nobody told her the truth about what happened?

She covered the wound on her neck, leaving her unanswered questions alone. After cleaning up, she headed down the hallway into the living room. The soap opera she left playing on the television had switched to the news and they were talking about the attacks again. With a frown, she grabbed the remote and muted the television. She watched the images on the screen, catching the captions.

Another person had gone missing. And there was mention of the animal attack that happened only four nights ago. Even though they didn't mention Candice's name, she knew they were talking about her. She supposed everyone would be talking about her for a while.

"Hey, Candice!" Mary called out when she stepped through the front door of the c-store. With a gasp, she added, "My dear! What happened? Are you ok?"

"I'm ok..." She started, approaching the counter with a bag of candy and a tall can of iced tea in her hands. She didn't really need the snacks, but she couldn't stay cooped up in the house much longer. "But I don't remember what happened."

"I'm sorry to hear that." Mary responded, her brows furrowing. She lowered her eyes and rung up her snacks when Alex appeared from the back room of the store. She let out a gasp when she saw Candice, but she didn't pay any attention to it. Mary placed her things into a bag and handed it over.

As Candice took the bag and turned toward the front door, Alex came around the corner and called out to her friend. When she turned to meet her gaze, she noticed Alex's eyes had landed on the bandage.

"Omigod! What happened?"

"I don't remember." Candice said, heading out the door. Unfortunately, there were a few more people present than when she first arrived. She knew their faces and tried not to give her attention to the glances towards her neck. She slipped into her car and drove home to rest in peace.

SATURDAY NIGHT ROLLED AROUND, marking a week since Candice had been attacked. She was starting to feel semi-human again, freshly showered and sitting on the couch in a fresh pair of pajamas with the rest of the family. It seemed to be one of those lazy days because her younger brothers and her parents were still in their pajamas. Even the dog was laying comfortably on the floor, no doubt dreaming about greasy cheeseburgers and tacos.

Empty Styrofoam to-go containers and cups from Troy's Tavern sat on the coffee table. Everyone was settled in front of the television watching a movie when there was a sudden knock at the front door. Nobody moved except her dad who paused the movie. Her mom reached over and smacked him, whispering. "Why'd you do that? They'll notice."

"No, they won't. The TV isn't that loud. This house is soundproofed."

"No, it's not, dad!" Cody sat up and spoke loudly. Her mom whipped around, putting a finger to lips.

"Someone should just go get the door. One of you kids that is." Her dad said, leaning forward to grab his beer bottle. Candice and Kevin turned toward each other with narrowed gazes. She glared hard, staring him down, determined not to get up. He eventually blinked and let out a loud groan.

"I'll get you next time, Candy." He rose from the floor and disappeared out into the hallway. With another grumble, the front door opened.

"Who are you? What are you doing here?" Kevin grunted at

their unexpected visitor. Her parents both groaned, but didn't leave the couch. That's when they heard the muffled voice at the door. "I'm here to see Candice."

Everyone in the living room turned toward Candice. Both she and her mom rose from the couch and started out of the room. The door started to creak shut when Candice jumped over the back of the couch, nearly tripping to the floor. Her mom beat her to the foyer when Kevin tried to shoo away their visitor. "Candice is busy right now. We're watching a movie, dude. She'll call you later I'm guessing."

"Wait! How do you know she has my number?"

"Don't worry, boy. I know who you are." Her mom shut the door in a hurry, shooing Kevin off to the living room. She leaned against the door, keeping Candice from opening it back up.

"Mom! What the hell! Who's there at the door? Who was it?"

"It's Zak, Candy. But I don't want you going out that door, you understand me? You may be a grown ass woman, but I'm not just going to let you go out there and speak to him. I'm very open-minded to all the things you want to do with your life, but not with him!

"I remember what he did to you and I won't have him around again! I've also heard plenty about him around town. And I forbid you from seeing him while you are living under my roof, Candice Anne!" Her mom said.

Candice huffed and spun on her heel to head back to the living room when her father appeared in the doorway. She stopped and stepped aside, turning her attention to her parents as her dad came out into the foyer.

"You mean under our roof, Kellie. You're not the only one who makes the rules around here. Let her speak to him. How do we know why he's here or what's going on?" Her dad spoke with a soft voice in very sharp contrast to her mom's commanding voice. Candice hesitated leaving.

"Jack, I don't want him to hurt Candy again!"

"I get it, Kell. But we didn't raise our kids to hold grudges. Maybe he's different. Maybe he's grown up since then. It's been five years and you know how people talk their bullshit around town. How do we know what's true? People change."

"And how am I supposed to trust that things have changed? How am I supposed to know things will be different, Jack?"

"I can't give you that answer, Kellie. We just need to trust Candice to make the right decision. She's a grown adult now and we should respect her enough to allow her that. And we should go back to our movie, anyway."

Her dad slipped an arm across her mom's shoulders, trying to guide her away from the front door. Candice backs away from them when they finally head back to the living room, her mother glancing over her shoulder but once.

When Candice finally opened the front door, Zak had stepped off the porch and was walking towards his little red sports car. Stones crunched under his canvas sneakers as Candice yelled out his name. He stopped and turned, his face brightening with a wide smile.

"Candice! If you're busy, I don't want to disturb you." Zak stopped and leaned against the front bumper of his car, watching her tiptoe across the sharp rocks and weeds in her bare feet.

He had hardly changed from how she remembered him except his normally spiky hair was slicked back with grease and those black baggy slacks weren't so baggy. His eyebrow and lip both had sterling silver rings now. And he had a colorful new sleeve tattoo on his left arm that stopped at his elbow. She wasn't looking at the design though. Not when she met those emerald green eyes.

"Don't worry about that." She was breathing a little heavy,

almost whispering when she spoke. "Sorry if my little brother and mom were being rude to you."

"It's alright. I wouldn't have expected anything less. Not like I left a great impression when I left town, you know?" He said with the ghost of a smile appearing at the corners of his lips. His undivided attention on her made her suddenly feel extra warm.

"What are you doing here, anyway?" Candice said with a smile. With her hand in her pocket, she pinched herself trying not to let on how happy seeing him made her. That sparkle in his eyes made her heart melt and her knees buckle.

For a moment, she forgot just why she felt such bitterness toward him. The feeling didn't last long though. The brief reminiscing of moments past faded quickly when she remembered how he left her broken-hearted. A sudden ache in her chest reminded her of the last time she saw him.

"I came to see you. Came to see how you were doing because I heard there was another attack. I heard people whispering about you. And I heard you survived, but I wanted to make sure you were ok for myself." Candice froze, unsure how to respond. He continued.

"I know you're probably still angry with me for what I did to you back then, but I still care about you, Ace. I don't want to see you hurt. I'm glad you seem ok considering what I heard." He took a step forward, slipping a hand to cup her cheek. She stared into his eyes for a long moment, feeling that warmth in the pit of her stomach again. His eyes drifted towards her neck, but he remained silent.

He caressed the side of her face and down the side of her neck, brushing his fingers over the heavy gauze. He frowned before lifting his eyes to meet hers again. "I'm sorry this happened to you, Candice. I'm sorry I wasn't there to protect you. I should've been there."

"Zak...you couldn't have protected me from a wolf. Not one that big."

He didn't respond. Instead, a gentle smile curled across his lips. There was a twinkle in his eyes that paused the world. She forgot about every ounce of doubt that creeped into her. As he leaned in and pressed his lips to hers, the moment their lips touched, that familiar spark ignited deep within her. Butterflies fluttered in her stomach and that ache in her chest disappeared.

CHAPTER NINE

When Candice walked through the front door of Troy's Tavern, she immediately scanned the dining area for her best friend in the dining area. The place was packed for an early Sunday afternoon. Not a single table was empty the moment she walked inside. She saw many locals seated, but there were many strangers.

"I'm sorry, ma'am, but there's going to be a wait for a table." The young woman with her long dark hair tied into a high ponytail took a step toward her, holding a clipboard. Candice glanced at her and frowned. She had no doubt that she was older than the young hostess, but she didn't think she was old enough to be called ma'am quite yet. "Is it just going to be you dining this afternoon?"

"Um, no. I am supposed to meet a friend here and she might already be seated." Candice spoke softly and glanced around the large dining once more—slowing down. She quickly spotted her, sitting in a booth near one of the front windows towards the back of the room. "There she is!"

Without another word, the young hostess turned and

grabbed a menu, escorting Candice over. Since Valerie was already seated, she had a tall glass of iced tea sitting in front of her, already sweating with condensation. She was lifting the glass to her lips the moment Candice walked up. A huge smile appeared across her lips when she finally set it back down.

"Hey, girlie! I was wondering when you'd show up."

"I was still lying in bed when you called. I had plans of getting out of my pajamas before you called. Especially after this last week." Candice said, picking up the menu that hostess had placed on the table in front of her. Valerie glanced in her direction and frowned, finally noticing the bandage on her neck.

"I heard there was another attack. People were saying it was you, but I didn't want to believe it." Valerie said. Candice lifted the menu, wondering what new dish she could try in the Tavern. She had a hard time deciding when much of the menu sounded really delicious. Too bad there were no pictures. Only descriptions.

"What happened, Candice?"

"You know I really don't remember very well. It was all... strange." Candice started, still glancing through the menu. "When I think about it, none of it makes any sense to me. People are always staring at me too and that doesn't help."

"I'm sorry, girlie. I'm glad you made it out on such a gorgeous day! A day like this is meant to be enjoyed outside! Out somewhere! Not sitting at home... reading."

"Whatever, Val. Ok. You got me out of the house for lunch."

"I know. My fried pickles should be here very soon too!" Val almost bounced and clapped her hands lightly out of excitement. Candice smiled to herself and lowered her gaze, taking another glance over the menu to make her final choices.

When the waitress finally came by, she took Candice's order of iced tea and a bottomless backet of fries with a side of ranch. When the waitress disappeared, she soon reappeared with

Valerie's plate of fried pickles and a tall glass filled almost to the brim with iced tea. A lemon wedge sat on the lip of the glass and Candice immediately plucked it, squeezing the juice into her drink.

"We haven't gone to lunch together in a while. Tell what else is new with you besides..." Valerie started, glancing at Candice's neck again. She picked up one of the fried pickles and dipped it into the ranch. "I heard Zak's back in town."

"I know. He stopped at my house last night during our family movie time. He said he came over just to see if I was ok."

"Shut up! Are you serious?"

"Yeah. I'm not sure I want to talk about it though." She said, taking a drink of her iced tea. She watched Valerie as she sucked down a few more fried pickles dipped in ranch before she finally spoke again.

"Tell me what's been going on with you. Was there something that you wanted to talk about, Valerie?"

"Oh yeah. Well..." Valerie started, sucking the dollop of ranch that had splattered across the plate with her finger. "You know it's hard for me to get out without the kid. As much as I love my boy, grandma needs a break once in a while. She has her own job too, and I just love hanging out with little Taylor. But I actually did want to talk to you about moving in together..."

"Yeah, of course. We've been talking about it since high school. Only..."

"Only we went in two different directions. You can see how well that's working out for me, Candy." She rolled her eyes and grabbed another pickle chip. "Do you really want to live together though? I know you've been wanting to get out of this place for a while now. And since you just graduated..."

"Why would you assume I wouldn't want to live together, Val?"

"I overheard what your band was saying about going on the

road and touring. Or something…" She spoke in a soft voice, lifting her eyes to meet Candice's gaze. Candice grabbed a fried pickle from the large, nearly empty basked, dipping it into the ranch before popping the whole thing in to her mouth. She paused mid bite when she finally had a moment to process Valerie's words and frowned hard.

She was waiting for this conversation to come up. She just didn't realize it would be so soon after graduation. She still didn't know where her life was going. She knew she would be touring with her band, but she didn't know more than that. Finally, she swallowed and placed her hands on the table in front of her.

"I was afraid you heard. We can't really leave until we have some money for gas and shit though so we're not leaving until the end of the summer. We're all working to save up some money. Are you sure you want to live together though? With Taylor around and our lives being so much different than before?"

"Yes! You're never gonna get rid of me that easy. Besides, I think it would be way more fun to live with my girl rather than some dumb boy." Valerie said, rolling her eyes as she slurped down a couple more fried pickles. Candice chuckled softly under her breath. She was so enthralled by her fried pickles that she wasn't even sure her friend was even paying attention to their conversation. That is, she thought so until Valerie's final comment about living with some dumb boy.

"Are you referring to Cyrus? Or are you seeing someone new?" Candice raised her eyebrow at Valerie who smiled wickedly. Except Valerie just shrugged and shook her head, her attention back on the basket of fried pickles.

"Not really. It's hard being a single mother as young as me and trying to date. There're guys out there with kids, but they have too much baby mama drama. Or those guys with no kids who want nothing to do with a kid. I swear there's never a guy who's somewhere in between."

"Well, let me save up some money first. We can figure out the details later."

"I told you not to worry about any of that, Candy —" Valerie said, picking at the last of the crispy fried pickles laying at the bottom of the basket. Candice met a familiar pair of warm hazel eyes and instantly wish she hadn't when Eric seemed to be interested in interrupting their otherwise private conversation. "Hey Candice!"

Valerie flipped her blonde hair over her shoulder, turning her attention to see who had interrupted their chat. A moment later, Eric rushed over from the billiards table, and slipped in the booth beside Candice.

"Well, hello...ladies." A crooked grin appeared at the corner of his lips, glancing between the two women. "What's up?"

"Just lunch, Eric." Candice glanced over at him, reaching for her glass of iced tea. She took a slow sip from the straw before she spoke again. "What's up with you?"

"I don't think I expected to run into you here, Candice." He started, turning his attention completely on Candice, but she just glanced away. She had too much going on to be dealing with him. Valerie just stared at him for a long moment, looking rather annoyed. She cleared her throat and spoke.

"I'm sorry, but who are you? I finally have a kid free day with my best friend and you're interrupting us. You can talk to Candy later. Eric, is it?"

"Of course." Eric said, turning his attention over to Valerie. Candice watched the two of them while they just stared at each other. Finally, he rose from the booth and took another glance at Candice. "I'll talk to you later, Candice. I'm glad you're doing ok."

Candice acknowledged his comment with a smile. When

Eric finally disappeared back toward the billiards tables, Valerie leaned in closer and whispered softly, watching Candice with a noticeable side eye. "What the hell was that, Candy? I thought you weren't talking to anybody?"

"I'm not." Candice said, but Valerie didn't seem convinced. Valerie lowered her eyes, pressing the tip of her finger down into the bottom of the basket for the crumbs. She didn't seem upset, but Candice wasn't so sure either. They may have been childhood best friends, but a lot had changed since Candice last lived in Hollow's Creek.

"Girl, it's all good. I get it. It's not like we've been able to spend a lot of time together since you've been away at college and I had Taylor. When I was with Cyrus, my whole life was about the three of us. I guess I should expect a few surprises." She shrugged, taking a long drink of her iced tea. A soft smile appeared on her lips. "We can talk more about this whole thing later on once you're ready. I know you have a lot going on. It's cool."

Valerie slipped out her wallet and counted the cash. Rising from her seat, she slipped her purse over her shoulder and leaned in to hug Candice. Pulling away, Candice leaned back and lifted her eyes, feeling horrible about what just happened. She never would've expected to see Eric at the Tavern.

"I gotta go pick up my boy. We have plans tonight. I got him a puppy!"

"Oh, that sounds great! I'm sure he'll be really excited, Val."

"I know. He's been asking for another dog for a while now. I figure he's old enough to learn about taking care of something other than himself. Goldie was already grown when he came along. We'll talk soon, I'm sure." Valerie said.

"What happened to Goldie? Did she pass or something? She wasn't that old, right?"

"That's because she wasn't, but uh. Something got Goldie a

few weeks ago." The smile faded from her lips and she tucked a lock of her hair behind her ear. She spoke in a soft voice. "I don't really want to talk about it, Candy. I can't really talk about it."

Candice frowned hard. She hadn't heard about Goldie and wondered if it was related to all the missing persons and animal attacks that had been happening lately. She wanted to ask more, but she wasn't sure she should. "See ya, Val!"

"Talk soon!" She lifted her freshly manicured hand and waved with a gentle smile curling over her lips, heading towards the front door. Candice returned her attention to the half-eaten basket of fries she had ordered that was still on the table. She grabbed the bottle of ketchup and squirted a generous glop out before putting it back. Grabbing a couple of fries at once, she swiped them through the large pile of ketchup and took a bite.

The saltiness of the fries was cut in half with the glob of ketchup at the end, but she loved every bite. She hadn't always been a salty fan, but whatever spice the cook used on the fries was perfection. Maybe seasoning salt, she thought to herself. When the waitress walked by, Candice called out to her with a smile appearing on her lips.

"Excuse me, miss? Can I get another order of fries, please? To go."

VALERIE HOPPED IN HER little old SUV and drove across town, toward the Native American reservation. Cyrus' parents lived just south of Hollow's Creek just outside of the boundaries of the reservation. When she saw the turn off, she pulled to the side of the highway to let the other cars traveling pass before she found a clearing to pull onto his parents' property.

Valerie parked outside by the fence instead of pulling into

the yard this time, just like Cyrus' parents asked her to do. She wasn't family. The only reason she was even allowed anywhere near their property was because of Taylor. They still had difficulty accepting that a blonde-haired, blue-eyed woman gave them their first grandchild by their only son.

His parents never approved of their Native American son dating a pale, white woman from outside of the reservation. She still remembered the way Cyrus' parents made her feel disrespected every single time they were together. And she hated it. She hated that most of their arguments had something to do with his family, their cultural, and racial differences. The fights never really ended well either.

They would break up and get back together every few weeks or months, if they were lucky. She never did understand it, but she always loved how different Cyrus was from the scrawny white boys they went to school with. She found him a mystery because she thought of him as the strong, silent type. She couldn't stay away from him no matter how hard she tried. Even when she ended up pregnant with his baby.

The worst part of it all wasn't just how they treated her during her relationship with Cyrus, but they wouldn't acknowledge her pregnancy when it happened. There was no way the baby could have been Cyrus'. Even after Taylor was born, they denied the child was his despite the striking resemblance and darker skin tone compared to her.

And now, here he was sharing custody of Taylor. Everything had changed. His parents even loved seeing the little boy every other weekend, but they wouldn't let Valerie inside the house. As long as she knew her boy was safe, she didn't care. She was just happy her son had the relationship with his father and his family unlike herself.

She stepped up on to the porch and took a seat on one of the old, sun-bleached rocking chairs, hoping Cyrus would bring

Taylor out soon. She pulled out her phone and opened one of her many puzzle games, bouncing her knee.

"Mommy!" Taylor yelled out when he came crashing through the front door. He attacked her with arms wide open, wrapping himself around her knees. The force almost knocked her off her seat. She laughed softly and rose, leaning down to pick him up. A wide smile took over his face.

Holding the young boy close, she glanced at the screen door that Taylor had just come running out of. She looked at her little boy, resting his head on her shoulder, and spoke in a soft voice. "Was daddy coming out with you, Taylor?"

Before the little boy could answer though, the screen door opened and Cyrus stepped out in a pair of gray sweats and a muscle shirt. His long, dark hair hung over one shoulder and he had a smile on his face. For a moment, Valerie remembered how she had been attracted to him, but she quickly pushed those thoughts from her mind. That wasn't their relationship anymore. All of that had changed, and they had both moved on. "Thanks for taking him for the day, Cyrus. He really missed his daddy."

"Yeah. Of course. It's fun hanging out with the little guy. I'm just sorry I can't be around much more than that, Val. Just work and stuff."

"It's fine, Cyrus. You don't need to explain anything. And I'd rather not talk about all that stuff in front of him." She turned closer to Cyrus, trying to keep her voice down with the sleepy little boy on her opposite shoulder. When she glanced over at him, she knew he would be out before she made it to the vehicle.

"Yeah. Of course, Val. I guess I'll see you and the little guy around again soon? Next weekend right?" He said, following Valerie down from the porch and across the yard. She spoke softly.

"Yeah. I mean, if you want to see him... that's up to you. If you want to hang out with him, Cyrus, just let me know. Give me a call or text me or whatever."

"I will, yeah." He smiled again, stuffing his hands in his pockets. Valerie smiled back and turned toward her car. Somehow, she carefully maneuvered the little boy into his car seat without disturbing him too much. Cyrus called out when she shut the back car door. "You two be safe, yeah?"

"Bye." She waved and climbed in behind the wheel. She glanced in the rear-view mirror and smiled, ready to go home and take a quiet nap. Later that evening, she had plans for the birthday boy just like she mentioned to Candice. She was probably looking forward to them even more than Taylor.

CHAPTER TEN

W hat do we get him, mommy?" Taylor said. He walked slowly toward the front door of the pet store, barely able to see in front of him. Valerie followed right behind, pulling her hair into a ponytail. With the long, hot summer days, she was grateful her hair was long enough to tie up again. She didn't even care if her hair stuck out all over like a cockatoo.

"We should get him some food and snacks, don't you think? Maybe a leash."

"And toys? The doggy needs toys."

They went down one of the dog aisles and turned the corner, finding plenty of rope and tennis balls hanging from pegs. The puppy yipped with excitement, struggling and squirming in Taylor's arms. Valerie stepped over to help. "Let me see the puppy."

"But mommy! I want the puppy!"

"He's not a tiny puppy, Taylor. He's going to get away, eventually."

"Okay," he pouted softly, stepping over to look at the colorful collection of dog toys. There were squeaky toys, bright colors and patterns, furry creatures, and even different sized plastic bones. He crouched down to those he could reach, sorting through the different options. A dark haired clerk, in her blue collared shirt, stepped over. Jasmine was printed on the name tag over her left breast.

"Hey, Taylor, Val. Did you get a new puppy? He's very cute!"

"Yes. My puppy." Taylor hardly looked up from the pile he had collected. She smiled softly and stepped over to Valerie, who had almost successfully calmed the whining puppy down. She lowered her head and spoke softly near Valerie's ear. "Does he know what happened to Goldie?"

With a sideway glance toward her son, thankfully still occupied, she shook her head. She leaned in closer and whispered back. "No, he doesn't. He's only four."

Valerie hadn't expected more than one person to ask her about Goldie in the same day. She had adopted the older grown golden retriever before Taylor was born, but the moment he came home from the hospital, Goldie became extremely protective of him. What happened to the dog was truly terrible. All that blood. The cops couldn't tell Goldie or the man apart. They also couldn't explain the presence of all the brown fur either.

"What do the cops say?" Jasmine spoke a little louder, but kept her voice soft and calm, not wanting to draw any further attention. Valerie stood silent for several moments, thinking about how to answer. Since law enforcement came out and checked out the scene, her father told her not to talk about it to anybody, but she didn't see the harm in saying anything here. She had even scanned the parking lot before stepping inside. At such a late hour, there weren't many people at the pet store.

"The sheriff tells me he thinks it was a large animal. A wolf or a mountain lion. Something like that, but Lieutenant Jones doesn't believe it. She thinks she knows who did it, but she has no proof either."

Jasmine raised a brow and parted her lips to speak but stopped herself when she noticed Taylor rising from the floor. He carried a blue and orange rope and a couple of tennis balls with him. "We need a basket, mommy."

"Here. Let me take them and you can go grab one, Taylor." Jasmine said, putting her hands out to receive the bundle in his arms. With a smile spreading across his face, he dumped the toys and went running to the front of the store. Jasmine looked over at Valerie when they were sure he wouldn't hear them.

"She thinks she knows who did it? What do you mean, Val?"

"I'm sure you've heard plenty of stories about Hollow's Creek. The supernatural stuff that goes on. You've lived around here long enough by now," Valerie started, but Jasmine frowned, shaking her head. "Werewolves prowl the forest. In fact, the richest family in town is a pack of werewolves."

"What? You mean the Grays? Are you going to tell me vampires exist too?"

"I haven't met one yet, but I'm in no rush to do so either. Just be careful about accepting a rose from a stranger. The darker the rose, the more dangerous the vampire. That's what I've heard, anyway."

Left speechless, Jasmine frowned, but Valerie was too busy watching Taylor. He carried a blue basket with him. There were a few more toys in the basket. A crooked curled over her lips, unsure she would get all of his choices, but for the moment, it didn't matter. The smile on his face was worth it.

From the corner of her eye, she thought she saw something or someone dressed in all black peaking from around the corner. She whipped her head around, but nobody was there. Not even a shadow. She could've sworn she was being watched, but it was already getting late. The shadows were growing in the pet store. Maybe her mind was just playing tricks.

She couldn't shake the feeling though. In fact, she could feel someone's eyes on her, but every time she turned, there was nobody. And she hated feeling so vulnerable when she was alone with Taylor. She needed to be strong for him.

Her and Taylor were almost to her car when her fears were finally confirmed. She noticed a pronounced shadow in the corner of her eye. She didn't want to draw any attention, but she wanted to get the three of them in the vehicle quickly.

"C'mon, baby. Let's get in the car." She spoke in a calm voice, getting Taylor and the puppy into the backseat. He was rambling on about all the things he couldn't wait to do with his new puppy except Valerie couldn't focus. She was listening and observing her surroundings without alerting Taylor.

She finally got them both strapped in and shut the door, glancing around the parking lot. That's when a cool blade pressed against the base of her throat. She tried to swallow, trying to remain calm, but whoever held the knife to her throat had a firm grip.

"Don't look at me." He spoke in a rough and modified voice like one of the robots on Taylor's cartoons. She wasn't going to do something stupid like get a better look at him. The odds of being stabbed were already pretty high, she realized. She closed her eyes and squeezed them tight.

"I know who you are. You need to keep your voice down in public. Don't you know you shouldn't gossip about things you don't understand? I know who you are, blondie. And I know what your father is doing—"

"I don't know wha—"

"Don't fucking interrupt me, bitch." He snarled in her ear. "I didn't ask you to speak. Just listen. If your father doesn't stop what he's doing... that only means trouble for you. And that baby of yours."

"Don't you touch him!" She said through gritted teeth, feeling the blade of the knife dig into her skin. The stalker just pressed the blade tighter against her neck, causing her to lean her head up. "I said. If your father doesn't stop what he's doing... that only means trouble for you. And that baby of yours. Nod if you understand me."

Her stalker released some of the pressure on her neck and she nodded slowly. She kept her eyes closed until she felt the blade disappear. She realized whoever they were wasn't a fan of her father and his politics. Unfortunately, it wasn't the first time that she had been threatened over her father's choices. She resented being his daughter because the two of them hardly saw each other let alone spoke. She didn't know what her father was up to this time.

Her stalker finally disappeared. Droplets of blood fell to the front of her shirt. She wiped the back of her hand across her throat, noticing the smear. She finally swallowed the lump in her throat, the sting of tears in her eyes. Closing them once more, she took a deep breath and quickly slipped inside the car. Her hands were visibly shaking when she set them on the steering wheel. After locking the car doors, she took Taylor and his puppy home.

As she drove, she wondered if she should mention the attack to anybody, but she wasn't sure who would be the best person to pass the information to. Her father would most likely try to convince her that she was delusional. Her mother brushed off anything having to do with him. And unfortunately, things were still tense between her and Cyrus, and Candice seemed to be having her own issues. There was nobody to confide in, but someone needed to know before it was too late.

CHAPTER ELEVEN

With both her bags slung over her shoulder, Candice tiptoed down the hallway and peaked into Susan's office. Her back was hunched over her desk, focused on a stack of papers in front of her. Candice took the opportunity to rush past her door, muttering farewell on her way out of the administrative building.

When she climbed into her car, she reached over and opened the glove box to grab the pack of cigarettes she kept hidden. She didn't smoke very often, but today was one of those days where she had been itching for one all day. Once she had the car started, she slipped one between her lips and lit the end. She took a deep drag before she finally shifted into gear and pulled out of her parking space, heading home.

Moments later, the first few notes of one of her favorite Lil Wayne songs came through the speakers. She turned up the volume. She could feel the beat vibrating through her body with each heavy bass drop. The trees whizzed by and the warm, sticky air floated in through the cracked windows as a bundle of storm clouds floated down from the other side of the mountain.

When she arrived home, the driveway was empty, but she still parked by the sidewalk. Her parents must've been at work. She popped her head in the living room, greeting her brothers who were hyper focused on the television screen. Of course, they were playing video games like every other afternoon when she came home. They probably didn't even notice her come through the front door either.

She shut her bedroom door and tossed her bags aside, peeling her clothes off. She had been looking forward to a nice cold shower since earlier that afternoon. It had been a hot one and she could feel the scorching heat radiate from her.

After a long cool shower, she went digging through her closet for something to wear. She quickly found a pair of stone washed boot cut jeans and her favorite purple lace blouse. She set aside a pair of ankle boots and grabbed her little makeup bag with hearts and lips printed on the fabric, pawing through the contents. Candice wasn't a girly girl and didn't have a huge collection of makeup, but she always kept a tube of mascara, a decent collection of eye pencils, and lip gloss just for special occasions.

Once she had her mascara, a dash of purple eye liner, and hot pink lips painted on, she headed back downstairs and popped her head in the living room again. Both her brothers were still glued to the television.

"I'm heading out. I'll see you two later... Kevin? Cody?" She waited only a brief moment and accepted Kevin's hand wave as acknowledgement before turning to head out the door. "Call me if you two need anything."

She drove down to Troy's Tavern. The parking lot was almost full, which she expected with half price drinks on a Thursday evening. Stepping through the front door, the air conditioning was a welcome change from the muggy summer day. People were laughing, cheering, and even a few having pleasantly mundane conversations about home life and how they hated their jobs. A quick glance told her most of the crowd was local people she knew.

Tonight there was no hostess, and she took a spot near the corner of the crowded area by the bar. Candice glanced around when she heard a loud cheer from nearby. All but one of the pool tables were occupied.

"Well, hey there, Candice." Troy with his salt and peppered auburn hair stepped over with a smile curling over his lips. "What can I get you tonight?"

"Hello, Troy!" Candice smiled, stuffing her driver's license back in place when he waved it off. She took a quick glance up at the menu hanging over the liquor shelves in the corner, but she already knew what she wanted.

"Let me just get a beer. The house beer sounds good." She said. Troy nodded and grabbed a freshly cleaned glass from the rack nearby, filling it at the tap. Troy handed her the glass, and she took a drink, savoring the skunky ice-cold brew. From the corner of her eye, she noticed someone come up beside her. They had a pool cue in one hand.

"Let me get one of those too, Troy."

"You got it, Eric!" Troy grinned and went to pour another beer from the tap. Candice turned to meet the familiar face, catching a twinkle in his dark eyes. A crooked grin appeared on his lips, setting his pool stick against the side of the bar.

"Well, well... I was wondering when I'd see you around again. I was really disappointed when you left the party." Eric frowned slightly. "And then I heard about what happened."

"I think you know where to find me, Eric. It's a small town and almost everybody knows who I am around here." She took another drink when Troy turned toward them, handing Eric his drink. He put his hand to his face and spoke directly to Candice in a whisper.

"Be careful with this one, Candy. He's a lady killer around here." Troy winked and disappeared to the end of the bar to fill more drink orders. Candice turned her attention back to Eric, her lips pursed slightly. With fluttering lashes and a ghost of a smirk playing at her lips, she spoke. "Bartender says you're a lady killer."

"Me? Nooo. Not me. I only have eyes for one girl here."

"Yeah, ok." She said, sarcasm dripping from her voice. She rolled her eyes, returning to her glass on the counter. She took another drink, keeping her hand cupped loosely around it. Eric glanced down at the way she held her beer close, but didn't say a word like she half expected for a moment.

"C'mon! You believe him over me? We went to high school together and you've known him, what, five minutes? If that?"

"More than five minutes, but yes! Exactly!" She never once lifted her eyes.

"Well, maybe one of these days, I can change your mind." He shrugged with a cute smile she had never seen before. "Hey. Do you wanna come join us for a few games of pool? One of my buddies didn't show up and we could use another person to make the teams even..."

Her heart raced in her chest when he said that, not sure she just wanted to play with a bunch of random guys she didn't know well. Thankfully, she hadn't seen Zak when she stepped inside, but she turned to double check. Luckily, he wasn't anywhere to be seen. Even though her heart was telling her otherwise, she didn't want to see him.

"If you were hoping to see Zak, he's not around tonight. His girlfriend is in town. Or whatever the fuck she is," he said, a hint of annoyance on his tone.

Girlfriend. Candice bit down on her bottom lip and

swallowed the hurt brought on hearing that word. She knew seeing him yesterday was too good to be true. With a nod, she slipped off the stool, taking her beer along. "Sure, I'll join you."

She followed Eric to the farthest corner from the dining area, just past the pool tables, and set her drink down. She grabbed a stick from the wall and prepped the end with the chalk nearby, directing her gaze in Eric's direction. "I wasn't looking for Zak."

"Oh, no? Then who were you looking for?"

"Well, I was looking for him, but I wanted to make sure he wasn't around." She said, really not wanting to share her feelings with Eric of all people. She had a seat and waited for her turn, finishing off her beer. Eric and his two friends glanced at each other.

After a few games between the four of them, the night grew old and eventually, Eric's friends left, heading home to their wives. Long before the end of the night, most of the bar patrons and pool players had left. Candice and Eric were the only two still playing.

She leaned in with her pool cue and took a shot, winning yet another game with a smirk curling over her lips. She let out a laugh. Even with several beers and a plate of nachos polished off between them, she was still the better player.

"Where'd you learn to play?"

"My dad taught me when I was younger. He used to play a lot more when I was a kid. Before he was recruited to homicide." She twisted the chalk, greatly feeling the influence of alcohol in her veins by now. He chuckled and went around the table, collecting the balls for a new game. Troy called out for last call and Eric setup the final game.

"How about we place a bet this round? To up the stakes a little. What do you think?" He said, taking a step toward her. She nodded, holding the pool stick between her legs, leaning up against the opposite edge of the table.

"Ok. And what should we bet? No money."

"No, no money." He paused. Even after a few drinks, his dark, sparkling eyes remained on her. A crooked grin appeared at the corner of his lips. He put a hand up, leaving a single finger in the air while awaiting her response. "If I win, I want you to go out on a date with me. Just one date."

"Ok. That's fair. And if I win?"

"If you win..." He started. She could see the gears in his mind turning. The pool stick thumped on the floor when she set the butt down beside her. She casually rolled her eyes and leaned over to grab her beer from the table, waiting impatiently for his response. She took a drink before he finally answered. "If you win, lady's choice at the movies."

"Wait—wh-what? That makes it sound like you'll win either way! That's not how this works here, Eric!" She squealed at him as he leaned down over the table. Aiming toward the perfect triangle of balls at the end of the table, he shrugged.

"Well, unless you have something better to offer, mine stands." He said with a wicked grin curling over his lips. With a satisfying crack, the balls scattered across the table and a couple of the striped balls sunk.

When it was finally her turn, Candice pocketed most of the solid-colored balls into the sockets, but by closing time, when the only ball remaining was the black eight ball, she missed leaving Eric with another chance to pocket the rest of the striped. Thankfully, he had just enough time to sink each one of them while Troy and his staff finished wiping down the tables. He even sank the black eight ball.

"Well...looks like you won." Candice pouted playfully and went to put the pool sticks back on the rack. She grabbed her things and glanced over her shoulder. "Are you coming?"

"Yeah. I'll be right back. I gotta go take a leak before we leave." A bashful grin appeared on his face and he turned away, jogging through the dining room. He disappeared down the back hall. Candice smiled to herself. She wouldn't admit it to him, but she had a great time playing pool with Eric and his friends—something she never would expect.

One of the waitresses appeared from the back and lifted a chair from the floor, placing it on the surface of the table. Candice slipped into her old jean jacket and went out the front door. She stood out on the front porch of the Tavern and looked up at the sky, waiting for Eric. As she stared at the twinkling stars in the darkness, a wolf howled in the distance.

CHAPTER TWELVE

D o you believe in monsters, Eric?"

"What do you mean by monsters, Candice? Wait. Don't tell me. You've been listening to the gossip about the murders up the mountain, too?" Eric asked, hopping down from the porch. A shy smile appeared across Candice's lips and she nodded. He threw his head back and laughed, reaching for the pack of cigarettes in his front pocket. Candice followed him as he started across the parking lot.

"How can you not hear about them? And after what happened to me, I have a hard time not believing in monsters, Eric." She said, her voice dropping slightly. A sudden silence hung between them and he slipped a cigarette between his lips. She glanced in his direction, taking a few more steps.

"I don't know the whole story about what happened to you. I don't really watch the news and I sure don't listen to gossip. I've had to deal with it most of my life being the rich boy." He started, mumbling against the filter. He stopped to light the end and took a deep drag. "Is that what makes you think there are monsters out there? You know they're all just stupid fucking stories our parents told us when we were kids. To keep us out of the woods away from the real beasts."

"What real beasts?"

"You know like wolves, coyotes, mountain lions, and other predators that may try to rip us apart no matter how big or small we are. But there's no such thing as the monsters you're referring to, Candy. And to answer your question, I don't believe in monsters, but I do believe that staying stuck on Zak is a horrible decision." He said, quickly catching up to her. Candice stopped and glanced in his direction, caught off guard by his response.

Candice stood silent for a moment. A wave of light flashed over his face and his hazel eyes glittered under the tall parking lights. An innocent smile appeared on her face and her cheeks flushed with embarrassment.

"How do you know I'm still stuck on Zak, Eric?" She said, following him through the parking lot to his car. He sat on the rear bumper, taking another long drag from his cigarette before offering it to her. She turned it down, and he took another drag, smoke billowing from his nose when he finally spoke.

"I don't listen to gossip, but Zak and I..." He paused for a long moment before he continued. "We're old buddies. We played sports back in high school together and we still talk once in a while. He told me he went to see you, but he's not a good idea. He has plenty of secrets to keep, not even including other girls, but I thought you already knew that when he left town with Quinn. All I'm saying is don't trust him because you deserve better than that, Candy." He said, finishing his cigarette and Candice sat beside him on the bumper.

"Who said I was getting involved with Zak again? I know he's bad for me. I've probably known since before I found out about Quinn." She said, watching those dark eyes of his. "Besides, didn't I win the chance to pick a movie on a date with you?"

"I'm glad to hear you say that. I haven't been able to stop thinking about that night when we kissed, Candy. I felt something and I know you did too." He started. A smile curled over his lips and he lowered his gaze for a moment, lowering his voice. "I don't want to lose a chance with you over someone who treated you the way he did."

"Who said you will, Eric?" She spoke in a soft voice, reaching for his hand, which he accepted. He lifted his gaze to meet hers with the ghost of a smile curling at his lips. With a gentle squeeze, he let her hand go and rose from the rear bumper of his vehicle.

"I should get going home, Candice." He said, stopping with a cautious, yet narrowed gaze in Candice's direction before turning to get in. She stepped away, crossing her arms over her chest when the engine came to life. Music came bumping through the speakers and he yelled back. "And stay away from Zak."

LATER THAT NIGHT, CANDICE woke when a thunder bolt shattered the quiet of the night. Lightning flashed brightly and suddenly rain started to pour. She shifted among the covers, listening to the rain hit the roof. Even over the roar of the pouring rain, the sound of howling wolves floated through her mind. Each howl louder than the last. Before long, she started to drift off to the music of the night.

Thunder rumbled and lightning flashed. The window overlooking the side courtyard creaked open, letting in several big fat drops of rain. A sudden low growl rumbled through the quiet room. A shadow appeared on the windowsill and slunk inside, crawling toward the bed where Candice lay among the blankets.

The shadow crawled forward, reaching the edge of the bed where her chipped pink polished toe nails stuck up in the air. Candice shifted and kicked a leg out but stayed fast asleep. The shadow stood motionless at the foot of the bed for a moment, hovering over her.

She shifted again. Her tank top curled over her torso to expose the smooth skin of her stomach, her naked breast peeking from the top. The shadow shifted into the familiar form of a large black wolf and lowered to the bed. She let out a gentle, sleepy groan, and the wolf snarled.

Thunder crashed. Lightning flashed. The animal crawled toward the top of the bed, its black fur brushing against Candice's exposed torso. Still, she stayed sound asleep, but when she shifted once more, the wolf lunged closer.

With barred teeth, the animal's claws grasped at her shoulders, drawing blood. She let out another sleepy groan. The obsidian furred animal lifted its head and with the crash of another bolt of lightning, bit into Candice's neck. She let out a deep moan and arched into the large animal holding her down.

Her eyes shot open. It was then that she saw a pair of glowing green eyes and a pair of bloodied canine fangs in the corner of her room. She had woken up, but the darkness had been replaced with the bright light of the morning sunlight.

Her hand went to her neck, but nothing was there. No blood. No cut. Just the bandage she still wore over her healing wound. She patted the sheets beneath her. She found no blood anywhere. From the shadows haunting her dreams to the blood that flowed from the wound on her neck to the scratches on her shoulder. Even the weight of the wolf. Every moment of that one single dream felt real, she found it hard to believe it hadn't happened.

Rising from bed, she went down the hallway to the bathroom. Locking the door, she stared at herself in the mirror. Everything seemed fine. She decided to take off the bandage, ripping it from her skin, noticing it came away clean. When she looked in the mirror, something had changed.

There was no scar. No blood. Nothing that convinced her she had been attacked by a wolf. She stood there, dumbfounded and confused. Between that strange dream, her conversation with Eric, and what she thought was the aftermath of being attacked by a wolf, there was only a strange mark on her neck that resembled a bruise. She leaned in closer to the mirror, convinced it was an illusion, and muttered to herself.

"What the fuck is going on?"

CHAPTER THIRTEEN

Candice sat sprawled in her old bean bag chair with a book in her hands. The moonlight shined through the bedroom window, but it wasn't enough to light up the page as she read. The lamp in the corner of her room gave her just enough. The cool summer breezed flipped at the curtains. Except for the wolf howling in the distance, it was a quiet night.

Suddenly, as she turned the page, the sharp wail of an ambulance truck pierced through the night. Candice lowered her book. The earsplitting siren only became louder with the passing moments. She stuffed the faded movie ticket stub into place and stood, stepping over to the window and stretched.

When she looked out the window, a few of her neighbors were outside in their sweats and night clothes. The lady from up the street came out in a silky pink bathrobe, holding the flaps closed against her chest. She rolled her eyes at the older woman. She was an idiot if she thought anybody would be looking at her when an emergency vehicle was rolling through. Something was going on.

After pulling on a pair of pajama bottoms, Candice slipped

out of the house when a couple of sheriffs deputy's vehicles and the ambulance turned down their street. Both her parents were already out on the lawn, observing the commotion brought on by the emergency vehicles. The vehicles had already disappeared around the corner, but the blue and red lights flashed brightly through the darkness.

"What's going on over there?" Candice said, crossing the lawn to meet her parents. They had stepped into the middle of the road to join the rest of their neighbors.

"Who knows?" Her father said.

"Maybe someone died." The neighbor with shaggy blond hair from across the road suddenly joined them. A hacking cough broke the tension and Candice turned. Their older next door neighbor sat on a lawn chair in his driveway. The garage door was propped open, a light spilling out. He held a can of beer in one hand and a cigarette in the other.

"Maybe there's been another murder."

"This far in the village? Haven't they all been happening on the edge of town? Like closer to the forest?" Candice's mother said. The older man just shrugged and took another drag from his cigarette.

"Anything can happen around here, Candice. I'm sure your mom and dad have told you plenty of stories about the supernatural and paranormal shit going on around here."

"Frank!" Her mother shouted.

"What? I'm sure your daughter is old enough to hear about shit, Kellie." The old man grumbled, throwing his head back, finishing his beer. Candice glanced in her parents' direction. Her eyebrows knitted into a frown as she wondered what he could've been talking about. She really wanted to know considering the rise in strangeness surrounding her lately. She was sure her parents wouldn't tell her though. "What's he talking about?"

"Candice. It's nothing. There're just stories my mom and dad told us growing up, but I never wanted to tell you those kinds of stories. They're not real." Her mom said. The old man let out another laugh, but when her mom directed her gaze toward him, he rose from his seat and disappeared into the house.

Later that night as Candice reached into the bag of cheese puffs she stole from the kitchen cabinets, she stared captivatingly at the television screen sitting on her dresser. Her undivided attention had been captured by the late-night movie she found. One about a young teen girl who was in love with the popular jock boy except he probably didn't even know she existed. To make things worse, she had family in town for her older sister's wedding, which was the same weekend as her sixteenth birthday.

Suddenly, the movie broke for commercials. Her attention now divided between the images on the screen and fingering at the last of the pulverized chip pieces and crumbs at the bottom of the bag. The commercial break was interrupted by a dark screen with the flashing words: breaking news. The camera cut to one of the studio reporters live on the scene. He was standing near the edge of the baseball field just outside of her neighborhood, where the emergency vehicles had most likely gone earlier that evening.

"Even the park is not a safe place to be when a young woman was found attacked. She must have been taking advantage of the cool evening weather and been out for a run when she made it out to this local park.

"Local law enforcement is still standing by and saying these attacks have been committed by an animal from the nearby forest just behind me here. Residents are skeptical though. They want answers and how this killer is going to be found. Whether human or animal, and with the summer in full swing, something needs to be done."

She rose and went to the open window, listening to the silence of the night. Crickets chirped, and the wolves howled, but she found it odd how often she heard the wolves' magical song lately. Could the growing activity be a coincidence or was something else going on that she was just now noticing? After her conversation with Eric, she knew there was something else going on. She just wasn't sure she was ready to accept it.

Candice grabbed her cell phone and opened her text messages, scrolling down to look for the thread with Valerie. She glanced at the time. It was just after midnight and she knew Valerie had been working the closing shift tonight when she and the rest of the family ran into her at Papi's Pizza Diner in town. She hesitated a moment, wondering what to say before finally tapping out her thoughts in a quick fury of thumb movement.

R U still @ work, Val?

Yes why?

Watching tv
Did u see news?

Yep. Bartender had the ball game on earlier.

Plz b careful out there 2nite!

Promise!

Call me when u get home

THE FOLLOWING DAY, CANDICE found herself preoccupied with the television when the dryer dinged down the hallway. She didn't want to move though. She was absorbed in her favorite soap opera. She finally rose from the floor when her show broke for commercials and headed down the hallway. An advertisement for diapers started things off. She wasn't interested in learning about how diapers absorbed baby fluids.

She opened the dryer and shoved the contents into the empty laundry basket nearby. With her basket on her hip, she hurried back to the living room just in time for her favorite oily dark haired hunk to appear on the television with that big-breasted woman he loved more than anybody. She still found it comical when the show revealed that he was cheating on her with an average Jane.

She sat down on the floor and grabbed a pair of leggings from the top of the pile. Her cell phone rang, startling her. She finished folding one of her old tattered band shirts and tossed it on top of the growing piles. She grabbed her phone from the coffee table and without taking her eyes from the television screen, she answered. "Hello?"

"Candice. It's Doreen. Have you heard from Val?"

"Not since last night. What's going on?" Candice said, rising to her feet. Doreen started squealing in a high-pitched voice that made Candice pull the phone away. "My Valerie! Something's wrong! I just know it!"

"What do you mean, Doreen?"

"Her boss called. Maybe five minutes ago. Valerie never showed up to work. She should have been in two hours ago. This is not like her, Candy! Something is wrong!"

"Ok, ok." Candice said, trying to calm the woman, but she was right about Valerie. Missing work wasn't like her. She wouldn't just disappear without telling anybody. Not without Taylor. "Can you think of where she might be? What about Cyrus?"

"No. I don't think so, Candy. She and Cyrus are civil to each other, but they don't spend time together unless it's with Taylor. They've both moved on. Do you know of anybody else who she might spend time with?"

Candice paused in thought. She realized Valerie's mom knew something she didn't. Unfortunately, the two girls didn't talk nearly as much as they used to and she felt like a horrible friend. Except how did you keep up with a friendship when you were both busy young adults with their own lives?

Valerie never shared anything about her love life anymore. She didn't seem interested in boys since Taylor came along. Instead, if she wasn't talking about Taylor, she always wanted to hear about Candice's new boyfriends. "She hasn't told me anything, Doreen."

"What am I going to do? What am I going to tell Taylor at dinner time when his mother doesn't show up?" Doreen was screaming. Candice had to pull the phone away again. The front door creaked open, and she glanced toward the door.

"Doreen. I'll look out for her. Just give me some time and keep Taylor busy, please. But I have to go get ready for work now." Candice hung up the phone before the panicked mother could say another word. It was bad enough that she was starting to think that maybe Valerie was in trouble, but she didn't need any added pressure.

"Hey, Candy. What's going on? Everything—" Her mom said, peeking into the living room. Candice went around her mom with a little more than a brief glance, frowning.

"I can't talk right now, mom. I gotta get ready for work." Candice said, her voice fading away as she climbed the stairs.

CHAPTER FOURTEEN

The very next day, sometime after noon, Hollow's Creek was rather empty and quiet while the rest of town was off working or even playing in the city. Kids were nowhere to be seen. The neighborhood parks would be quiet with most of the kids in summer school or camp.

A red luxury sedan with gold rims pulled off Main Street and into the quiet parking lot in front of the county sheriff's department building. The driver parked with the windshield facing away from the sun before popping the door open.

A man with expertly groomed light brown hair stepped out from behind the wheel. He wore a nice pressed pair of slacks, a light blue button-down shirt with the sleeves rolled up and a pair of Ray Bans sunglasses. He crossed the parking lot and headed inside the building. He took off his sunglasses and folded them, tucking them into his shirt pocket. He approached the front counter, clearing his throat.

"Can I help you, sir? Are you here to see somebody today?" The deputy sitting behind the computer monitor glanced up, lifting his attention to the man who had walked in. He grabbed a pen and placed it on top of the clipboard sign-in sheet.

"Yes, hello. I'm here to see Lieutenant Maggie Jones." He said, grabbing the pen.

"And you are?"

"Allan Gray. She should already know what my visit is regarding." The man said, not lifting his eyes.

The young deputy swallowed a lump in his throat and sat back down, rolling to the other end of his desk. He picked up the phone and dialed a four-digit number, placing the receiver to his ear. He wasn't going to impede the richest man in all of Hollow's Creek; the great-great-great-great-grandson of the founding father.

"Yes, Lieutenant. This is Garcia down at the front desk. I have a Mister Allan Gray here to see you. He says you should already know what his visit is regarding."

With a simple nod, the young deputy hung up the phone. He rolled back to the end of the desk, looking up at Allan. With a smile on his face, he addressed him. "Lieutenant Jones says you can just head right in. She's almost done with her meeting and is looking forward to speaking with you."

"Thank you." Allan said with a quick nod and a smile.

Allan went around the corner and passed through the carousel leading him toward the back of the building. Every deputy in his path turned and watched him, silent. Allan was used to being treated like a celebrity throughout the Hollow Valley though. Everyone knew him and his family well because of their reputation and Allan continued that legacy.

When Allan's mother passed away, he not only inherited Gray mansion standing proud on Gray Mountain, but he also inherited ownership of many of the shops surrounding the village square; two coffee shops, the old bookstore, the hardware store, and two grocery stores between Hollow's Creek and Juniper.

The Gray family had the money to help keep local residents running their businesses without ever thinking about selling out to corporate chain supermarkets and shops. He cherished the local shops and would champion for any of the Valley's citizens including law enforcement, but he was otherwise a recluse.

Allan stepped up to the door and knocked. Through the glass door, he saw Lieutenant Maggie Jones handling a phone call and waving him in. The moment he stepped into her office and shut the door, she smiled, setting the phone into its cradle.

"Mister Gray. I didn't expect you to come in. Please do come in. Seth, no calls, please." Maggie stepped up and went over to lock the door; she cursed the fishbowl office with wall-to-wall windows and shut the blinds. She leaned down and unlocked the bottom drawer, pulling out a small stack of old files. "I take it you got my messages then?"

"Yes, I did."

"I was hoping to talk on the phone about this. You know how the town feels about you and blames you for your mother's death."

"I don't know how I could have killed my own mother and gotten away with murder. Nothing happens without everyone knowing, but the accusations are absurd. My mother was very sick, and she didn't survive." He closed his eyes momentarily, steadying his voice when it broke for that brief moment. When he opened his eyes, they flickered a faded silver and burned with anger.

"You know as I do how the people of this town get with whispers of supernatural activity. Some of them don't believe it and others believe we're lesser beings than humans. I've dealt with it my whole life because of ignorant people who have boring lives and must make up stories about others."

"I've done my best to quiet down the whispers of this

department and this station, but I can only stop these bored people so much, Mister Gray."

"Please. We know each other better than this. You can just call me Allan."

"Allan. I can't tell you how very sorry I am about your family's loss. I've known you since we were kids, but I do need your help with this. Even with all the supernatural talk, there is truth in some of it.

"I know your kind doesn't normally form relationships or friendships with humans. There are codes in place to protect both human and supernatural. However, I need to figure out who is kidnapping and killing people. I need to figure this out before someone else gets kidnapped, killed, or worse."

Allan narrowed his gaze in her direction, but there was no animosity in his eyes. He quickly brought a gentle smile to his face. Lieutenant Jones glanced down at the folders on her desk, patting them as she kept her eyes lowered.

"I need to figure out who is behind these attacks before Sheriff Loveland gets involved. He is determined to get rid of all dual natured creatures in this town. He has been backing a secret society of slayers calling themselves the Rayers. They believe humans are a superior species. They're separatists. And the sheriff and this group are both going against our historic codes in hopes of wiping all supernaturals off this earth."

"Who are these people? These Rayers as you've called them."

"I don't know much about them yet except that they don't believe in mixing human with supernatural. I'm not sure where they're from or who they are. I only just recently learned of them because of some other situation that has been kept quiet by this office, but I know the Sheriff is working with them. He's going against the codes, but against his own oath as sheriff. So, I could use your help to save human and supernatural lives alike."

"What do you need from me, Maggie?" He said, lifting his eyes to meet hers when she lifted them once more. She opened the file at the top of the stack. She spread the grisly crime scene photos across her desk and glanced up at Allan.

He stared silently at the photos. He linked his fingers and rested his chin on them. His brows furrowed into a deep frown the longer he analyzed the collection. He remained silent for several moments, picking up a couple of the photos to analyze them much closer.

"I need you to tell me whether this was an animal. I'm hoping you recognize these bite patterns. And if it's not an animal, what can we do to stop this offender?"

He lifted his eyes to hers once more. She could see the hurt in his eyes, but the look quickly disappeared. He cleared his throat, his hands still clasped, and let out a heavy sigh. He spoke in a quiet voice. "Yes, I recognize these bite patterns. The killer isn't an animal. It's a werewolf, but which werewolf, I do not know."

"Do you think it could be..." Lieutenant Jones started. Allan put up a hand and shook his head before finally responding. "No, these bite marks are too small to be my son's."

CHAPTER FIFTEEN

On her way to work the next morning, Candice stopped at the c-store, hearing muffled yelling over the rumble of her engine. She didn't recognize the voice. Nor could she see who it was with all the deputy vehicles parked and blocking most of the view.

She hesitated getting out of the vehicle, but she really wanted a pack of smokes. She really didn't want to drive to the other edge of the valley where the next closest c-store that sold her favorite brand of smokes was six miles south.

She stepped out of her car and the yelling across the parking lot became much louder and clearer. She shut the door behind her, almost wishing she had just stayed in her car. She knew the voice yelling across the parking lot. And she hated that voice. But she hated the words coming out of her mouth even more.

"You came all the way down here to see her? The fat loner bitch when you have someone like me? How could you, Zak? You know I've always loved you and wanted you!"

Quinn was in town. The girl who Zak ended their relationship over and brought along with to Denver. The girl who always made her feel a little inadequate back in high school. She was the total opposite of Candice. She saw her standing at the end of the lot and just the sight of her made her heart bitter.

Quinn was a tall, slender girl who had been a top athlete in her graduating class. From softball to basketball, she was the team captain for many of the girls' sports teams. Her long light brown hair still glimmered under the sun. Her bright blue eyes could rival the blue skies of New Mexico.

Candice turned, hoping the bitch hadn't actually noticed or recognized her. Yet, it was hard not to recognize someone you spent many of your formative years around. She stepped inside when she heard Zak yelling.

"I've always known you were a whore! You sleep around with everyone because I don't give you enough fucking attention. And yet, you're still following me around like a lost little puppy! You can have anybody else you want. I'm tired of fighting like this, Quinn. You following me all the way down to Hollow's Creek? I'm done. I can't do this anymore!"

The yelling and shouting continued, but after hearing Zak's words, she tuned their words out. She didn't need to be listening to their relationship problems when she was part of the whole fight. Suddenly, several more county deputy vehicles pulled into the parking lot with their sirens blaring. She walked over to the counter with a freshly poured Styrofoam cup of coffee and glanced toward the front of the store.

"What's going on out there? Why are there so many cops?"

"Who the hell knows? All I know is it looks like she pulled out a gun." The dark salt and pepper haired clerk who she didn't recognize, stood behind the counter near the end of the counter. He was stepping on his tip toes to get a good look at the outside scene.

After getting her coffee and smokes, she headed out the

door, but a deputy stopped her from stepping out the door. Candice tried to step around him, but he quickly dodged to block her, holding out his hand.

"Ma'am, are you sure you need to get out now? We don't want to risk anybody getting hurt in this situation right now."

"You're arresting her, aren't you?"

When the sheriff's deputies finally hand cuffed Quinn and loaded her into the backseat of one of their vehicles, Candice stepped around the deputy and away from the c-store. She crossed the parking lot to her car sitting beside one of the gas pumps. She glanced around, looking for Zak's little red car, but she didn't see it anywhere—unsure if she was hurt or relieved.

She pulled her keys out of her pocket and slipped in behind the wheel, staring out her rear view and slipped the key in the ignition, starting the engine. When she lifted her gaze out the front windshield, she was startled by a familiar face that had suddenly appeared with a smile on his face. Zak had lifted his hand to knock. The old tint crinkled near the top edge of the window when she rolled it down. "Hi, Zak..."

"I was wondering when I would run into you again."

"I've been busy, Zak."

"It's still a small town, Ace."

"Don't call me that..." Candice muttered under her breath and closed her eyes. She remembered how he used to call her by that nickname many years ago. He rarely ever called her Candy unless they were having dirty sex in his old childhood treehouse. Only now hearing him call her by that name made her heart ache.

She lifted her gaze and met his deep green eyes, daggers pierced her heart, leaving her speechless for a moment. She took a deep breath and whispered, "You have no right to call me that after what you did."

"Well, maybe I can earn that right back? Let's hang out

sometime soon, Candice."

"Don't you have somewhere else to be? I heard Quinn was in town and it looks like she was arrested."

"Yeah, but I'm really in no rush to get to the police station."

"Yeah, well, I have somewhere else to be, Zak. I don't have time to stand around and catch up. What are you even doing in Hollow's Creek? I thought you were done with this place."

"I—uh. I'm back now. And I'm uh...staying with my dad for a little while until I find my own place. I need some space to figure some things out after Quinn cheated on me. And she nearly destroyed my art career back in Denver."

Candice didn't know what to say. Her first reaction was to gasp because she knew how passionate he was about his art. She quickly snapped out of that thought and the perfect thing came to her. She bit her tongue and glanced away, keeping the remark to herself.

"It didn't sound that way from the way she was screaming at you."

"That doesn't mean you know what happened either. You only heard this one fight, if that's what you can call all her screaming."

"Yeah. Well, maybe you deserved what you got, Zak. After what you did to me." Candice snapped back. The venom on her tongue was sharp and the look on Zak's face told her it was felt.

"It was complicated. It's always been complicated, Candice." Zak lowered those vibrant green eyes, fiddling with the ring on his thumb. A moment later, he lifted his gaze again, still fidgeting. Candice glanced at his hand and rolled her eyes at his response because she heard it many times before.

However, she still remembered those nights she laid in bed crying about what he had done, resisting the urge to reach out and demand an answer from him with her mom's support. She longed for an answer, but she knew it would never come. That alone was the hardest part of it all. He didn't deserve her sympathy.

"Right, whatever." She reached down and put her hand on the gear selector, shifting into drive.

A few drops of rain fell from the sky, hitting the windshield. She glanced over at him standing just outside her window for a long moment. She ignored the hurt pout that appeared and gestured for him to move out of her way.

"C'mon, Candice. Don't do this."

"Zak, I don't have time for this shit. And I don't want to talk about it either. We're done. We're over and maybe you should move on because I already have. And I thought you had too for that matter."

"Can't we just talk about it? Once?"

"Maybe. If I run into you again. I really should get going now, Zak. I gotta go. Some of us have jobs."

"Of course. I hope you know nothing has changed. My feelings for you never changed." She rolled her eyes and rolled up the window. Zak finally backed away from the side of the car when she revved the engine.

"If you're heading north of here, you're probably gonna be waiting awhile. Deputies have the Hollow's Creek bridge blocked off on both sides. Directing traffic and all that. They found a car in the arroyo."

She remained silent, peeling out of the parking lot and out onto the highway. Big fat drops of rain fell from the dark, cloudy sky. She drove past the high school where a group of teenagers were walking down the hill. She could hear them laughing and cheering outside while the rain continued to fall. A couple of the boys still had their baseball uniforms on.

She drove into the canyon at the other end of town, leading her north, and in the distance, she noticed a pair of lights flashing. Police lights. Her heart was racing in her chest. She could feel it pounding in her throat. She pressed her foot down on the gas, taking the nearest curve much sharper than she thought, but right now all she could think about was Taylor and Doreen. How would she tell them if this was Valerie?

The road was blocked before the bridge. Candice parked to the side of the highway and got out of her car, heading toward the barricade. She wasn't the only one sitting on the side of the road, waiting to pass.

"What's going on?" Candice asked, approaching the bridge, hoping she was panicking for nothing. She couldn't see past the barricade of sheriff's deputies. She knew that somebody would know something, but nobody said a thing.

"Ma'am, you need to get back in your car."

"Why have you barricaded the bridge? Some of us are trying to get home, asshole!" Another woman yelled from the other side of the road. Her kids peeked out from the back seat of her truck.

"Both of you need to get back in your vehicles and leave."

"What's happened?"

"There's been an accident. They won't tell us what though." One of the high school teachers came up beside Candice, putting a hand on her shoulder. Just then, she noticed a vehicle sitting on the slope of the riverbed. The front bumper crushed against a tree, but she noticed a sticker on the rear bumper. Those stick figure family stickers that some parents proudly display on their vehicles. That's when she went lightheaded.

Suddenly, helicopter propellers whipped through the air. Candice fought the sick feeling that washed over her. She rushed toward the railing, yelling out as the sheriff deputies tried to hold her back from the railing.

"Valerie!"

CHAPTER
SIXTEEN

Candice's eyes were red and filled with tears when she knocked on Doreen's door. She felt horrible. Her heart sank in her chest when she saw the worry etched across Valerie's mother's face, but she owed it to her oldest friend to deliver the news herself.

"Tell me, Candice! Where's Valerie? Is she ok?" she said, grabbing Candice's hand with desperation. With her gaze lowered, she told them how Valerie's car was found on the riverbed just north of the Hollow Canyon.

"They're still searching for Valerie. She wasn't in the car, Doreen," she started, tears rolling down her face. "I don't know where she is."

The older woman shoved Candice's hand away. A wave of mixed emotions had flooded over her face. Anger and sadness twisted Doreen's face leaving Candice unsure what more to say, but nothing came to her. Tears welled in her eyes.

"You need to find her, Candice. Find her before the sheriff does. Promise me! You need to promise me!"

"I don't know if I can promise that, Doreen..."

"Promise me you will find her, Candice! I will not have

Sheriff Loveland find her and keep her from me!"

"But why would he do that?"

"You don't know her father like I do. Just find her, please! I beg you. For Taylor's sake. A boy needs his mother," Doreen said, her face soggy with tears. She grasped Candice's hands again and held them, looking up into her eyes, pleading. Candice frowned.

Valerie's parents divorced when Valerie was still a toddler. And unfortunately, he didn't get involved with his daughter's life beyond paying the court-ordered child support. Doreen never talked about him much and she despised him, but why would Sheriff Loveland get involved now except to bring justice?

"Promise me, Candice! I can't let her father find her! Sheriff Loveland isn't the man either of you think he is. He isn't who he says he is."

Candice nodded. She didn't know what to say. Her mind swirled with plenty of unanswered questions that she hoped to have an answer to. She could only hope and pray that Valerie wasn't out there alone suffering somewhere. Or worse.

CANDICE STEPPED THROUGH THE front door of the admin building when Susan, Maya, and a few other camp counselors scattered. She knew they were probably gossiping again. Zak and his girlfriend fighting in the parking lot at the gas station became the talk of the town. By now the murders were old news, but nobody was talking about Valerie's disappearance.

Candice raised a brow slightly when Maya came fluttering toward her like some kind of hummingbird zipping through the air. She bounced with excitement as she spoke. "Did you hear about what happened at the c-store? About someone pulling a gun out in the parking lot? Did you hear?"

"I did hear about it." Candice said, disappearing down the hall. Her suspicions were confirmed; nobody was talking about Valerie. Maya followed a few moments later, practically floating on air. Candice stuffed her bag and the rest of her things in her locker. It wouldn't be much longer before the kids showed up. She took a quick glance over her shoulder. "I had to stop for cigarettes on my way to work."

"So, you were there?" Maya's face lit up. She stepped across the room, still bouncing with excitement, pressing her hands together. Candice just nodded without saying a word. She shut her locker and spun the dial. Finally, she turned toward Maya, who spoke faster than she could keep up. "What did you see? Did you hear anything? I heard she had a gun and was waving it around in the parking lot."

"I didn't hear everything. I didn't see any gun either, but that older dude who works down at the c-store sometimes said he saw the whole thing happen." She stepped across the room, turning away from Maya, and grabbed her coffee and took it toward the microwave, trying to remove herself from the gossip.

Maybe it was because her dad has been a deputy for so long, but she never wanted to get involved in police business. She was used to not getting involved. Her dad did his best to keep from bringing police work home saying he was doing so to protect them, but there were times it wasn't always possible. He would only tell them enough to keep themselves safe when absolutely necessary, which wasn't that often.

"C'mon! You had to have seen or heard something juicy! Tell me! C'mon, Candice!" Maya begged and pleaded following Candice around the back room, but Candice ignored her. With a glance at the clock over the kitchenette sink in the corner, she started toward the door. "Please, Candice! You probably hear all that juicy news with your dad being a deputy."

"Maya, we don't have time right now. The kids will be here soon. We should get up front to help out Susan."

When they returned to the front room, Maya fluttered over to Susan. The two of them twittered with the other counselors. Candice didn't care though. She didn't get a job to stand around and gossip. If that is what her co-workers wanted to, that was their business. Thankfully, the kids would be arriving before much longer.

THE FOLLOWING DAY, NEWS reports were released about Valerie's disappearance. They also revealed that the sheriff's office removed the barricade only to reduce the canyon bridge and the surrounding area to a single lane. They brought in officers from Craven Hill to help conduct their search of the area.

"We are still on the lookout for the culprit of these horrible crimes. Kidnapping and murdering are unacceptable in Hollow's Creek." Sheriff Loveland said to the news reporter on the television. "I am uncertain at this time whether these murders and Valerie's disappearance are related, but I do ask that my personal life not be brought up again. My family matters are not something I wish to discuss on television."

The camera cut back to the studio journalists. Candice rolled her eyes, shoving another large spoonful of cereal in her mouth. She grabbed the television remote from the coffee table, startled when the front screen door slammed shut. Her dad popped his head in and she glanced up at him with a frown.

"Sheriff's got some nerve talking about family on TV." He muttered.

"Dad! I thought you were gone with mom or Kevin and Cody for the day."

"The sheriff continued by announcing there will be a curfew starting at eight pm and there will be a deputy on guard to direct traffic through the area. Until deputies have finished searching the canyon, the weekend traffic will be limited to local residents only." the news reporter said.

"Me? Go with your mother? Or one of those two ungrateful brats while I enjoy my day off from work out in my garage? Never!" He scoffed, stepping into the living room. He sat on his recliner with a crisp bottle of water in his hand. "And it's hotter'n hell out there."

"Then why are you working out there?" Candice finished off her cereal and set the empty bowl down. She gestured to the bottle in his hand and turned attention back to the television, surfing through channel after channel. Only she found not a thing on.

"And what about you, little miss still in her kitty cat pajamas? What are your plans for the day?" Her dad said. She shrugged, rising from the floor, taking her bowl to the kitchen. She only hoped her dad would head back outside before she got back. She just wanted to stew in her laziness for a little longer.

Later that evening, she laid on her bed and scrolled through her call history, trying to find the log for the last time she spoke to Valerie. Nearly a week had passed since their last shared text messages. She never messaged when she got home from work. She hesitated for a very long moment before finally dialing her number. She knew she was taking a shot in the dark. The chances were likely slim to none that Valerie or her assumed kidnapper had her phone, but an answer, even brief may help find her.

The phone rang for an eternity. Candice closed her eyes, hoping someone would answer, but the call went to voicemail. Even the inbox was full. A queasy feeling washed through her. Rising from the bed, she stuffed her phone in her pocket, and left her bedroom.

She headed down the hallway, passing the kitchen with a quick glance through the darkness of the doorway. The digital numbers on the clock over the stove glowed blue. It was 10:31 PM. The silence was palpable. Even her parents would be in bed.

As quiet as a mouse hiding from the cat, she grabbed her purse and headed out the front door on tiptoes. With a glance up at the sky, the moon beckoned to her. The first full moon since she was attacked was still days away. She had never been one to pay attention to or even notice the different phases of the moon, but something felt different. Some sort of electric energy in the air yearned for her attention. She could feel it down to her bones.

She made it down to the canyon bridge. Except for a few lone cars cruising down the highway, there was virtually nobody out on the road this late at night. When she pulled up to the bridge and parked, the county vehicle and the sheriff's deputy that was supposed to be watching the bridge were nowhere in sight.

Candice grabbed the flashlight from her glove box, silently thanking her father for being such a pain in the ass about road safety. Without it, she may never have found the courage to go out looking for Valerie in the dark. She unscrewed the top of the large bulb and dropped a couple of D batteries inside.

She slipped out of her car and locked up, flipping on the switch on her flashlight. She scanned the horizon, facing the towering shadows of the forest that swallowed the glow of the nearly full moon. A few beams of light peeked through the pine needles, leaving her in almost absolute darkness.

Walking carefully down the side of the mountain to the edge of the cliff, she flashed the light across the canyon trying to plan her route on the fly. She climbed over the guard railing, a few feet away from the damaged section where Valerie's car must've gone through, and rushed down the side to the riverbed toward the low rushing river.

Candice frowned softly when she saw Valerie's car still crushed up against the tree. A bittersweet pang in her chest had her lifting the palm of her hand to her chest. Maybe Valerie's phone, a grocery receipt, or something was still in the car to point her in the right direction. Hope wasn't totally lost, she thought. She approached the vehicle.

Lucky enough, the car door was unlocked. The hinges creaked when she pulled the driver's side door open just enough to climb in. She did a thorough search of the front seat, checking in ash trays and even under the seats, but she found nothing useful. Even the back seat had nothing. Only a few toys, a pair of white work sneakers, and old takeout bags and cups littered the floor. Whatever hope she held had been crushed.

Candice stepped out of the car and locked up. She didn't want some vagrant making the car a home while Valerie was missing—that is if the old car was still usable. She stood on the riverbed and scanned her surroundings, knowing the sheriff's deputies had likely searched most of the area already, but there was one spot she doubted they knew about. A spot she had only just remembered.

When Candice and Valerie were still in high school, they snuck out of the house many times. They both had moments where they would run from home in the middle of the night, usually after a fight with their parents. And even after a few fights with boyfriends. One night, they found the cave and dubbed it their safe space in case they needed to clear their mind. Or just have some quiet time alone doing whatever they needed in private.

Candice walked along the edge of the river and around the curve of the mountains. With careful steps, she walked up the hill to a large pile of rocks. The rocks were too large for the average person to move, but somehow Candice pushed one of the larger ones to the side, revealing a hole in the ground.

With a glance at her surroundings, she climbed down into the hole. Candice dropped from the surface into a small cave. The flashlight fell to the ground with a crash and rolled away. She followed the faded path of the flashlight. The light flickered randomly a few times. She grabbed it and hit the base against her palm, correcting the flickering beam.

The small cave was dark and absolutely silent except for what sounded like a few rocks dropping to the ground somewhere off in the distance. The beam of light didn't give her enough visibility in the darkness, but she knew she was alone. She didn't feel any other presence in the vicinity. If Valerie was here, surely, she would have appeared the moment she dropped down into the cave.

"Where are you, Valerie? What happened that you couldn't take Taylor with you?" Candice whispered aloud. She scanned her surroundings one last time, running her long fingers through her auburn hair. Tucking the flashlight into her arm pit, she grabbed the ladder still leaning up against the nearest wall and lifted herself back up to the surface.

CHAPTER SEVENTEEN

When she reemerged from the cave, the first thing she noticed was the sudden silence. Not a cricket chirped. The silence was broken with a snap. Candice froze and ducked behind the nearby bushes, holding her breath. She hoped nobody heard her, if there was anybody out there tonight.

Her heart pounded in her chest. She was certain she would face absolute danger if she dared move or even turn around. When she could no longer hold in her breath, she wet her lips with her tongue and slowly poked her head around the bushes.

"Who's there?" Candice croaked, swallowing back the lump that formed in her throat. "Valerie? Is that you? Are you hiding from me?"

There was no answer except for a couple of small pebbles smacking the back of her heel. Someone was approaching. Although her heart pounded in her ears, she focused her attention on the quiet steps behind her. Candice squeezed her eyes shut, her hands shaking. She muttered, hardly audible. "Please don't hurt me."

"If we wanted to hurt you, we would've done it already.

We're not here to hurt you, little red." A voice floated through the silence. Rocks crunched under the man's boots. A sudden gust of wind brushed against the back of her arms. She stood there in the dark, frozen with fear, when she noticed a man with salt and pepper hair approaching her.

"Then what do you want from me?" Her voice trembled.

"Why are you all alone out here? After curfew even. You know what happens when people disobey us or even the sheriff?"

"The sheriff has nothing to do with this."

"Oh, little red. You are mighty wrong about that." Said the salt and pepper haired man. The moment he took another step in her direction she bolted across the side of the mountain. The salt and pepper haired man followed. She let out a scream when he yelled out after her. "Get back over here, you fucking bitch!"

She ran as fast as she could. She tossed a glance over her shoulder only to realize the man was not alone. There were two other men chasing her. The sudden presence distracted her. She didn't watch where she was running and slipped on a large rock near the ledge.

She tumbled and went sliding down the mountain. Her heart jumped into her throat. The three men gained on her. She fell hard and landed on a rock, hitting her tail bone and the back of her head. The blood rushed from her head and a wave of nausea washed through her. Those three men came down over her when everything faded to black.

When Candice woke once again, she could hardly lift her head it felt so heavy. The loud ringing in her ears slowly faded away. When she laid her head back down, she closed her eyes and stretched her limbs, testing herself. Tiny little pebbles and rocks scratched against her palms. She was alive, but she couldn't remember all that happened or how long had passed.

Her fingers brushed against the blacktop and she lifted her head. The back of her head was pounding, but so was her behind. She carefully rose from the pavement, hardly able to perceive anything around her. Suddenly, a car came out of nowhere blaring the horn.

Candice turned and shielded her eyes from the bright headlights. The pickup swerved to keep from hitting her in the middle of the road. Leaving the vehicle running, a man not much older than her jumped out. He ran a hand through his light brown hair and shouted as he approached. She stumbled; her mind still fuzzy with confusion. "Are you ok, miss? Can I give you a ride somewhere?"

"Yes. If you wouldn't mind." She said, trying hard to fight the terrible migraine or concussion that was brewing. The man approached slowly and the passenger side door opened. The man turned and yelled out. "Sally, can you give me a hand to help this lady get in the car?

"Do you remember what happened to you? Why are you in the middle of the road?" He finally asked, but when Sally and the man approached, she remained silent and let them carry her aching bones to their truck. She was too exhausted to do anything.

HER FATHER DROVE OUT to the police station when the station operator called him on his cell phone. Sally and her guy, Ted, had dropped Candice off hoping she would be safe there. They hadn't seen any hospitals in the area, but she was conscious.

Her mom sat quietly in the living room when she and her dad arrived at home. The moment he burst through the door carrying Candice, she shut off the television to help him carry her upstairs to her bedroom. They stripped her bloody clothes and pulled a blanket over her. She was half asleep, but still breathing when they finally left.

It wasn't long before Candice woke in the darkness of her room, staring up at the faded glow of the stars on her ceiling. The pain at the back of her head and ass had finally faded, leaving only a distant memory. Carefully, she sat up and glanced around, wondering how the hell she made it home and into her underwear.

She moved carefully to the side of the bed and swung her legs over. Rising, she grabbed her robe and opened the door. When she stepped out, she could hear her parents talking down at the end of the hallway. Candice tiptoed towards her parents' bedroom door, and listened.

"Candy can be so damn stupid sometimes! I cannot believe she snuck out after curfew! After dark! What the hell was she thinking, Jack?"

"Kellie... isn't this what you wanted her to do?"

"To be an idiot who could get hurt again? Or possibly even killed?" Candice's mom almost squealed at the top of her lungs. She glanced down toward the end of the hall. Her brothers' bedroom doors were still closed thankful that they slept like the dead. She whipped her gaze back toward her parents' bedroom.

"Dammit, Kellie! You know damn well that's not what I meant!" Her dad rose his voice slightly, but he continued. "What I mean is, didn't you want her to be an independent adult? She just graduated college. You wanted her to get out there and experience life. Did you want her to have experiences?"

"Yes, that's what I want for her! That's always what I've wanted for that girl, but I didn't mean for her to be running around Hollow's Creek with that fucking boy again!"

"Boy? What boy are you talking about?" Her dad's voice fell

almost to a whisper and Candice took a step forward, still listening. She moved carefully, hoping the floor wouldn't creak like it was wont to do at the most inconvenient times.

"You know exactly what boy I'm talking about! The boy she dated. The boy who came up to our door a few nights ago asking to speak to Candice. He's back in town."

"How do we know that she's running around with him? What if she was out there for another reason? The deputy down at the station said that the couple who brought her said they found Candice lying on the side of the road. How do we know what she was doing? She could've just been out there on one of those nighttime runs of hers."

"I'm having a hard time believing that, Jack. I know my Candy. I remember how in love she was with that boy. And I know what he did to her back in high school. I don't want to see our girl hurt by him again."

"I know you don't, Kell. Neither do I, but we need to let her be an adult. She is going to live her life how she wants and we need to trust that whatever path she chooses is the right one for her. Not for us, remember?"

That's when Candice turned and headed to the bathroom, grabbing some pain killers. She locked the bedroom door behind her and crawled back on to her bed, pushing aside a few lavender and black striped pillows. She leaned back and pulled one into her arms, hugging it close. That's when her minded wandered.

She remembered Zak when they were still back in high school—when things were much different. Old, blurry images popped into her mind of him with his dark brown hair, green eyes, and black eyeliner. She even remembered the old black electric guitar he carried almost everywhere with him.

She laid back on her bed and curled up on her pile of pillows. The warmth of tears welled in her eyes when she thought of how he treated her back then. Even now, she knew he had taken advantage of her to get laid. He never wanted to go out in public with her. And it still made her angry because she thought they were more than just friends with benefits.

She just wished he could've told her the truth instead of lying about leaving town on his own. Life was shitty sometimes. Wiping the tears from her cheeks, she pulled a blanket over and cried herself to sleep.

DAYS WENT BY AND there still wasn't a word about Valerie's disappearance, but local law enforcement hadn't yet given up looking. Candice tried to avoid Doreen during that time and having to work made it easier. She had no clue where Valerie was and she couldn't bear to face Doreen again.

Candice just kept her head down and worked, ready for the upcoming holiday. She couldn't wait for the fireworks, baseball, and her dad grilling in the backyard, but as the long weekend approached, she had started to realize that her family life was changing.

She, her parents, and her brothers weren't spending nearly as much time together as they used to. Kevin had his summer job, a girlfriend, and friends he would hang out with when he wasn't playing video games at home. Her mom and dad were both working all the time, which meant Cody was off with his own friends doing whatever young boys do.

Since graduation, she started to notice that other parts of her life were changing too. Even the small town where she spent most of her childhood was changing with the addition of Troy and his Tavern.

She had that strange feeling in the pit of her stomach that

her favorite summer holiday—or rather her favorite in general —wasn't going to be anything like she was expecting. Nobody had mentioned anything about Fourth of July plans. Candice made it to some new crossroad, but nothing had really changed.

Yeah, sure, she just graduated college less than two months ago, but she was back home living with her parents. Her old boyfriend was back in town, trying to get her to talk about their relationship. Then there was Eric who was the same old party boy trying to hook up. Currently, life spelled trouble and she could see the possibility of getting stuck living in Hollow's Creek for the rest of her life. That wasn't the life for her. She wanted to see the world, but she would have to leave behind everything she knew.

Candice understood that when they found Valerie, the young mother wouldn't have the time to be a friend like the past. Even if they finally decided on living together, their friendship wouldn't be the same. She missed the good old moments of their friendship. The late night talks. Beauty nights. Shopping trips. She would've done anything to have Valerie back, even if only for a phone conversation

CHAPTER EIGHTEEN

Thursday evening, Candice knew she was about to be disappointed when she came to the table and saw the large pasta serving dish filled with her mother's infamous portobello mushroom parmesan pasta. Her mom almost never made it unless it was to break some bad or life-changing news. As much as Candice wanted to love the pasta especially the thick, creamy sauce, she knew mom and dad had some news to drop.

"What do you mean we're not going to the baseball game together this year? And no barbecue?" Candice's face distorted into a deep frown, lowered her gaze, and put her elbow on the table, picking at a thin slice of portabella. Her mom shrugged.

"Cody asked to go camping this year. It would be a nice change from the ordinary."

"But it's tradition, mom!"

"We know that, but we didn't know your plans this year. You don't really talk to us lately. I guess it's because you're an adult now. Maybe you should go out and do adult things." Her mom said. Candice hardly glanced up, slurping up a mouthful of noodles.

"Maybe we'll be back in time to make it up to you," her dad said, putting a hand on her shoulder. Candice didn't know what else to say. She just sat silent, picking at another mushroom slice swimming on her plate.

"Candy, I can't believe I'm saying this to my grown daughter, but quit playing with your damn food." Her mother snapped, but Candice continued, resting her chin in her hand. Candice finally took another bite and looked toward her parents. "Can I just be excused?"

"Of course." Her mother said.

Once upstairs, Candice grabbed her cell phone and searched through her contacts, unsure who to call. Valerie was still missing and many of her other old high school buddies had long since left Hollow's Creek to pursue a life of their own, unlike herself.

She still had Zak's old number in her phone and hesitated dialing for fear that his girlfriend would answer. She wasn't sure she believed him about his girlfriend being the cheater in their relationship. That was just too easy, but Candice caved and dialed his number, listening to the line ring over and over again until the voicemail picked up. She disconnected the call and set her phone aside, grabbing her book from the side table.

The rest of the week flew by. Friday morning of the long summer holiday weekend came. Candice rose from her bed sometime just before seven am. When she opened her bedroom door, Cody with his fully loaded backpack strapped on was dragging his suitcase. He was making quite a ruckus with his things ready for the camping trip with their parents.

When he finally noticed her, he gave her a grin that made her want to slap him, but he was only eight. He stuck his tongue out at her, but she just shut her door. After all, her little brother was the whole reason she would be alone for the first time on her favorite holiday. Maybe her mom was right; she needed to find some adult friends.

After crawling back into bed to sleep for a couple more hours, Candice took a quick shower and changed into a clean pair of sweatpants and a t-shirt. Cody and her parents were already gone on their trip. Her mom's SUV was no longer in the driveway. She turned on the television and made herself some coffee and a bowl of cereal for a late breakfast. She plopped down on the floor behind the coffee table and flipped on the television.

Between bites of her frosty corn flakes, while waiting for her television show to come back on, she checked to see if she had any new text messages waiting. Suddenly, her attention was drawn to nothing other than a television commercial for the upcoming Independence Day game down in Craven Hill. Bright fireworks shot across the screen and popped through the speakers.

Just like every summer for as long as she could remember, Craven Hill Stadium hosted an extra special patriotic baseball game complete with fireworks. The Mountain Wolves played a home game on Friday and Saturday night. She wanted nothing more than to attend, even if it meant she would be going alone.

The following evening, she dressed in one of her favorite summer outfits, her red white and blue t-shirt and white jean shorts complete with blue stars all over. She put on a little mascara and her favorite pink lip gloss before heading out with a smile on her face.

When she arrived in Craven Hill, the parking lot was packed. She recognized a few vehicles on her way across the lot to the stadium. She knew she would run into a few familiar faces, but there were still plenty of strangers.

Candice strolled through the stadium lobby, navigating her way through the meandering crowd, and took a detour to one of the nearby concession stands. There she grabbed herself a Chicago-style hot dog, light on the onions, and an ice-cold beer. She took a sip from the red plastic cup, letting out a sigh of satisfaction. This was exactly what her soul needed.

She stepped away from the counter, balancing the beer and hot dog and attempted a bite off the end. Happier than a kitty cat with catnip, she kept her eyes on the delicious foot long she cradled in her hands and walked slowly through the crowd.

"Oops…" Candice muttered, licking the mustard from her lips. Beer slopped over the rim of her cup. She stepped carefully over the spill, glancing around for someone who may be able to clean it, but when she looked up, she met a familiar pair of emerald green eyes.

"Watch where you're g—Candice?"

"Zak? What are you doing here?"

"Just getting some drinks for me and my friends. What are you doing here?" Zak glanced around a moment before redirecting his gaze back to her. He took a sip of his beer with a frown. "Are you here alone?"

"Yeah. My family decided to go out camping this year, and they didn't invite me. So here I am! I wanted to see a little baseball and some fireworks. It's my favorite time of year. I want to enjoy it." She spilled more of her beer and glanced over at Zak with her hands too full. "Let's find somewhere else to chat?"

The two of them quickly scanned the area and found a spot tucked away from the crowd wandering near the concessions. She finally had the opportunity to set her dog and beer down. She sighed, not ready for whatever Zak was going to say to her. What were the chances the conversation would go well?

"So, isn't this what you wanted? Some time to talk. And here we are. Let's talk." Candice started, biting back the sarcasm, hoping that he didn't notice. "What's on your mind? What's been going on with you?"

"You mean besides coming back to Hollow's Creek to pick myself back up again after a horrible experience back in Denver? My girlfriend cheating on me with one my oldest friends? Nothing really too exciting." He gave her a tight-lipped smile.

"You drop a bomb like horrible experience and don't even explain? What the hell?"

"Hey, one question at time! I asked you a question."

"Fine." Candice rolled her eyes slightly and took another bite of her hot dog before she finally spoke. "What have I been up to? I just graduated from the community college here in Craven Hill and I'm living back home for a little while, you know. Trying to save up to get out of this bumfuck town."

"I'm surprised to see you still around here. I figured you woulda left here the minute you graduated high school." Zak started, taking another sip of his beer. Candice shrugged, keeping her eyes on her food. "Are you still playing with your band? What were they called?"

A huge grin appeared on Candice's face when Zak asked about her all-girl band, surprised he even remembered. "You mean Paper Dolls? Yeah, but our other guitar player dropped out and went out to Hollywood herself. It's just the three of us."

"Wait. So you're their only guitarist now?" He said. She only nodded, taking another big bite of her hot dog and washing it down. She waited for his response, but he remained silent.

"But uh—Ramona wants to go out to LA or New York together, but I'm not so sure I'm ready for that yet." She lowered her eyes, wiping the mustard from her lips.

"Why not? I thought that was your dream? To get out of here and travel the world, playing your music. At least that's what you told me before."

"Yeah, I know, but sometimes things change, Zak."

"And what could have changed, Ace? Don't tell me some guy is keeping you from leaving?" Zak asked with a crooked grin on his lips and Candice lifted her gaze with a frown. He glanced down at his hands again, fidgeting with that black ring on his thumb.

"What? What did I say?"

"You already know. Please, don't call me that, Zak." She lowered her own gaze, feeling that familiar ache in her heart. There was nothing she could do to prevent that feeling in her heart, but the least she could do was ask him to stop. She lifted her eyes again to find that he was gazing at her. She bit back a smile of her own and debated lying to him about someone else, but wasn't sure she could. She still cared deeply for him.

"There is no boy, Zak. It's Valerie. She's gone missing. And I can't just leave without knowing she's been found, and she's safe."

"And why can't you just leave, Candice? People leave this shit hole all the time. There's more to life than this valley and the people in it. Why do you care so damn much?" He barked. Candice didn't know how to respond, but his words stung. A wave of anger washed through her and she bit back at him.

"Maybe it's easy for you to do, Zak, but some of us don't want to leave our family and friends behind. Because we know we have something good here and sometimes, it's not worth leaving."

Zak chewed on the hoop ring at the corner of his lower lip without a single word. Candice glanced up and watched him for a moment, biting her tongue. For a moment, she wondered if she had bit back too hard, but she knew he deserved every bit of sting. She still didn't understand why she even said yes to chatting with him.

She lowered her gaze and finished the last of her beer, which had started to become warm. She couldn't look him in the face. She couldn't believe she had the courage to tell him what had been sitting in the back of her mind.

"I'm sorry...I shouldn't have..." Candice muttered under her breath, biting down on her lip. She glanced down, tracing the outline of the chain links on the table's surface.

"No, it's cool. I guess I deserved that after leaving town with another girl, but I didn't know how to tell you at the time. I was a confused kid. I still love you, Candy."

"Zak, please, don't. Not now."

"Why not? I'm telling you the truth. I swear it. Candy...I miss the hell outta you and I wish we could just be together, but shits always complicated for me."

"Zak, your friends slept with your girlfriend."

"I've always known she was sleeping with my buddies. Long before Denver," he said, nodding. A shy smile appeared across his lips and Candice frowned. For a moment, she wasn't sure she heard him right, but she waited for him to continue. "Like I said, Candy, it's complicated for me. You wouldn't understand because it's not your life. Not your family that you have to deal with."

"Try me. Maybe I can understand if you just tell me what I don't know. Don't I deserve that much from you?"

Zak didn't respond. Instead, he gazed off into the distance without another word passing his lips. The moment their eyes locked, she could feel the weakness in her knees. Her heart ached when he glanced into her eyes with that familiar sparkle.

She shook her head, biting down on her lower lip to keep the tears from appearing. She excused herself, hoping he would get up from the table, and stop her, but she rushed through the crowd without any acknowledgment. She wasn't sure what hurt more.

Candice's heart ached worse than before. The pain was somehow worse than when she first found out about Zak's new girlfriend—that she had been replaced by Quinn. She never would've thought the pain of heartbreak would hurt this bad the second time. She could've sworn she was over it, but she was very wrong.

She wiped a few tears from her cheeks, glancing at her wrist to check for smeared mascara, but there was only a dampness left behind. She rushed through the parking lot, dodging a few latecomers to the stadium.

Zak called out her name, but she continued across the parking lot toward her car. Only a few steps away, she pulled out her keys when she heard him call out once again. "Candice! Come on, babe! Stop and talk to me!"

"Go away, Zak! I'm tired of talking about nothing! And I'm tired of just remembering old painful memories. Leave me alone!" She stepped up to the side of her car and lowered her eyes, fumbling with her keys. Tears rolled down her cheeks, and she swiped them away.

She wanted the pain to go away. She just wanted to go home and not have to deal with Zak anymore. What a way to spend my favorite holiday, she thought to herself. With a sniffle, she finally found the right key and unlocked the door when Zak finally caught up to her.

The next thing she knew, a pair of hands grasped her gently, but firmly, and turned her around. She came face to face with Zak. Those gemstone eyes were even brighter beneath the long shadows of the late afternoon sun. She hated it. She hated how fucking attractive he still weas. He still looked like the eighteen-year-old boy she was once in love with.

For a long moment, Candice stared into his eyes and he didn't dare look away from hers. Silence hung heavy between them until she started pounding on him. He held her arms, and she continued to pound on his chest, her long auburn hair flying in her face. Her keys eventually dropped to the ground and Zak reached out to grab her wrists, but she yanked them away from his grasp.

"How could you?! How could you have done that to me? How could you just choose another girl over me, Zak? We were supposed to spend the rest of our lives together! You told me you always wanted me there by your side. You promised me forever!"

Without a word, Zak finally grabbed a hold of her wrists and she didn't fight him. She stopped. Her wavy hair a mess from swinging at the very object of her desire. Her chest heaved. Her face burned. She stared into his eyes, waiting for him to say something. Except he didn't say a thing.

An electric charge sparked between them. One that Candice hadn't felt in a very long time. She had been on other dates here and there since starting college, but nobody compared to Zak. Nor did any other man make her feel the warm flutter of butterflies in her stomach like him. And she hated it. She hated feeling such an intense charge of emotion towards him when all she really wanted was to forget him.

Suddenly, he leaned in and captured her lips in a deep, sensuous kiss that filled her with a static that sparkled through every limb. She let out a gentle moan when she felt the warmth of his tongue press against her lips and dance with hers.

When the kiss finally broke, her eyes slowly fluttered open to meet his again, but this time he was frowning hard. He held her hands tight. "You think I wanted to tell you about Quinn? You think I wanted to give up what we had for what my family wanted for me, Candice? Quinn is nothing like you! Nothing! But I had no fucking choice! You wouldn't understand! You wouldn't get it because you didn't grow up with a family like mine! We're from two different worlds and I fucking hate it more than you can imagine!

"I never stopped loving you, Ace. And I was fucking stupid for what I did. If I had the chance to take it all back and repeat history, I wouldn't have done it because family expectations are shit! No matter what I do, I'll never do the right thing in their eyes. I might as well find what makes me happy, and that is you! Not Quinn."

"Wh-what? What are you trying to say, Zak?"

"I want you to be with me! I want to be with you. And only you." He growled and Candice caught sight of the ball on his lip ring. For the longest moment, she just stared at it, until those lips met hers in another deep kiss that shook her down to her very core. And it made her whimper with frustration when he finally pulled away.

CHAPTER NINETEEN

Work kept her busy when the long weekend finally came to an end. Between the kids indoor and outdoor activities, lunch, snacks, and even the occasional paperwork at the end of the day, she really didn't have time to sit and mope around or think about everything going on around her. She welcomed the calm in her mind while she was working.

When the day finally came to an end, Candice stepped into Troy's Tavern and went straight to the bar to have a beer except another patron told her the bartender had just stepped away. She pulled out her cell phone, checking for any unread text messages or missed calls while she waited for the bartender. When he reappeared, Candice nearly jumped when he spoke. "Well, Candy. Didn't think I'd see you out here tonight. Your usual?"

"You scared me." She screeched, placing a hand on her chest and setting her phone down. She gazed at Troy who waited patiently, leaning against the bar. "Yeah, I know, but I needed a drink. It's been a rough few days. Yes, please."

"You got it," Troy winked and headed to get a fresh glass

from the dishwasher. He filled the glass and brought it on over to Candice within moments. She lifted the glass to her lips and took a drink from the foamy head, thankful for the quiet night. She knew most of town was probably down the street at Miguel's for Tacos and Tequila.

The moment she brought the glass to her lips for another big gulp, she heard a familiar voice reach her ears. He laughed aloud, but the sound of a billiard ball crashing across the table quickly drowned out his voice. She set the glass down and ran her hand over her face in a swoop.

"Eric's here tonight?" She whispered, leaning in closer to Troy who had stopped right in front of her to check in. He gave her a crooked grin like she was asking a dumb question and she knew it. "I really can't go anywhere in this town without running into someone I know, can I?"

"You're telling me? I learned that pretty quickly, Candice. I don't think he'll bother you tonight though. He's got plenty of company." He chuckled. "You need anything else to go with that beer?"

She thought about it for a long moment, sitting silently while staring into the foamy concoction of dark beer. When she finally glanced up at Troy, she smiled and shook her head. He smiled back and tapped the bar top before moving along to the end of the bar where the waitress approached. "Let me know if you change your mind, Candy."

With a quick glance in Eric's direction, she realized he seemed to be too occupied to even notice she was even there at the bar. She hoped he wouldn't wander to the bar for drinks anytime soon because she needed a little peace. She took extra care to keep her head down when a group of his friends headed towards the front door, but a sudden wave of disappointment washed over her when she didn't see Eric among them.

"Can you put that one on my tab, Troy? I'm gonna get going

home now." She said, grabbing her purse. He waved his hand in acknowledgment, keeping his focus on the waitress at the end of the bar. She stepped out the front door and crossed the parking lot when someone whistled. She paused and glanced over her shoulder at the group of guys, smoking cigarettes at the end of the property.

She turned and headed towards her car when she heard a few obscene remarks float through the air. Candice stopped and looked over at them with her hands on her hips, wondering where Eric was. One or two of them whistled and then they broke out into a chorus of laughter. She crossed the parking lot over to them. "What the hell's your problem?"

The group of guys all just ignored her question. A couple of them shrugged while others looked intensely at their nails and others simply looked away. Nobody would answer and she placed her hands on her hips again. A few of them moved off to the side. Eric stood and walked over to her while the canvas top rolled back into place. "You're my problem."

"You're being childish, Eric. Trying to pick a fight with me in the middle of a parking lot? I don't have time for this game." She said, starting to turn away, and that's when Eric reached out and placed his hand on her shoulder. She darted her gaze in his direction and frowned hard. "What do you want?"

"Who said anything about trying to pick a fight? And you know what I want, Candy. I just wish you could see it and stop falling for that asshole's mind games and stupid little pity party." He spoke in a soft voice, just above a whisper. A few of the surrounding guys chuckled and whistled, but Eric wasn't going to deal with it either. He reached out for her hand and pulled her away from the group, only encouraging more whistles and howls from the crowd.

The moment they found a spot far enough away, Candice pulled her hand back and was ready to tear into him, but he interrupted her before she could get a word out. "Just calm down for a minute. I'm not trying to make you upset and get in a fight with you. I just wanted to talk with you."

"Then why the hell did your friends whistle and make lewd comments at me? You could've just come over to talk to me."

"I'm sorry about that. We all get a little rowdy when we've been drinking." He said. She crossed her arms, her eyes locked on him. She didn't say anything though. She just turned her gaze away.

"He told me you two finally talked. And kissed" Eric said, completely accentuating the final word with his whole mouth. She frowned hard and leaned forward, punching him in the arm as hard as she could, but she hardly made a dent. Eric was corded with muscle in a way she hadn't noticed before. "You really think he's not gonna tell me?"

"When did you talk to Zak?"

"He stopped at the c-store to grab some snacks and drinks while I was working. We didn't really talk long though. The place got busy after that." He said, watching her for a moment. "Why would you kiss him though? He's only going to keep treating you like a door mat because you fucking let him, Candice! You deserve so much better than that."

She lowered her head, trying to gather her thoughts. Finally, she lifted her gaze, meeting those sparkling hazel eyes that seemed to be on fire. A sudden gust of butterflies fluttered in her stomach and she bit her lip.

"I appreciate you looking out for me, Eric, but I'm a grown woman and I can take care of myself. I know what I'm doing and I don't need your input." She said, turning away to head toward her car, but he never followed her. Her heart sank and she glanced in her rearview, watching him head back to his group.

The following afternoon when camp let out for the day,

Candice stood outside beneath the shade of the nearby tree with the children while they waited for their parents. She was absolutely miserable and she couldn't wait to escape the scorching temperature. No matter how much water or sugary sports drinks she drank, she could still feel the first bit of a nagging headache creep up on her.

Suddenly, loud music bumped through a set of high-end car stereo speakers and Eric's little black convertible pulled into the gravel parking lot where Candice and the kids waited. The tires kicked up dust when it came to a sudden stop. Candice and Maya both waved the dust from their faces, coughing. Eric rolled down the windows and yelled out. "C'mon, Jared! Hayley! Let's go home."

Both Hayley and Jared looked over at Candice, who frowned with concern. She knew Eric was no brother of the year, but at the very least he wasn't one who seemed to make them uncomfortable. Still, she followed them over to the car.

When the kids walked to the back of the car, Eric stepped out of the vehicle. He had a cigarette in his mouth. He narrowed his gaze in Candice's direction with a sour expression on his face. Blowing smoke in the air, he pointed in her direction.

"Not you. I don't want to talk to you."

"What? What did I do?"

Eric took another long drag before crushing out the cigarette beneath his foot, helping his little brother and sister into the back of the car. Candice had started to approach, but she stood back with her arms crossed over her chest. Hayley shouted over the loud music. "Turn it down, Eric!"

Eric leaned forward and turned down the volume, leaving Candice a little surprised, but over the summer, she noticed that he seemed to have a soft spot for his much younger siblings. Even if he was rough on the edges, he was always there for them more often than their father. What did she know about being small town royalty though?

"Daddy said be nice, Eric!" Hayley grumbled at her older brother as he finished tightening his little sister's belt. He let out a chuckle and slipped out of the car, glancing in Candice's direction. "Thank you for being here to help my brother and sister into the car."

Candice glanced in his direction, but she didn't respond. She knew why he was acting like a jerk and she wasn't going to stroke his bruised ego by trying to save face with him. They may have experienced a moment of strange attraction one night, but he needed to realize that she wasn't interested in him the same way he wanted her. She didn't care that he came from a rich family or that he would one day inherit a small town empire. Sure, he was attractive and protective, but he was still the Eric she remembered from high school.

After helping Jared and Hayley into the backseat, she crossed the parking lot back to her spot. Maya had left hers to walk a few more kids to their parents' cars. Candice ducked under the low-hanging branches and had a seat when she heard Eric yell out her name. Maya glanced over at her with a crooked grin curling over her lips. "I think that hottie over there is trying to get your attention. That guy in that loud car."

She rose from her seat and stepped over to where Eric stood just outside his car, leaning over the top. Now that she was able to see him face to face, he appeared pretty beat up with a couple bruises on his cheek and jaw, which she hadn't seen the night before. There was a long cut over one eye, which looked red and angry despite the stitches. She flinched slightly at his appearance.

"What happened to you? You look really bad."

"Don't worry about me. It's none of your business." He said, glancing away from her. A car pulled out and went around Eric's car. And then another. At least he wasn't completely holding up traffic.

"What is it, Eric? I thought you didn't want to talk to me?

"I know what I said. And I still don't wanna waste my time, but there's something important I feel I need to tell you about." He started and she crossed her arms over her chest, leaning slightly while she waited for him to respond. "It's got nothing to do with you and me or Zak for that matter."

"And what would that be?" She lowered her eyes, waiting for his response. She wasn't sure what to think or if he would become angry and insult her in front of the kids and her co-worker. She didn't expect him to let out a snort.

"You better watch your back, Candy. There's a white wolf prowling the forest. She's a feisty one and if the pack hears about a new hybrid werewolf in town, they'll come find you."

Before she even had the chance to respond, he slipped back into his car and took off.

CHAPTER TWENTY

Later that evening when the sun was starting to sink in the horizon, Candice sat in the middle of her bedroom, dressed in her old purple kitty cat pajama bottoms and an old tube top, with her feet tucked into her old pink kitty slippers. She sat with her eyes closed and headphones over her ears, bobbing her head to the rhythms flowing through her ears, and tickling her brain.

When the song finally faded away, she paused the song and sat, and waited for a long moment. She thought she heard someone knock at her bedroom door. Lo-and-behold, they knocked again. She rose from the floor, setting her headphones down. Cody stood just outside in the hallway. He spoke softly. "Your friends are here, Candy."

With a frown, she stepped out into the hallway. Voices floated from downstairs. She didn't recognize the voices. Not right away anyway. She headed down the hallway and took the stairs. The voices grew louder as she walked towards the front of the house.

Candice stepped into the living room to find her mom

chatting with her band and one of their boyfriends. The boyfriend's piercing blue eyes caught her off guard for a moment, realizing just how attractive he ways. She recognized him from somewhere around town, but she couldn't think of where or what his name was.

The three of them sat comfortably on the couch, their attention on her mom who sat with a sweaty glass of water in one hand. The shortest one of the bunch, Ramona, with her long, two toned black and white hair was leaning forward and resting her elbows on her knees. Stars sparkled in her eyes.

"Being in a band was everything to me back in high school. Making music. Just being creative! That was my life. We played up at the Silver Dollar once a month back before it became the Graffiti Heart. We hoped someone from Hollywood would come out to scout us and take us to California.

"Oh, I do miss being out on that stage. I enjoyed it so much, but I had other more important things to focus on when the producer came and discovered us. He wanted to take us to Hollywood, but I couldn't leave my family behind. My little girl was only a couple years old. I had to be able to come home and take care of my family.

"They spent years trying to replace me with someone who had my style. Unfortunately, they never recovered from it and eventually broke up. That's why I say you kids should wait until you've lived long enough on your own before having kids."

"I never want kids." Tommie said.

"That's what you say now, Tommie, but things change. Just be careful about who you spend time with. You can never really tell until it's too late." Candice's mom said. Ramona ripped her gaze from Candice's mom and glanced over her shoulder at Tommie with a quirked brow.

"Are you giving my old roommates the facts of life, mom?"

"Candice. How nice of you to join us. Come. Sit." Her mom

scooted to the cushion on her dad's recliner in the corner of the room. She patted the cushion for Candice to join, but she sat on the arm of the chair.

"I didn't expect to see you two. Or the new boyfriend." She glanced toward piercing blue eyes and smiled. He smiled back with a moment of recognition flashing across his face. Except it disappeared much too quickly to confirm. Ramona glanced up, dropping her hands to her sides.

"We haven't heard from you in a while, Candice. I've tried to call you several times, but you haven't returned my calls. What's going on with you. We thought you were ready to leave this small town and do something bigger with your life! Do something big together in LA!"

"I've told you already, Ramona. And I thought we all agreed that we need money before we can leave town. We can't just drop everything and leave Hollow's Creek right now. I have a job."

"You mean you don't want to leave your boy toy behind." Ramona said in a sarcastic tone, her face pinched with disgust. Candice's mom glanced at her with a narrow gaze, but Candice shrugged and rose from her spot. "I can't believe you! You said that you would never let some boy get in the way, Candy!"

"Who said anything about a boy? That's not why I haven't called. I have a lot more going on that you wouldn't understand. More serious things that you wouldn't know anything about!" Candice said, her brow furrowed.

When Ramona stood up, she towered over everyone sitting in the living room in her tall spike heeled boots. Her face still pinched with disgust; she crossed her arms over her small chest. Everyone in the room, including Candice's mom, sat silently staring at Ramona for a long moment.

"You know, Candice. If something is bothering you...if there's something you need to work out, I told you I'm here to help you and talk through it. I'm not ready to just give up on this band! You heard your mom's story! I don't want to end up like that. We've been through too fucking much just to throw this all away!"

"And that's my cue…" Candice's mom rose from her seat and excused herself, disappearing down the hallway. Those still in the living room looked away from Ramona and Candice.

"I thought you said you were willing to wait around for me until I was ready to leave and go touring with you around the country? Are you telling me you're not willing to do that anymore, Ramona?"

"And how long is that going to be? What are me and Tommie supposed to do while we wait around for you? It's not like there's much out here to keep us entertained! You're telling me you don't know if you want to pack your shit and get the hell outta here? Outta this bumfuck town? Do you really think I want to keep working at the old burger joint and wait for you? Why are you being such a goddamn flake?" Ramona growled, stomping her foot on the carpet. A loud crash came from down the hallway. Tommie and Ramona both glanced out the doorway when Candice's mom yelled out only moments later. "Sorry!"

"I'm not trying to be a flake, dammit! But what am I supposed to do? I'm working to make sure we have money. Valerie is missing! And I can't just leave town until I know she's safe! I can't do it. You know what she means to me, Ramona!" Candice said, raising her voice slightly.

"That's not your job to be looking for her though! That's the sheriff's job! You don't owe her anything, Candy! She has her own life to live and so do you. The county deputies can look for her and you can't just wait around for these dumb fucks to find her!"

"And what if they don't find her? I couldn't live with myself after that!"

"Then that's your decision. But I'm not just going to wait around for you to do nothing while those lazy fucking cops do nothing trying to find her." Ramona pulled out a mocking voice and gesture, rolling her eyes. Suddenly, Candice's father cleared his throat and made his way down the hallway toward the kitchen, muttering. "I'll be in the kitchen then."

"I don't believe that's the only reason you just sit around. We're not stupid. We've seen Zak in town. That's not you, Candice. If there's something else going on—whatever it is— you can't just keep it inside! Come practice with us again. Please. Then maybe you'll remember just how much you love playing and remember why you wanna leave this valley."

"What? Why would you think he would keep me from practicing with my band? He's got nothing to do with any of my decisions, I've told you. I need some time to warm up. And shouldn't we spend some time practicing before we leave town?" Candice said, her hands balled up into fists. The energy in the air surrounding them was filled with tension, except for Tommie, who was most obviously on another planet of her own cuddled up beside piercing blue eyes.

"You need time to warm up? That's all you had to fucking say!" Ramona started. "Come on, Candy! I may not know you as well as Val does, but I know you pretty fucking well. You're a part of this band and if there's something we need to do, you need to tell us instead of ignoring my calls, because if you aren't ready to leave, we need to know so we can find someone else who is ready." Ramona closed her eyes and turned away. She patted Tommie on the shoulder and whispered something in her ear. She crossed the room and stopped in the doorway, turning in Candice's direction.

"We'll give you to the end of the summer. If there's any part of you that still wants this as bad as we do, like I know you do, then come with us. We'll tour around the state and make some cash. We'll go to Hollywood, just like we talked about. By then, maybe they'll have found Val. But if there's something else keeping you from leaving, you have to let us know because we won't wait forever."

Ramona turned and headed out the front door, following Tommie and her boyfriend out to the old van. Candice let out a heavy sigh and plopped down on the recliner, slouching. She stared at the frayed fabric print at her knees. She wondered for a moment what she was doing. Was she really waiting for the sheriff's deputies to find Val or was there something else going on that she wasn't ready to admit?

"She's right you know. Your mom too."

"What?" Candice glanced up at her dad. He looked younger than she was used to. He was dressed in a pair of old jean shorts and a tee shirt. He stepped over and had a seat on the couch, facing her.

"It's not your responsibility to be looking for Valerie, sweetheart. That's my job. And if you don't do it now, with that boy in town, something is going to happen that you'll regret. Then you won't have any chance to do this again. Do you really want that?"

"No, but I promised Doreen that I would find Valerie. I need to find her! She's my best friend and I think she's in trouble somewhere." Candice said, sitting up in her seat.

"Candy, let me take over that worry. I want you to live your life. Don't get yourself stuck in this small town with a baby like your mother or even like Valerie did. Don't you think she would want you to live your own life?"

"Yeah, but what about Doreen?"

"Let me worry about that, ok? Now you get your ass out of that chair and go rock!" Her dad lifted his hand into the air, his fingers forming the devil horns. He grunted and Candice laughed. She finally slipped out of the chair, but by the time she made it to the front door, the old van was already gone. She hesitated, wondering if she should go after them.

She turned and headed back inside the house, heading up to her bedroom, where she shut the door behind her. Sitting on her bed, glancing toward the window, she thought about what her dad said. And even Romana and her mom. What was she still doing here and why was it taking so long? After all, her summer job wasn't keeping her there.

She glanced over at her guitar sitting in the corner of her bedroom. She grabbed the case and placed it in the middle of the floor, opening the latches that kept it closed and locked. She felt excitement the moment she lifted the lid. An excitement she hadn't felt in a long time. She wondered why she had taken so long to open the case.

Suddenly, there was a knock. With a slight frown, letting the lid drop on the guitar case, she rose and opened the door. Her dad stood there with worry written all over his face. She frowned. "Dad? Um, what's going on?"

"I need you to have a seat now, Candice." Her dad gestured, stepping inside the room. She did as her father said and he sat beside her. She shifted and adjusted a couple of times, waiting for her father to continue.

"Dad, will you tell me what's going—"

"I just got a phone call. There's been another attack." He said, shifting uncomfortably. Candice gasped, covering her mouth with her hands, waiting for him to continue. Her mind was already jumping to conclusions about her best friend. "Was it...Did they find..."

"Well. We haven't found Val yet, but um," He paused, lifting his gaze to Candice. "That boy? Zak? He was taken to the hospital."

CHAPTER TWENTY ONE

You mean Zak? Are you sure, dad?" She let out another gasp.

"Yes, I'm sure. Sherry described a handsome-looking rocker boy with green eyes. I figured I'd tell you before you hear about it all over the news." He said. Candice rose from her bed and slipped into a pair of her worn-out slip-on canvas sneakers. She grabbed her purse, keys, and cell phone and headed out the door. Her dad followed, leaving the bedroom door open.

"Candice, where are you going?" Her dad shouted as she flew through the house.

"Candy! You better get back in this house and change before you leave! You don't look appropriate going out like that!" Her mom yelled, suddenly darting from the living as Candice bolted toward her car. She needed to see what had happened to Zak and nothing was going to stop her. Not even her parents. She could still hear her mother yelling out when she peeled out on to the highway.

Candice drove across Hollow's Creek like a bat out of hell. She flew to the far end of Juniper where the local clinic was located. Thankfully, the road was free of sheriff's deputies cruising this late, managing to keep from getting pulled over on her way.

When she finally arrived, she barely parked her car and shut off the engine before spilling out to the parking lot. She flew through the front doors of the urgent care lobby, pushing past a few others patients waiting anxiously. Many of them watched her march through the small crowd.

She went straight to the nurse's station, pushing aside a young mother who was signing herself in. The older female nurse behind the counter narrowed her gaze over her glasses. Candice had never seen this nurse before, but it wasn't often that she ended up in the urgent care clinic either. She quickly realized she must be new to the area.

"Can I help you?"

"I'm here to see Zak Trujillo. My dad said he was brought in last night. My dad, sheriff's deputy, Jack Olson. He said that Zak was attacked and was brought here to the clinic..."

The older woman held her glasses further down the bridge of her nose and eyed Candice suspiciously. With a narrowed gaze, Candice glanced at the woman's name tag, which simply read, "Nurse Rosie."

"And how do you know the patient, ma'am?"

"We, uh—He was my high school boyfriend."

The older woman stared at Candice for another long moment before pushing her glasses back up her nose. She turned her head slightly before smiling at Candice with a hint of amusement playing on her face.

"I don't think so. I don't care who you think you are; you're not going to see any of my patients tonight if you're not on his chart! Do you understand me?"

"But my father is a sheriff's deputy! He was the deputy pres —"

"Again. I don't care who you are, young lady. You're not going into any of those rooms to see any of my patients tonight. So, you can leave this waiting room." Nurse Rosie lowered her gaze and pointed toward the door, but Candice wasn't just going to give up and leave. Instead, she walked away to find a seat in the waiting area.

Glancing at the time, she realized visiting hours were already over, but she heard a familiar voice coming down the hallway. A tall, lean brunette came through the swinging doors, holding used tissues in one hand and a Styrofoam cup in the other. Quinn. She must've been here to see Zak, wondering if she was on his chart. Candice lowered her eyes, trying not to draw attention, and waited for her to disappear.

The door leading to patient rooms slowly dragged across the linoleum floor, the crack in the doorway growing smaller and smaller. Candice took her chance and snuck down past the counter and through the door with medical staff only painted on. Luckily, Nurse Rosie was occupied with another patient.

She headed down the hallway and glanced through windows and cracked doors, trying to find Zak. She dodged behind a corner when she heard a voice approaching. When she turned the corner, she slammed into someone head on.

They both let out a groan on impact. Rubbing her head, she opened her eyes only to find she didn't just run into anyone. She had run into Zak. He had several bruises and deep cuts. That's when she thought of Eric, who had looked rather beat up when he came to pick up his siblings. Could he have been lying about meeting up with Zak?

"Candice! What are you doing here?"

"I came to see you."

"How did you get past that nurse in the lobby? Or Quinn for that matter?"

"Really? You don't remember sneaking around in the middle

of the night with me back in high school? Well, that hasn't changed." Candice said with a crooked grin on her lips. He mirrored her smile with a slight wince. She frowned hard.

The cuts and scrapes on his left cheek appeared flaming red and swollen. And the bruises on his face were such a dark purple that they appeared to be black. That's when she noticed his hands at his sides. Several cuts and scrapes decorated them. She reached down and lifted one hand between hers. "I heard you were attacked! What happened?"

"Well..." Zak started, lowering his gaze with a frown. He lifted his hand to the back of his neck. Candice could feel her heart melt when those emerald green eyes met hers once more. "I don't think that it's a good idea for you to be getting involved right now. Not with Quinn around. And there's some other stuff going on with Eric, and his dad."

"Wh-what do you mean?"

"There's a lot that goes on around Hollow's Creek that you don't know about. That you're not a part of. There are things around here that I don't want you getting involved with, Candice. Because it makes life a little more complicated and a little harder than you would expect in a place like Hollow's Creek. I—But I think it might be too late, anyway."

Zak glanced over her. An unnatural glow flickered in his eyes, revealing a glimpse into an animal nature that Candice had never been aware of. She was frozen in place, staring into his eyes when a low vibration rumbled in his chest. He spoke in a low growl.

"I can smell him on you, Ace."

"What are you—" Candice stood there, confused. She didn't understand what he could've meant by that. Was he referring to Eric? He turned to walk away, getting only a few feet before Candice reached out.

"Zak! Don't walk away from me! I'm tired of you leaving me

in the dark about this shit! Stop being so fucking cryptic! You've kept enough secrets from me in the past and I'm not just going to let you walk away without an answer this time, dammit! I don't care that you're trying to protect me anymore because if you loved me, you wouldn't keep all these fucking secrets. If you ever fucking loved me, you would tell me what the fuck is going on."

Her heart raced in her chest, adrenaline pumping through her veins. She couldn't remember the last time she found the courage to stand up to someone she loved. In fact, she wasn't even sure she had ever stood up to him. All things considered, they had been good at communicating. Just never about their relationship.

When Zak turned, something in the air changed. She could feel a thickness that she never experienced before, but a sudden sense of déjà vu washed over her. He rushed toward her with another rumble of anger in his chest. His lip curled up to reveal several extended, sharpened teeth much like a wolf. She gasped and before she knew it, the moment disappeared. Zak stood before her. His green eyes blazing with anger. He whispered through gritted teeth.

"What do you want me to tell you, Candice? You want me to tell you that werewolves exist and that I'm dealing with them because I am one? That I'm dealing with Eric and his father because we used to be part of the same pack? That Eric and I got into a fight? And that everything is too complicated because you're not one of them?

"You're human. It may sound insane, but it's all real. Maybe not everything you hear about in the movies or in books, but all those crazy stories about the supernatural presence in Hollow's Creek? It's all fucking real! And I tried to protect you from all of it, but it's already too fucking late for you!"

"Zak...that doesn't explain anything to me! Why is it already too late? I don't understand what is going on! What do werewolves have to do with it? Or even Eric for that matter? What are you trying to tell me that you can't just fucking say?" Candice said, putting her hand out to Zak's shoulder in an attempt to bring his attention back to her.

"I can't explain it. Not now. We have to wait for the full moon in a couple of nights. It will be easier by then. I need you to meet me up the mountain at Camp Gray and I'll be able to explain everything to you."

Zak yanked his arm back from Candice and started down the hallway to the lobby, leaving Candice alone and speechless. She didn't know what to say. She didn't know how to process all the information he just gave to her about werewolves and him and Eric. None of it made sense to her, but deep down, something told her it was all the truth.

CHAPTER TWENTY TWO

Candice left the hospital feeling unsatisfied. When she looked up at the moon, it was nearly full. She was sure that the new moon had only passed a few days ago, but she didn't pay attention. From what Zak said there was nothing more she could do except wait for the inevitable. She had a hard time wrapping her mind around the possibility of werewolves lurking through the forest.

She had been bitten by a wolf at the last full moon, but was it really just a wolf? Or could she have been bitten by a werewolf like Zak had alluded? That thought blew her mind. From what she remembered, the wolf looked nothing like a werewolf.

Most of the wolves she had seen in the movies were big and ferocious and they were bipedal. They looked like monsters. The wolf Candice had seen that night looked like a regular wolf except it was much larger. They must have been the size of Irish wolfhounds that she would see in those old King Arthur movies her parents loved to watch.

Were these werewolves behind all the attacks around Hollow's Creek lately? If she had been attacked by a werewolf, why had she survived and nobody else had? Had those been actual wolf attacks or was somebody trying to cover up more secrets that she knew nothing about? She also wondered if someone turned her into a werewolf for some nefarious reason? Above all, was it all connected to Valerie's disappearance?

"YOU GOTTA DRIVE ABOUT five miles north of the camp. That's the elite grounds where people of influence camp every year. You'll find me there." He said. That was all she remembered from her earlier conversation with Zak. She watched the mile markers closely and right after mile marker five, she found the turn off. A dirt road to be exact.

She followed the road from the highway until a sudden alcove opened. There right in her headlights, she saw the cabins that Zak mentioned on the phone. There were already several cars parked. She shut off her headlights, taking in a deep breath as she wondered why there were so many cars this late at night. Was it just a bunch of locals? Was she even supposed to be here?

She found a place to park under a canopy of large evergreens. She didn't want to park too close to the large group of vehicles, many of which were much nicer than her dad's old patinaed Chevy. There were Jeeps and fancy Land Rovers she wanted to stay far away from just in case. Hopefully nobody would call the cops. Or her dad.

It was a quiet night except for that slow ticking sound of the engine cooling off. Nothing was going on. There was no sign of anybody nearby. There were a few porch lights on and the smell of smoke in the distance. That's when she realized there must be a bonfire nearby.

She started toward the campgrounds, following the smell of

smoke. The smoke became thicker as she crossed the property. She glanced up at the moon as several bundles of clouds floated by. Tendrils of smoke reached into the night.

A loud scream and several low groans broke through the silence, echoing through the valley. She crouched down and listened carefully, hoping to hear another scream or something more that would lead her to the source, but instead there was only silence. Adrenaline started to pump through her veins.

The groaning started again, but quickly faded away. Candice flattened herself against one of the nearby cabins and went around to the front, but found nobody there. Still, she moved slowly, carefully. When she glanced around the corner, she saw the flicker of flames from behind the wooden fence further out.

A sense of dread fell in the pit of her stomach. She could hear the voices of others on the property. From what she could tell, there was a generous crowd of people standing by the edge of the creek. It wasn't just going to be her and Zak tonight. She listened, hearing their voices, but she didn't recognize any of them.

Candice crouched behind a nearby evergreen and gazed toward the group that appeared to be worshipping a natural deity that resembled some kind of animal. Maybe a canine, she thought. No, it is a wolf. Behind them, she noticed an old iron gate that stood open to a path in the forest.

Silence hung over the area and she carefully moved closer when she noticed something happening. A strange energy seemed to rise from the deity, shimmering through the small crowd. Candice gasped watching one individual in the crowd shift into the form of a wolf before her very eyes. Then another and another. This large gathering of people was a pack of shapeshifting wolves. Werewolves!

She kept still, crouched, watching each of them to shift into a wolf, and run into the forest. She took a few steps closer and stepped on a tree branch. A familiar face appeared from the crowd and walked toward her. Zak. He was still human. He stopped and whistled at her, signaling for her to keep watching, she assumed.

The beautiful rocker boy she had grown to love was now a large dark brown wolf standing by the heat of the roaring flames. The animal padded toward her and she backed into the tall evergreens. She watched the animal sit on his haunches and arch toward the full moon, letting out a long, deep howl.

Candice was dumbfounded. Even though she had witnessed it, she still couldn't believe what she had seen. It was one thing to see strangers all turning into wolves, but Zak shifting too was the strangest part of it all. That's when the realization came to her.

Zak had invited her to see what happened to many people on the full moon. He wanted her to see other humans shapeshifting. He confirmed there were werewolves lurking around the valley. She watched them dart up the side of the hill, counting at least a dozen wolves disappearing into the forest.

Candice rose to her feet and ran in the opposite direction, heading back to her dad's truck. Her mind was spinning. For someone like her, who had been sheltered from the supernatural, she couldn't wrap her mind around the truth.

Fear clouded her mind. She wasn't just afraid; she was completely alone. Her heart was pumping wildly in her chest. She knew what Zak had been trying to tell her, even if it was subtle. She had been bitten by a werewolf and she would turn just like them.

She was almost to the truck when the energy surrounding her turned hot and prickly. The sensation of hot needles poked at every inch of her body. She groaned in agonizing pain, dropping to the ground and cried out Zak's name as a tear rolled down her cheek. He was nowhere to be found. She curled up into a ball, wailing with pain. She whispered to the silent night, her eyes fluttering as she fought to stay awake or alive, whatever her body was going through. "What's happening to me?"

Candice let out a scream due to the excruciating pain. Tears poured down her face. Everything went dark.

CHAPTER
TWENTY THREE

The blinding light of the morning sun woke Candice. She didn't want to open her eyes. Her cell phone was vibrating on the nearby table. Eventually, she peeled her eyes open and reached for her phone only to feel a sudden tug at her wrist. She was hindered by a pair of cuffs. Confused, she glanced around the room, but found she was all alone.

She laid back, finding herself in a hospital bed, no less. She reached for the call button hanging nearby, smashing it repeatedly. Eventually, she let it drop from her hand and stared up at the ceiling. Closing her eyes, she took a deep breath, and waited for the nurse to come. Moments later, the door creaked open.

"I wondered how long it would take for you to wake up and realize what has happened to you." Except it wasn't the nurses voice she heard. For that matter, it wasn't Zak, Eric, or her dad either. Her eyes shot open, and she sat up to see a cruel grin curled over Sheriff Loveland's face. He was the last person she wanted to see enter the room.

"You're not the nurse." She muttered, laying back against

the pillows. She closed her eyes once more and waited for the Sheriff to continue speaking. His boots clicked across the tile flooring. He stepped up to the side of the bed and pulled the nearby chair closer. The legs dragged across the floor with a horrible screech before he sat just out of Candice's reach.

"That's right. I am no nurse. I told them to tell me when you were finally awake and mashing that damn call button. They fought me over it, but they finally gave in when they remembered who I am."

"You're just the sheriff of this town, Mister Loveland."

"That's Sheriff Loveland to you, missy." He said, adjusting in his seat. Candice glanced over at him, noticing the gun and handcuffs at his belt. She caught a whiff of his chewing tobacco and turned away in disgust. With a chuckle, he leaned back.

"We finally caught you. And you're going to pay. You're also going to tell me where my daughter is at, low life." He growled low enough for only her to hear, leaning closer to the hospital bed. She whipped her head to a tilt in his direction, frowning hard.

"I don't know what you're talking about, Sheriff! I was attacked too so how could you even think it was me who hurt all of these people? Or even—"

"That's enough out of you! You know what you did. I know what you are. Candice. I can sense a bastard supernatural when I see one." He said, a crooked grin curling over his lips. He leaned back again, watching and waiting.

"You don't know shit, old man." She said, tugging the hand cuffs. He let out another chuckle. His eyes blazed with pride and anger, a dangerous combination. Still, she didn't know what was going on. She grabbed the nurse call button and pressed it a few more times, hoping the nurse would actually come this time.

"Watch your tongue, young lady. You forget the power I

have in this town. I can destroy you and your little pack. I can destroy your family too, but that would be a waste. They're all human as far as I know."

Candice laid there silent, unsure what to say to this man accusing her of killing people, but she didn't know why. She couldn't even remember what happened the night after she passed out. She didn't remember how she ended up in a hospital bed. Or even how she ended up in cuffs.

"Whatever you're trying to prove, Sheriff, you're wrong. I may not remember what happened, but I didn't hurt those people. And I never kidnapped the daughter you abandoned, Sheriff!" Candice snapped, tugging at the hand cuffs. If she pulled any harder, she was sure they would break. She also saw the anger flare in his eyes.

He pulled back his arm and tightened his fist, ready to punch her or maybe pull out his gun. She hardly flinched at the threat. The door creaked open once more. A crooked grin curled over her lips when a nurse finally came in, shooing him away.

"It's time for you to get out of here, sheriff. You had your time with her. No matter what you think she may or may not have done, she is still my patient here, and she needs our care. Go on now. Get out of here."

With a grumble, the sheriff left the room. Candice leaned back, grateful she didn't have to worry about him any longer. Except now she was starting to worry about being attacked by the man who swore to protect the Hollow Valley seeing that anger in his eyes.

She wondered what he meant by calling her "a bastard supernatural". She had never heard that term before. Not even by Zak. She didn't really care about what he said. Not after all the damage he had done. She finally understood that she was part supernatural. A hybrid. But there was no way she was the werewolf stalking people around town. Maybe it was the white wolf Eric mentioned watching out for, but who was the white wolf, she wondered.

She glanced at her cell phone, resting on the bedside table. Someone must've called her parents when Candice woke. Her mom came through the front door of the hospital, fuming with anger. She didn't waste much time speaking with the nursing staff though. She wanted to see Sheriff Loveland and confront him. She may have been much smaller than him, but her temper was unmatched when it came to her children.

"If you aren't going to charge her, Sheriff, then there's no reason for the handcuffs! Her doctor and the nursing staff said she is fine and can be released so back off!"

Candice heard her mother growl at the sheriff out in the hallway. The sheriff mumbled a little something meant only for her ears. Even though he barely whispered, Candice found she was able to hear what he was saying. "Her time will come and she will have to answer for her sins."

The hospital staff helped convince the sheriff to take the hand cuffs from Candice's wrists and let her go home. The sheriff could grumble all he wanted, but there was nothing more he could do. They knew he had no evidence that she was the killer murdering people. He had nothing except for his own personal bias.

When Candice finally exited out the front door of the hospital with her parents flanking her sides, Sheriff Loveland stood waiting in the parking lot. He was leaned up against the side of his patrol car with his arms across his chest. He sucked and chewed on his tobacco, spitting in their path.

"Tsk, tsk, tsk."

"Is there a problem, Sheriff Loveland?" Candice's father glanced over his shoulder, telling his wife and daughter to head to the car. He knew he was the one who needed to take care of the judgmental fuck standing by his patrol vehicle. After all, the sheriff was his boss.

The sheriff's boots clicked across the pavement as he approached Candice's father, spitting on the pavement near his feet. His voice was hardly more than a growl. Still chewing on the wad of tobacco, he sighed.

"I knew you were going to try to get her out, Deputy Olson. Playing favorites with your own child is violating the oath you took when you first joined the county law enforcement. I should have you arrested for betraying the law like you have. After what this young hoodlum daughter of yours has done to my daughter and others around this town."

"Henry Loveland!"

"That's Sheriff Loveland to you—" The sheriff said. Candice's mom turned with a wide-eyed gaze and stepped over to where the two men stood. If anybody was going to face him, it was going to be her whether or not they liked it.

"I don't give two shits, Henry! I wouldn't give two shits if you were the Queen of England herself! Or the Pope for that matter!" She growled at him. The Sheriff let out a chuckle and glanced at Candice's dad, but before the sheriff could respond, her mom started in on the sheriff again.

"Henry Loveland, you're a goddamn hypocrite! You go to church every Sunday and preach to others about freedom and the right to own guns. America this and America that! Get your guns! Protect yourselves and everyone around you! Except you're protecting the wrong people! I hear what kind of people you hang out with! And they're not interested in protecting the people of this town. They are here to handle your political agenda against the dual natured!

"And clearly you can't accept the thought that my daughter is innocent of hurting or murdering anybody. I know my daughter, sheriff. I know she would never hurt a fly let alone murder! You have no proof that she did anything.

"If I didn't know any better, I would say your daughter ran away from this town to get away from you, but I know without a doubt that she would never leave that baby of hers behind!" Her mom yelled. Candice's dad didn't make a motion to try to silence her either, but the anger was visible on the sheriff's face.

"You just want to pin it on my daughter because she's different from yours. She's not the image of the perfect daughter by any means. She's a convenient choice for you. A scapegoat! You already know who's been doing this and for someone who seems so concerned about protecting his daughter and this town, you sure do a heck of a job fucking that up too."

"Deputy Olson! You better handle your wife before I arrest her for assault on an officer!" The sheriff spat out another clump of something nasty on the pavement. Her mom's eyes were blazing with anger and she lunged forward, ready to get into the sheriff's face once more. He stood there with a crooked grin appearing on his face.

"If you want assault, old man, I can give it to you! Get back, Candy!"

"Kellie, Kellie!" Her dad finally stepped forward to restrain his wife from whatever she was about to do. He pushed her toward the car a few steps back and although she tried stepping around him, she stood back. "We're not going to do this, Kellie! Not today. That's my boss!"

"I don't care who the hell that man thinks he is! He needs to know he's not the only person in this town who could..."

"Kellie! Let's go home!"

The old sheriff stood chuckling with his arms crossed over his chest, leaning against his car. He stood watching and waiting while Candice and her parents all climbed into the family vehicle and shut their doors.

CHAPTER TWENTY FOUR

om? Do you really think he's more concerned about pinning the murders on me than he is about finding Val?" Candice stared out the window, putting on her seatbelt. She watched the Sheriff at the other side of the parking lot.

Silence hung for a long moment before her mom finally turned toward her and spoke, smiling softly. "I think you already know the answer to that, Candy."

"Residents from Juniper reported another animal attack near the high school baseball stadium. Police will not release the identity of the victim at this time. The family has yet to be notified. Local neighbors in the area have their own ideas of what happened and what is going on around town."

Shirley Jones with her blonde hair tied up into a ponytail turned from the camera to an older woman with graying hair and a young boy standing off to the side, waiting patiently. Candice had seen the young boy before, but she couldn't remember. She thought he looked a little too young to have attended Camp Gray though.

Candice scooted forward on the bed, setting the bowl of half melted cookies and cream ice cream to the side, hoping it wouldn't spill. She was the only one in the house who was still awake. Everyone else was already in bed for the night. She had been waiting for the replay of America's Next Top Model when a breaking news report interrupted.

"It was the full moon. These things happen. That's what my daddy tells me! And my grandma! Didn't they tell you the supernatural come out to play during the full moon, lady?"

Candice snickered, idly listening to the reporter continue with her report after turning away from the young boy. She wondered what the young boy really knew about the supernatural coming out to play under the full moon. Were there children that young who knew about werewolves? Were there children that young who were werewolves? She assumed it was possible.

She wondered what Zak knew at that age or if had still been of the belief that the only monsters were the ones under the bed. Or in the closet. She wasn't sure she was ready to know that truth. After what had happened, she was starting to accept that the world of the supernatural lurked in the shadows. She couldn't help wondering why a supernatural would be attacking people. Everyone seemed to get along.

Had something recently changed that she was about to be thrown into? Was there some kind of supernatural war going on? Most importantly if it was werewolves attacking people, why was she the only one that had survived? Not understanding why had been the most difficult part.

She realized Zak and Eric's situation was different. If they were really werewolves, was it one of them who saved her? Or did one of them attack her? Or maybe it was all just a coincidence? She didn't see Zak or even Eric being a serial killer in their hometown. She wondered if one of those wolves were responsible for all these "animal attacks".

She also wondered about Sheriff Loveland who seemed to be cold and callous about his own daughter's disappearance. He seemed suspicious, but why would someone like him kidnap his own daughter and try to blame someone else for her disappearance? Maybe he was somehow behind it all. Being sheriff, he had a whole staff of deputies under his authority. They would do anything he said considering he was just a bully of a man who treated women and supernaturals like they were less than human.

Candice grabbed her cell phone and opened up her text messages. She sat there and thought for several long moments, tapping the edge of her cell phone against her temple. She really didn't want to talk to Zak, but he was the only one she could think of when it came to this supernatural business.

If there was anybody who would know anything about the supernatural, it was going to be him, but with Quinn around, finding answers would be a little difficult. Getting Zak alone was going to be tough period, but she needed to find Valerie. If not for Doreen, for her young son who didn't understand why his mom hadn't come home yet. She sighed and opened a new text message thread on her phone, typing in Zak's name for the contact. She quickly typed out and sent a message.

Zak. Can we talk? I could use some help.

Candice set her phone down, not expecting a response back for a while. After all, Zak still had to deal with Quinn and her shit. She wondered for a moment who had bailed Quinn out of jail. If anybody were to do so, she hoped it wasn't Zak considering Quinn had been arrested for having a gun and aiming at him. She needed to stop thinking of Zak.

She glanced down at her guitar case, still laying in the

middle of her bedroom. She glanced over the different stickers and patches. Many of them were faded and torn. A few smiley faces were altered to look dead or emo, which made her think of Ramona. She had been right that it had been too long since they practiced together. Thankfully, she still had their address in her phone.

The next morning, Candice headed out the front door, carrying her guitar case in one hand and an old tote bag with a few necessities over her opposite shoulder. Suddenly, her phone buzzed. When she pulled it out of her pocket, she noticed a new text message waiting. She smiled when she read Zak's message.

I can always make time for u. Let's meet

The message would have to be left read for now. She had other relationships and promises to keep up with. She tossed her phone aside and placed her guitar in the front seat of her dad's old truck, climbing in behind the wheel.

Nearly an hour later, she could see the outskirts of Craven Hill in the distance. She followed the highway until the first exit appeared, leading her to the main road. The late morning sun started to warm up the truck cab, and she rolled down her windows as she reached the first red light.

After a quick pit stop, at the gas station to fill up, she followed the side streets to the main road, St Francis. Once parked, she pulled out her cell phone to check the address again. Thankfully, building H wasn't too far of a walk.

After grabbing her guitar, she crossed the parking lot into a courtyard that took her through a xeriscaped garden with yuccas and a large cactus plant. A sudden wave of déjà vu washed over her. She had walked through the courtyard and to Ramona's second-floor apartment many times before she moved out.

When she knocked, piercing blue eyes answered the door, but she still couldn't remember his name. He knew who she was though and yelled over his shoulder for Ramona. The door swung wide open and Ramona appeared, dressed in an old pair of pajama bottoms with bats and cats and an old concert tee. Ramona glanced over her shoulder as piercing blue eyes disappeared.

"I didn't expect to see you." Ramona said, leaning against the door with her arms crossed over her chest. She glanced over Candice and her eyes lit up when she noticed the guitar case in her hand. A smile appeared on her lips. "And you brought your guitar?"

"I told you, Ramona. I need a little warm up and practice before I'm ready to go out on the road with you guys. I've had work and other shit going on." She started. "Mind if I come in? This thing isn't getting any lighter."

"Oh, shit sorry." Ramona stepped out of the way, leaving the door open. Candice stepped inside and shut the door, setting the guitar case down. She then took off her zip up hoodie and glanced around for a spot to put it, but Ramona was more prepared. "You can just set your hoodie on the chair by the door."

Candice took a seat in the brown overstuffed chair and glanced around the living room, which hadn't changed much since she had moved out a couple months ago. When she left, it had been the three girls living together. Her, Ramona, and Tommie, but now it seemed piercing blue eyes had taken her spot. At least, that would explain the balled up pair of dirty socks nearby.

She made a face, ignoring them, and directed her attention toward Ramona who went to the kitchen. She was getting a pot of coffee ready to brew and Candice smiled. When the coffee maker started to percolate, Ramona crossed to the living room, shuffling her stocking feet across the tile floor. "You arrived right on time, Candy. I was just about to hop in the shower so we can get ready to leave. Is there anything you need before I get in?"

"No, I think I'll be fine, Ramona." Candice said, leaning back into the cushions of the old familiar chair. Ramona smiled and disappeared down the hallway, leaving Candice alone. She leaned her head back and stared up at the ceiling, listening to the coffee brew. The fresh scent inspired a smile to appear across her face. She closed her eyes, enjoying the moment of peace and quiet.

Suddenly, something soft and furry brushed against her arm. She jolted up only to be greeted by a large ginger cat sitting on the arm of the chair, staring at her. Candice reached out to pet the cat, but he backed away, analyzing her hand. The cat started sniffing, opening its mouth to taste her smell.

"Soda pop!" Piercing blue eyes came down the hallway dressed in hardly more than a towel wrapped around his waist. His dark hair dripped in his eyes and fell to his muscular chest. Candice grew warm from the inside out and glanced away, feeling ashamed.

"He's ok. Really. Just wasn't expecting him to pop out of nowhere."

"Sorry about that. He's not mean or anything, I promise." He chuckled, glancing down at himself when he stepped into the living room. "Sorry. I should probably get dressed first. I'll be right back."

The rest of the morning wasn't any less chaotic. After grabbing a mug and pouring herself a cup of coffee, Candice stayed put on the overstuffed chair and simply waited for everyone. The ginger cat, Soda pop, even joined her, which she enjoyed immensely.

Candice always liked cats, but growing up, she couldn't keep one because her stupid younger brother, Kevin, was allergic. Candice had started getting a little jealous of the new baby. Her parents brought home a small ginger kitten only a few weeks before her mother was due to give birth. Unfortunately, Kevin wasn't even a full month old when they realized his strange new rashes were due to all the cat hair flying around.

She still remembered how upset she was when they told her they couldn't keep the kitten and that a nice family on a farm would be taking him in. If it hadn't been for that incident, she might not have been led to her first guitar. It was a bright pink electric from the music shop where her mom regularly bought new sheet music for her piano. Thus, her love of music was born.

Once Ramona, Tommie, and piercing blue eyes were all dressed and had drunk at least one cup of coffee, Candice grabbed her guitar case and followed them down to the van. Ramona was much more animated now that the whole band was back together.

"I'm so excited you finally made the time to join us, Candice! I'm so ready to jam with you again!"

CHAPTER TWENTY FIVE

I'll have to think about it, Ramona. I mean, if we're planning to leave for California soon anyway, what would be the point?"

"Maybe, you're right." Ramona started, wrapping her arms around Candice in a quick hug. She kissed her cheek before pulling away. "We'll see you soon for more practice?"

Candice responded with a smile and a quick nod. Ramona pumped her fist and spun into the air, cheering with excitement. Candice watched her run across the parking lot and rejoin Tommie and her boyfriend, Matthew, with the piercing blue eyes. They stepped inside their apartment before she finally turned away.

She stashed her guitar in the truck and checked her phone, finally responding to Zak's text message from earlier. She slipped her phone back into her pocket and climbed into the truck, heading home.

Later that night, after a scorching afternoon, her dad brought home takeout from Troy's Tavern. Her family were settled on the couch with their takeout burgers and fries when she came into the living room. Both her brothers were already a few bites deep into their cheeseburgers. Cody discarded the large section of onions with a gooey mess of ketchup and mustard on the wrapper.

Candice's attention was drawn to the television when the familiar tune of one of her favorite movies started playing. She feigned a pout and grabbed the last bag, which held her order. A mushroom Swiss burger and fries with a couple of sides of ranch at the bottom. She landed on the nearby recliner in the corner when suddenly, a phone started ringing. Her mom tore her eyes from the television and glanced around with a narrowed gaze.

"Who forgot to turn off their phone?" She asked while the phone continued to ring. Candice and her two brothers shrugged. None of them had any interest in checking their phones. That's when Candice's dad slipped off the couch, and darted out of the room.

"Oh shit!"

"Jack! I thought you were off tonight?" Her mom yelled when her dad disappeared down the hallway to the kitchen. He grabbed the phone and took one glance at the caller ID, sighing heavily. He stared at his phone with a grumble, hesitating to answer.

"I'm supposed to be, babe, but you know how this shit goes." He yelled back, but received no further response. He dreaded answering, but he learned that things were different working in the homicide division. Swallowing the lump in his throat, he finally answered.

Back in the living room, Candice and the rest of the family were enjoying their food and the movie that had barely started. The back door suddenly opened and shut. She glanced at her mother, who audibly sighed knowing he would be a little while.

One by one, they finished their meals. When Candice rose from the couch not long after finishing, her mom looked over at her with concern. Both of her brothers were leaning back on the couch, appearing half asleep. Finally, her mom spoke. "Where are you going? I thought this was one of your favorites?"

"Yeah, but I'm kinda tired, mom. I'm just gonna head to bed."

"Everything ok?"

"Yeah. Just feeling exhausted and worn out. It has been a long week up at the camp, you know?" Candice started. Not to mention everything else going on, she thought to herself.

"And I'm sure that heat all week didn't help either, did it?" Her mom frowned, putting a hand out and wiggling her fingers. She approached and crouched down, letting her mom put a hand on her forehead. "You feel fine. Sunburnt. But you feel fine. Go get some rest, Candy."

"Night, mom." Candice said, disappearing down the hallway. She headed up the staircase and overheard her father talking out on the back porch. Quietly, she crouched down and listened to the conversation.

"While I'm enjoying a night in with my family." He raised his voice, pacing back and forth. His head was lowered with a frown etched on his face. He let out another heavy sigh and Candice stayed as still as she could, trying to catch more of the conversation. "Can't this wait until the morning?

"In the gorge? I thought we searched that whole area already? And her vehicle."

A floorboard creaked and Candice gasped, turning to dash up the stairs. Her dad popped his head up just as she ascended. She shut the door and stood there for a long moment. The summer heat was quickly getting to her, almost suffocating. Sweat trickled at her temples. She crossed the room, unlocked the window, and cracked it open. A cool summer breeze slipped through the nearby trees and rushed into the room. She sighed with relief.

Her phone buzzed in her pocket and she slipped her phone out, finding a couple of new text messages from Zak. She smiled to herself, reading them silently. He couldn't talk tonight, but maybe she could come by when Quinn was away tomorrow. Finally, she crawled onto her bed, grabbing the book from the nightstand. Before long, she was falling asleep.

The cool breeze didn't last long. The night air was just as warm as the last several nights. The summer had turned out to be the hottest she could remember. Nor was there a single storm cloud anywhere in the sky, leaving no hope for a late night shower to bring even a few moments of relief. She shifted and kicked the blanket off to the bed in her half asleep daze.

Strange images played through her mind as she slept. A blood halo around the moon. The evergreen trees. A purple mist. A pair of green eyes. The sound of howling wolves. Yet another dream about wolves that would only leave her confused. Dreams seemed to be telling her more than anybody else lately, but what it was trying to tell her was unknown.

When she woke once more, the room was still dark. The window was cracked, and everything around her was silent and still. The faint glow of the waning full moon was enough to cast shadows from the trees against the window and walls.

She stared into the darkness; her mind too busy for sleep. There was something powerful about that dream that filled her with an energy she didn't understand. Something had been stirred within her and there was only one solution.

She rose from bed and in the shorts and old tee shirt she wore, slipped on her running shoes. Candice hesitated and grabbed her cell phone, heading downstairs. She was as quiet as she could be. When the stairs creaked, she froze, and glanced up, but the sound of her dad snoring continued. Her mom didn't appear, and neither did either of her younger brothers. Letting out a heavy breath, she continued down the stairs and out of the house.

She needed some fresh air. She needed to go out for one of her nighttime runs. The urge only grew stronger when the light of the moon touched her skin, something that seemed to be growing since her very first shift only days ago.

Once outside she glanced up at the sky. Clouds floated across the waning full moon and that's when she felt that strange, yet familiar electric feeling in the pit of her stomach. The very same feeling when Zak first introduced her to a side of the night she had never known before. Except nothing seemed to be happening. Is this what it was like to be a hybrid werewolf when the moon wasn't full?

CHAPTER TWENTY SIX

Candice woke late the next morning, feeling almost hungover in some strange sense. The dizziness. Angry buzzing bees in her skull. And the migraine from hell that made her feel like crawling under a rock to die. She rolled to her side, not wanting to move from the safety and comfort of her bed.

After pulling the sheets over her head, she fell back asleep for a few more hours. When she finally rose once more, it was nearly midday. The rays of the sun weren't nearly as blinding. She headed downstairs, in an old pair of sweats, making a beeline to the kitchen to make some coffee. She needed at least a couple of cups before having to deal with Zak.

She hadn't heard back from Zak, but at such a late hour of the morning, she thought Quinn would be away. She should be safe driving to see him even if every part of her was telling her not to. She didn't know what else to do though. Zak was the only werewolf she knew, and she needed to talk to someone about it.

The moment she pulled on to Cherry Wood Lane, she spotted his little red sports car parked along the sidewalk a few houses down. She let out a heavy sigh of relief that she didn't realize she had been holding and pulled up behind his car, shutting off the engine. Luckily, the driveway was empty. Zak was home alone.

She walked up the driveway and opened the gate to the front yard overgrown with weeds and littered with toys. A small neon pink plastic pool was propped up against the side of the house. She stepped carefully, dodging a few overripe apples lying in the grass and passed a few others crawling with worms, causing her to look away with disgust.

She stepped up to the front porch and took a deep breath, listening to the silence. Except for a few dogs barking off in the distance, the neighborhood seemed strangely quiet. Finally, she made a fist and knocked. The next door neighbor's dog came to the fence and barked at her, but she was unphased.

Candice didn't wait long when Zak appeared in a sudden rush, opening the door. He was dressed in a pair of old gym shorts and a band tee. The frown on his face faded, leaving a ghost on his face when he caught her eyes. A moment of hurt pinched at her.

"Ace? Was that just—why are you pounding on the fucking door like that? I thought it was the fucking cops. Jesus Christ."

"You expecting the cops to come pounding at the door?"

"No, but that's what you sounded like... You never know in this town." He stepped outside in his bare feet, shutting the front door behind him. Another frown appeared on his face, rubbing the sleep from his eyes. "What's going on, anyway? I didn't expect to see you around. Not here."

"Seriously? You said I could stop by. I need to talk and figure out what's going on around, Zak. I need the whole truth. Not some vague version." She turned toward him, catching sight of the chipped black and pink nail polish on his toes. She glanced at him with a smile. She never knew him to wear any girly colors especially pink, but it had been a few years. People changed.

"Tell you the truth about what?" He said, stepping into the yard. He offered his hand to help her. "Let's go over to the treehouse. My dad could be home at any time."

Candice took Zak's hand and followed him across the yard, dodging a few toy cars, and trucks laying haphazardly. They passed a pink play house and kitchen set complete with a bunch of stuffed animals and dolls at a little table tucked around the corner.

She wondered who's kid's toys they passed out in the yard, but she was afraid to ask him. After all, they hadn't spoken in at least five years and a lot could've happened. It would break her heart to learn if he had a child with Quinn.

"I meant to call you sooner, you know, after the other night up at Camp Gray."

"It's ok, Zak. It's been an interesting couple days to say the least."

"I know. I heard Sheriff Loveland tried to arrest you at the hospital. Do you remember what happened that night?" Zak stopped at the base of the tree and climbed the ladder, disappearing into the treehouse. He popped his hand out to help her up inside.

The smell of old, moldy beer hit her nose the moment she popped her head inside. She took a glance around the treehouse, which really hadn't changed much since high school. The old blue futon and reading chair with cigarette burns were still standing against the opposite wall. The old tube television where they played video games stood nearby except now there was a new system she didn't recognize.

A warmth spread through her when she remembered back to the good old days. Back when they would spend many Friday nights making out and feeling each other up between go cart races. How long ago that all seemed. Curse those old memories. She blinked those thoughts from her mind and joined Zak on the couch, leaving a cushion between them.

"I don't know what happened, Zak. I don't remember much of that night, really. I remember the pain was so bad that I passed out in the parking lot. And you disappeared into the forest somewhere. You left me to go through all of that alone." Candice started.

"Candice, I never—"

"Shh. Please, I need to finish what's on my mind. I need to figure this out. I don't know why the Sheriff arrested me. I'm sure the rest of town has their own thoughts about what happened. But when I woke up in the hospital, he said a few things that didn't make much sense to me."

"Do you remember what he told you?" Zak leaned back at an angle, propping his arm against the back of the couch. His brows furrowed into a tight frown, waiting for her.

"He made a comment about me being a bastard supernatural. And I remember what you said about how it was already too late for me. I didn't understand what you meant at the time either, but now? I think I might understand now though."

"Understand what, Ace?"

"Well, this is all gonna sound fucking crazy, but—"

"Try me." He said, closing his eyes. An amused grin appeared, keeping his attention on her.

"Werewolves are real, Zak. And I'm one of them." She leaned in closer, whispering as he put a finger to her lips. Zak didn't say a word. He just smiled, still leaning against the corner of the couch, and waited for her to continue with her story.

"There are supernatural creatures around here. There are werewolves and shape shifters out there. For all I know, there are fucking vampires, demons, and angels out there too. That witches aren't just people who use crystals and manifest energy and sage their houses. That it's all fucking true! There's magic in Hollow's Creek."

Zak sat there silent and waited for Candice to finish. He watched her twiddle her thumbs in her lap. A nervous, anxious tick. When her fingers started moving faster, he leaned forward and put a hand on top of hers. She stared at his thumb nail with its black nail polish, and the silver wolf ring he wore.

She frowned, but she didn't push his hand away. Instead, her twitching, anxious movements came to a stop and her eyes welled with tears. When she lowered her eyes again, she spoke softly. "I... am a supernatural, Zak. I turn into a fucking werewolf and I don't even remember what happened while I was...turned?

"There's more though. I think all of this supernatural shit is the reason Valerie is missing. And that's why the sheriff is trying to blame me, Zak. That's why he tried to hold me responsible for Valerie's disappearance. He knows all about it and I don't know shit. And I need you to tell me that I'm not crazy because I know you know the truth of it all too. Because you're still keeping secrets from me! I saw you shift into a wolf!"

Zak leaned back once more when Candice pulled her hands away. She frowned hard. Her eyes narrowed. Rising to his feet, he started pacing. A long lock of his dark, greasy hair fell between his green eyes. Candice watched him. A palpable tension filled the air.

"Zak! Stop, please! Just talk to me. I fucking hate it when you do this. For once, just fucking talk to me!" She said, rising from the couch. He did stop and met her gaze. A gentle smile tugged at the corners of his lips. He reached for her, stepping in close, but she stepped away and pulled back her arm.

"I never left you alone, Ace."

"Don't!"

"I didn't leave you alone that night up on the mountain. We were together all night long. Just you and me under the full moon. In our animal form. Maybe I wasn't the one to turn you, but you're the one I need by my side. I can feel it. Fuck Quinn. And fuck your maker. We were always meant to be together, Candice."

"Don't fucking lie to me!"

"Why would I fucking lie about this?"

"Then why did you leave me for Quinn?"

"Because I was expected to be with another werewolf! I was pressured to be with someone who could carry on the werewolf genes. Being with a human is forbidden by pack laws. It's forbidden being with someone who isn't part of our species. Why do you think my dad raised me and my sister alone?

"I was still a baby when my mom tried to leave, but the pack still found her and killed her. They almost killed me and my sister too because neither one of us are pure blood. My dad didn't want to see that happen again. He left the pack after her death and that's how we ended up out here in this fucking hick town!

"My dad. He also told me that if I really loved you, that I needed to leave you and be with someone who would be accepted by the pack. I needed to be with someone from this pack. And that if I really loved you, I needed to let you live a normal human life away from this supernatural shit. I was protecting you from the pack!"

Candice stood there contemplating his words, but she felt like she was drowning. Everything he said was just too much. Her hands started shaking and tears rolled down her cheeks. Her heart ached with conflict and she dropped to the floor. "I don't know what to say..."

Zak pulled her trembling body into his arms. He gently

rocked her back and forth, and stroked her hair, trying to calm her down. Her tears fell freely, soaking both their cheeks. He lifted his hand and wiped some of the wetness away with the pads of his fingers. His touch alone had started to calm her.

The tears were fading. She was no longer shaking from the wave of emotions surging through her. He leaned in and kissed her forehead. She lifted her gaze, wiped the tears from her face, and took a deep breath. Her voice hardly more than a whisper. "Why couldn't you tell me any of this before?"

"Because being a hybrid is almost just as bad as being a human to a werewolf. You don't want to live a life where you can't live your truth, Candice. Living as a hybrid, you can't live your truth because you're too human to be wolf and too wolf to be human."

"But...you said it was already too late for me."

"Yes. Because I was there that night you were attacked. I was there to protect you even as a beast. I had hoped you hadn't been bitten. That the stupid fucking legend of the full moon with the blood halo wasn't true, but it's not just a legend. I was born like this so I didn't have that choice. You didn't deserve any of that, Ace, and I'm here to protect you."

"What about the pack? And Quinn?"

"How about you let me worry about all of that? Fuck the rules. I'm tired of having to hide who I am. And I'll be here to help you through all of it. I promise, Ah—"

A crooked grin curled across her lips. She lifted her hands to the sides of his face and leaned in for a kiss. His lips found hers and she melted into him. Her hands slipped from his face, but their kiss never broke, stumbling over to the couch. Over and over, they kissed. Soft sweet kisses lingered and became deeper.

She let out a gentle groan against his lips. Their tongues met in a dance they fell into all too easily. His hands slipped over her full figure and down to her waist. Soon, his desire for her became apparent with the bulge in his jeans. Candice laid back, and he slipped between her thighs, closing the small gap between them.

He leaned back, removing his shirt. She lifted her hand to brush over his chest, peppered in fading bruises. She frowned hard, remembering Eric. She noticed an older tattoo Candice didn't remember. A full moon and stars hovering over the mountains. Looking close enough, she could see a howling wolf. He leaned back in and trailed kisses down along her neck and to the top of her breasts, peeking out from her low-cut top.

She discarded her top and her bra, letting them fall where they may. His kisses found the path down her naked torso. She arched close against him, slipping a hand into his dark hair. Her body responded to his every touch and kiss. The passion flowed through her with a familiarity that coaxed another moan from her lips. The anticipation was agony.

His hands slipped to her waist where he undid her belt and jeans, pulling them from her legs. She arched her body, helping him remove the last bit of her clothes. She moved her hands to his waist to remove his belt, but he pushed her hand away, slipping his hand between her thighs. She obeyed the silent command.

He slipped low between her legs. Moments later, she was arching her body against him. His tongue and lips danced over the warmth of her sweetness. She moaned deeply, and he continued to tease, building the tension of passionate electricity between them. Gripping his hair tight, she nearly screamed out his name.

Zak slipped out of his jeans and without another word, they became one just like old times. Every moan had been worth the wait. She was his again. The way her body conformed to his, Candice lost herself in the moment.

She let out another moan, barely whispering his name. When he leaned down to kiss her neck, there was a magnetic pull in the air. A passionate energy she never experienced before. She briefly wondered if it had to do with their dual nature. When her body arched into his, the air suddenly shimmered with a mystical energy.

She let out another moan, whispering. "Oh Zak. I am yours…"

And so, he took her in a flash of sweaty passion. He finally landed, trying to catch his breath. He rested his head against Candice's bare breasts. She glanced down over him and watched his eyes close with a smile on his lips. She leaned her head back and smiled, enjoying the warmth of his skin against hers. She even loved the feeling of his unshaven face rubbing against her soft skin. Nothing could've ruined their post-coital moment.

CHAPTER TWENTY SEVEN

Candice's cell phone started to ring. Her eyes shot open, and she tapped Zak on the arm. He leaned back on to his heels, still very naked. He smirked at her, running a hand through his dark hair. She glanced at his semi erect member for only a moment, but quickly made herself turn away. She wasn't trying to be distracted into another romp. Finally, he laid back on the couch. She rose to her feet, slipping on her vibrant pink panties, while she scanned the area for her cell phone.

She quickly spotted it, tossed haphazardly on the floorboards, and snatched it. When she turned the newly cracked screen toward her, she saw her dad's number. Carefully, she answered. He never called her in the middle of the day when he was supposed to be out at the office. "Dad? Is everything ok?"

"I didn't want to tell you this over the phone, but we found Valerie."

The phone dropped out of her hands and she turned toward Zak. She was speechless and overwhelmed with a multitude of emotion. It was like a huge weight had been lifted from her shoulders. She was barely able to contain the tears that welled in her eyes.

"What's wrong, Ace?"

"It's Valerie. I need to get home. I'll...we'll talk more later, ok?" Candice said, picking up her phone and the rest of her clothes off the floor. She rushed to get her jeans and tee shirt back on, fumbling a few times. A thick silence hung in the air. Other than Zak rising from the couch to dress himself, she was oblivious to everything else. She was anxious to get home.

Candice jumped back into her vehicle and raced across town, kicking up a few clouds of dust on her way. Upon pulling into the driveway, she barely turned the engine off before running inside. Except when she got inside, she couldn't find her dad. She peeked in the living room, kitchen, and the back porch. With a glance at the clock, she went back down the hallway and spoke aloud. "Dad? Are you here? I thought you would be home."

"I'm up in my office, Candice." Her father's voice floated down the hallway stairs. She went up, stopping at the cracked door of her dad's office. She knocked and waited for her dad to push the door open. "What's going on?"

"I raced over here because I couldn't believe I heard what you said on the phone." She said, examining him as he sat behind his desk. He still wore his full uniform. The brown button-up shirt, tan khakis, and his hiking boots. Her dad's old hat sat upon the desk.

She wondered how long ago he had arrived home because he rarely stayed long in his work uniform. Not intentionally. Candice had a seat in the chair across the desk from her father. He turned away from the computer screen with a smile.

He seemed busy, but she needed confirmation about what he told her on the phone. The anticipation grew quickly. She only hoped that she hadn't imagined what he said on the phone only twenty minutes ago. "We found Valerie. We found her alive last night."

"Y—you found her?! How's she doing? Where did you find her?"

"One question at a time now, Candy."

"Then tell me what happened, dad." She said, shifting in her seat. Despite her late morning rendezvous with Zak in his treehouse, she was still filled with anticipation for her dad's story.

WHEN HER DAD FINALLY left the house the night before, Candice and her brothers were already asleep. Her mom was lying in bed watching the nightly news when he left the bathroom, dressed in his work uniform to patrol up the mountain. Neither one of them was happy about it, but they knew it was a part of his position in supernatural homicide investigations.

Being a traffic cop only three years earlier wasn't nearly as exciting, but there were days he missed being county highway patrol. It had been much less responsibility. Even the paperwork for the tickets he wrote were easier. Out-of-towners going more than five miles over the posted speed limit. People with half empty beer bottles in their laps or three-foot-tall bongs in the backseat were the extent of what he saw on a daily basis.

When he wasn't out patrolling the highways, he had time to listen in on cases while he tried to stay focused on his paperwork. That was the first mistake he made. All because he was able to provide some additional intelligence on a case that the squad wasn't already aware of. That was the whole problem with being in a small town for a lifetime. One knew too much about how things worked. Back before joining the squad, he knew Lieutenant Jones was right about the sheriff's hypocrisy.

Along with the sheriff. many of the citizens of Hollow's Creek didn't believe that supernatural beings belong in the human world. A radical point of view considering the history of the small town, which many of the older generations including the sheriff denied. Behind closed doors, there was suspicion the sheriff was using his power to control the supernatural population in order to keep the citizens under his control. Only nobody was sure how he was doing it until the Rayers showed up.

The sheriff needed to be brought to justice. And now, facing new murders on a semi-regular basis, he could see how many of them were supernatural in nature. They even had a confidential informant that was a werewolf, but their identity wasn't exactly something he could share with Candice. Thankfully, she didn't stop and ask further questions.

Her dad continued recalling how he was falling asleep behind the wheel of his vehicle, watching the old buildings, just up the highway from Camp Gray. The Gray family owned most of the mountainside, which was why Lieutenant Jones wanted him to stake the place out for any signs of strange events that might occur. The Silver Coin was the last place that the lieutenant could think of that hadn't been searched.

The Silver Coin was an old boarding school turned hotel turned warehouse that the Sheriff owned at least in part from what her father knew. He didn't see the appeal of the area. Even the Graffiti Heart didn't seem very exciting. If he didn't know that the place was a music sanctuary, he wouldn't understand why Candice enjoyed spending so much time there. Hopefully he wouldn't have to, but he was stuck on a stake out in the middle of a Thursday night.

He reached over and grabbed the travel mug sitting in the center console, popping the top. He tilted his head back, closed his eyes, and let the last few drops of coffee fall to his tongue. He was going to need more if his lieutenant expected him to sit here and watch the abandoned warehouse all damn night. He placed the cup back down and leaned back in his seat, just watching the horizon from under the protection of the evergreens.

His eyes were fluttering with sleep deprivation when his radio crackled on. A familiar voice came through the speakers. He shot up, ready and mostly alert, listening to the call, catching a quick glance at the glowing numbers on the dashboard clock. It was just before one am. He grabbed the microphone and waited.

"Unit five and unit seven. What is your current twenty?"

"This is unit five. I'm still up in area six watching north of Camp Gray. Nothing exciting going on tonight." He spoke into the speaker. He cleared his throat and spoke once again. "If anybody is nearby, I could use a coffee run up here."

"This is unit seven. I'm patrolling through town in area three. Quiet night. Nothing's going on down here either. A few crickets. I think I saw Bambi's mom on the edge of the woods though..."

"This is unit ten. Unit five, I can head up that way with some coffee." A woman's voice came over the radio. One of the younger deputies who had recently joined the force in Hollow's Creek. She wasn't a rookie fresh out of the academy, but she didn't have much experience with the supernatural either. Only the more supernaturally seasoned deputies patrolled the highway through the forest this late at night.

"That would be great, unit ten. You know where to find me. Over." A crooked grin curled over his lips when he spoke. He could almost taste the hot, fresh coffee on his tongue and he couldn't wait for it.

"Ten four, unit five." The younger deputy said. He placed his radio microphone back into place on the dashboard and leaned back in his seat, scanning the less dense areas of the forest across the highway. He watched and waited for something to move among the cars or even closer to the building. It was a relatively quiet night though.

Suddenly, a pair of headlights appeared from down the highway.

He slouched down in his seat and waited for the car to pass, but instead the vehicle pulled up beside his just beneath the brush of the trees. He heard a voice yell out to him and he poked his head up to see the young deputy smiling.

She held a large coffee in one hand and a paper bag in the other. Suddenly, a sleepy smile appeared across his lips. He rolled down his window to take the coffee and the bag of cream and sugar from her hands. "You're my hero tonight, Sherry."

"Yeah, I know. You need it sitting up here all night watching this creepy place. I don't know why you're up here all alone. What happened to your partner?" She turned off her car engine and hung her arms over the side of the vehicle. He shrugged, carefully removing the lid from his coffee to dump some packets of cream and sugar in the steaming brew he balanced between his legs. "Mind if I join you for the night?"

"You don't have any other assignments tonight?" Jack tossed the bag with his trash on the floor of his car, and took a sip of his coffee, feeling the warmth flow down his throat and warm the late summer night chill from his bones.

"Nope, I sure don't, but I wasn't in the mood to stay at home tonight either. My roommate is having some kind of party. And none of them wanted to have a cop sitting around the place, anyway."

"Mhmm. They never want us folks around unless someone is doing them dirty. You'll get used to it or you'll find yourself hanging out with more of the force than the public around here.

"I don't mind you joining me. Just stay away from the highway. You don't want to blow our cover and chance someone seeing us out here." He took another drink of his coffee and reached down, unlocking the vehicle doors. Sherry rolled up her windows and slipped out of her car, ducking beneath the canopy of trees on her way over.

"Why are you out here, anyway?"

Nearly half of the coffee from his cup was gone by the time Sherry slipped into his cruiser. When he turned to answer her, a bright light across the street flickered on. A light that stood near the old building that was the Silver Coin. He put a finger up to his lips. They silently watched the movement across the highway.

A large group of people slipped out from the north end of the building, which had been blocked from view by a large pile of old wooden crates and palettes. There were men and women walking toward the parking lot and many of them were talking and laughing. He had no doubt they had a few drinks before leaving the property.

They watched the group disperse through the parking lot and slip into different vehicles. Some trucks, cars, and even a few sport utility vehicles. And a motorcycle or two. But those bright lights on the front of the building never came on. He had patrolled the area long enough to know those lights usually came on when with motion, but something seemed off. Ever since the mayor ordered safety lights be installed in the area, he had never once seen them off. He doubted the occurrence was a supernatural event though.

He took another sip of his coffee as he and his partner

slouched in their seats. Bright headlights flashed over the trees and through the pine needles. Engines roared through the night, tearing down the mountain. Soon, Deputy Lucero would be having a good old time chasing after a few rowdy individuals driving through town and toward Juniper. And maybe he would catch a drunk.

He and Sherry waited until they heard the last vehicle zoom down the highway, heading south east toward the lower end of the valley. Both he and Sherry noticed the lights on the building across the highway were still off. He frowned and finished the last of his coffee, placing the cup back into place. He pointed toward the passenger side of the vehicle. "In the glove box, can you grab the flashlights?"

She grabbed them without any questions and handed them over, frowning. "Jack?"

"Deputy Wilson. Are you ready to go investigate that property with me? And hunt for a little supernatural tonight?"

"What? Are you kidding? That's why I came out here, sir!" He hated it when younger people called him sir, but there was something more important going on he quickly reminded himself. He slipped out of the car, dropping his keys into his pocket in exchange for the gun sitting at his waist. Sherry followed suit a few steps behind him, unholstering her own weapon.

They made it across the highway and past one of the side parking lots, heading toward the building with haste, dodging a few tree branches on the way over. The scent of smoke tickled the air, which was not a good thing in the middle of a high desert forest like the Hollow Valley.

The summer had been hot and dry, leaving the area at risk of wildfire. Her dad swore under his breath and rushed down the path leading toward the Silver Coin. Several hundred yards from the back door of the building, he found the smoking remains of a recent campfire. Whoever had been in charge of putting out the flames hadn't finished the job. He lowered his gun slightly and with a glance over his shoulder, he called out to the young deputy.

"Sherry! Back here!"

Before long, Sherry appeared. Jack had extinguished the last of the burning embers in the pile of charred wood, which had their undivided attention. Suddenly, they heard a strange sound in the distance. They both paused and surveyed the area.

"Did you hear that?" Sherry said.

He didn't say a word though. He approached the end of the property, where the banks of the nearby lake separated the Gray's property from the forest. The waning gibbous moon shined on the surface of the small lake. Sherry walked to the edge of the water and listened, waiting, but the night was silent once more.

He stepped away from the banks and led Sherry across the property, toward the back door of the large building that was the Silver Coin. He stopped at the northwest corner and waited, holding his gun close, listening to the quiet of the night. He glanced back at Sherry who crouched down, still following along behind. She appeared nervous with the lines of concentration on her face, but he thought she was trying to mask her fear of the unknown.

A muffled scream came from somewhere inside the building. Sherry's eyes widened, and he frowned harder, speaking in a whisper that was almost silent. "Don't you give up on me now! I need you here in case I need backup, Sherry! You understand me?"

Silent, Sherry nodded. He tried the back door to find it locked. He was going to need a little help getting inside the building. The door knob appeared brand new, almost like it had recently been replaced.

"You better stand back, Sherry."

CHAPTER TWENTY EIGHT

He lifted his leg and kicked as close to the door knob as he could get. The door didn't swing open, but he heard a muffled crunch on the other side. He lifted his leg once more and kicked the door again. This time, the door slammed against the inside wall, hitting a solid concrete wall. He took one step forward and stood there for a long moment, a sinking feeling growing in the pit of his stomach.

He finally glanced back at Sherry. She stood there, waiting for commands. He remained silent for several moments and she lowered her weapon. His stomach started feeling queasy, but he stepped inside the building. Without a glance over his shoulder, he spoke. "I need you to stay up here and watch out for someone that may show up."

"But what if you get into trouble?"

"Sherry, I'll be fine. I need you to keep watch. This is very important for you to remember. If someone shows up, I need you to call for back up and come find me. Do you understand?"

"Yes. I understand."

That's when he nodded and turned into the darkness of the

building. He waited a moment, allowing his eyes the time to adjust. Another muffled scream rang through the building, much louder now that he was inside, almost echoing. He had never stepped foot inside the Silver Coin, but now that he stood inside, it was much different from what he expected.

He stood near the entrance of a large area that had been turned into a bar complete with pool tables and a juke box in the far corner. On the front wall, someone had painted a mountain forest with a wolf howling up at the full moon. The smell of beer and cigarettes clung to the air. A set of neon lights with the words Silver Coin hung over the bar, but there were no lights on.

He quickly stepped out of the bar area back into the hallway. With his gun cocked, he cautiously stepped forward, not wanting to alert anybody to his presence. He was sure he did more than enough of that by kicking the back door open.

At the farthest end of the hallway, he found a set of doors leading to what appeared to be a kitchen. When he peered inside the small window, he saw a dark room, but the beam from his flashlight caught a few stainless steel workstations complete with a few sinks.

Catty corner from the kitchen doors, there was a door leading to a staircase. One that went up into the upper and lower levels of the building. That's when he heard that scream even louder than before. He stepped forward, gripping his gun tight.

He opened the door and stepped forward. He heard something rustle nearby and a voice call out to him. He stood there, frozen in place, and listened to the hoarse voice, which somehow seemed familiar.

"Is someone there? Please. If somebody is there, please help me. I'm trapped down here. I've been trapped for weeks. I need help please! Please get me out of here! I have a family. I need to see my child!"

He lowered his gun and re-holstered before grabbing his flashlight to explore further. He entered a dark, hidden room. A couple of large cells lined the wall, and they were empty except for a couple of beds and a table holding large trays of food and water.

"Can you help me? Please!"

He lifted his flashlight. The beam of bright yellow light landed on her face. She squinted bright blue eyes and lifted her dirty arms to shield herself. He lowered the flashlight. "Valerie?"

"Yes?"

Candice was left speechless once he finished his story. An overwhelming wave of relief surged through her. Tears filled her eyes. She had been insistent on finding Valerie before she could leave Hollow's Creek, but hearing that she had been found was a little surreal for her. Life had changed quickly in the matter of months.

Zak was back in town. She had been turned into a werewolf. Ramona and Tommie were still planning to drive out to Los Angeles, and they wanted her to come along. Zak finally revealed his true feelings for her. Moving in with Valerie had been pushed further down her list because she had forgotten all about their plans. The feeling wrenched her heart.

With tears trailing down her cheeks, she rose and wrapped her arms around her dad. Another wave of conflicting emotions washed over her and when her dad wrapped his arms around her, she let it all pour from her, sobbing on his shoulder. She finally whispered a few words in her dad's ears. "Thank you, daddy. Thank you for finding Valerie."

Her dad remained silent though. He just held her, rubbing her back, for as long as she stood there, sobbing against his shoulder. Whatever she was feeling was so much more than finding Valerie alive though. Candice had been through so much of her own since Valerie's disappearance that she didn't know how to stop.

Eventually, she pulled away, wiping the tears from her cheeks and smiled at her dad. He smiled back at her and leaned in to kiss her forehead without a word exchanged between them. She gave her dad a kiss on the cheek and finally turned out of his office. She needed a little time to herself before she could face anybody else. She disappeared down the hall to her room and grabbed her Walkman, drowning out the world with a CD.

That night, Candice hardly slept. That strange dream with the purple mist and those glowing emerald green eyes haunted her dreams once again. This time she was able to see a large, beautiful gray wolf that seemed to appear out of nowhere. Before it had only been the raven haired wolf that followed her. She wondered if it was all supposed to mean something. Was her subconscious inner wolf trying to tell her something about her dual nature? Or were these strange dreams just a part of being a hybrid?

After an eternity staring up at the ceiling, she slipped out of bed. There was one other thing she could try to help her sleep better. The tried-and-true night run. She slipped into the pile of clothes lying on the floor. A pair of old gym shorts with the Craven Hill community college logo and an old black tank top she had worn to death; the fibers were starting to come through.

She sat on the floor and laced on her shoes, glancing up at the clear night sky through her bedroom window. The stars twinkled, and the moon was waning. A full week had passed since the full moon. She was starting to feel less achy beneath the glowing light, which was enough to light her way on a quick midnight run.

Candice snatched her cell phone and Walkman sitting on the bedside table, clipping it to her waistband before heading out the door. The stairs creaked on her way down. Chopin barely glanced up from his spot on the couch in the living room, which she found odd. The old family dog usually slept in Kevin's room, but he must've been away tonight. Luckily, he wasn't much of a barker. Even he was getting too old to care about things changing.

With her keys in hand, she slipped out the front door and jogged up the highway. When she reached the top of the hill, she stopped and glanced around. Something seemed off. Something wasn't normal. She had taken runs late at night before to clear her mind, but tonight felt different. Shadows crawled everywhere along the forest. An eerie feeling seemed to linger in the air. Strange feelings seemed to be becoming the new normal for her and she wasn't sure she would ever get used to them.

With every bit of caution she could muster, she started jogging up the road toward the mountains. She slipped her head phones back on and pressed play, turning the volume down low. She scanned the surrounding area. That strange feeling followed her up the mountain. Something was watching her. The curfew hadn't been lifted yet, but she was sure someone was following her.

Ever since that night when she had been caught by those strange men down in the canyon where Valerie's car sat on the river bank, she had the strange feeling that she was being watched. Many mornings she noticed a strange black car following her down the highway until she pulled into the gas station. And on the way home from work there were several times where she could've sworn that very same car was following her home.

She started to feel more anxious about her drive home and even the drive to work. She wondered about reporting the incident to someone at the sheriff's department, but she didn't want to worry her dad or her mom for that matter. She knew her mom would make a huge scene over something she couldn't physically prove.

She couldn't shake the feeling that she was being watched from somewhere deep within the forest. Whenever she glanced toward the forest and the mountain tops, there was nothing there except for the towering evergreens, several junipers and pinon trees. Many times it was just the shadows dancing with a light breeze slipping through them.

Halfway up the mountain, she stopped and sat on the edge of the nearest boulder. She scanned her surroundings, trying to find who might be watching her. For a moment, she remembered feeling this same way the night that she was attacked by that wolf, but she wondered to herself, why would a wolf attack twice? Was there something about her that was attracting wolves or was it all just a coincidence considering her dual nature?

"Who's out there?" She whispered, still scanning her surroundings carefully. There was no answer though. Sitting on top of the boulder, a strange sound drew near, drawing her attention from the music flowing from her headphones. When she paused her music to listen, it sounded like someone breathing or panting nearby. She popped her headphones completely off and listened to the quiet, but whatever she heard had stopped. With a shake of her head, Candice stood and started back down the hill.

Heading back home seemed like the better choice. It was definitely the easier choice to head downhill. This time though, she kept her headphones off and turned off the Walkman, listening to the late night wilderness. Crickets chirped. An owl hooted. A nightingale cooed. She didn't once hear that strange breathing noise the whole way downhill.

When she finally made it to her driveway, a bright flash of movement passed her peripherals. She whipped around, hoping to catch the culprit as the night went dead silent once again. Deeper into the forest behind her parents' house, a white wolf darted up the side of the mountain. When the animal reached the top, they sat down and watched Candice intensely. Suddenly, their tongue slipped out and hung from their lips.

Candice felt the urge to approach the wolf and took a few steps forward. Eric had warned her about this wolf, but why? Before she could even leave the driveway, the wolf snarled, barring their large teeth in a gentle warning. The wolf stood on all fours now, making them appear much larger. At least so she thought. She had never been so close to a wolf.

The wolf took a few steps forward, but Candice hesitated. The wolf had already warned her to stay away, but now the wolf had decided to start approaching. She wasn't sure what to think of the sudden change. A gust of wind slipped through the trees. A whisper slipped through the air and Candice listened for it sounded like someone whispering to her.

Stay away. Know your place, hybrid.

The wolf turned and dashed up the mountain, disappearing among the shadows. Candice stood in the middle of the driveway and frowned. She knew this was no ordinary wolf. She had just met

CHAPTER
TWENTY NINE

eeks passed by. The summer was coming to an end. The colors of the leaves were starting to fade and turn yellow. A breeze whipped through the trees and a few more apples fell. The kids and teens started the new school year. College kids were returning to Craven Hill and Albuquerque for their new semester.

There was a chill in the air now, but by the early afternoon, Candice would be wishing that she wore a pair of shorts instead of pants, but she wouldn't be out long. Once dressed, she disappeared in the bathroom with her small box of makeup and finished getting ready for the day ahead. Valerie was back from house hunting with her mom and Candice was going to meet her for breakfast at Maple's Pancake Hut just at the edge of town.

When she walked through the front door of Maple's, she greeted the hostess, searching for Valerie and Taylor. Valerie waved until Candice spotted them sitting in the furthest corner, near the window. The hostess led her through the dining area to their table where she sat, ordering herself a coffee to drink.

"I'm so happy to see you, Candy!" Valerie rose to her feet

and wrapped her best friend in a hug. The hug went on for several moments and the girls wiggled as they swayed side to side. It was the first time they met since Valerie had been rescued. They had talked a few times, but it took sometime before Valerie could go out in public.

"I'm so happy to see you too! How's the hunting going?"

"It's not too bad, I guess. I've found a few places outside of town, but nothing that I'm happy with just yet, you know. I want a place where I can take Taylor out in the yard and not worry about... well, you know." She said, lowering her voice. Candice only responded with a nod, reaching over to grab the sugar and cream.

"I'm still incredibly grateful to your dad for finding me. I owe him my life for breaking me out of that cage so I could come back home to my baby." Valerie leaned over the table and brushed Taylor's cheek with the back of her knuckle. A gentle smile appeared on her lips when he smiled back at her, placing his plastic cup down on the table.

"Then why is it you won't tell law enforcement the truth about what happened, Val? The sheriff and the whole county sheriff's office need to know who did this to you so they can arrest the man. Or men! And if you know why they did this to you, my dad and the rest of the deputies can use that information to help you."

Valerie lowered her head, twiddling her thumb against the side of her coffee mug. The sunlight came through the window and lit up her face, revealing a couple of old fading scrapes and cuts. The contours on her face also appeared much sharper, but Candice hadn't found the opportunity to ask her about what happened during that time.

"You have no idea what I went through. And I still don't even understand why they choose me to torture to get to my father. My father hardly gives two craps about me and whatever they wanted, I'm sure he won't give it to them either. My father is an asshole."

Candice lowered her face, ashamed for causing her to think about that time. Valerie turned to the waitress when she appeared with a fresh thermos of coffee. Taylor sat quietly with his crayons and the large paper place mat in front of him, coloring in peace.

He lifted his foot on to his mom's thigh, almost like he was afraid she would leave again. Valerie glanced over at him with a gentle smile and ran a hand through his dark hair in an attempt to smooth it down. An unruly patch stuck up at the back of his head, but the more she tried, the less cooperative his hair became.

"He hasn't left my side since I got home. And it's been almost two months. Oh, I missed my little boy very much. Mama's never going to leave you again." Valerie spoke in a soft voice, smiling at her son. Candice took a drink of her coffee watching the two of them. Mother and son together once again. It made her heart swell with happiness.

After ordering breakfast, Candice cleared her throat and took another sip of coffee as she tried to come up with something to say. She knew her friend had to be traumatized from the whole ordeal. Maybe now wasn't the best time to talk about it, but she didn't want to see another person go through the same thing. There had been enough murder and strange activity going through Hollow's Creek.

"Valerie, I'm sorry for pushing you to talk—"

"I don't even really know why they kidnapped me, Candice. I wasn't part of those conversations at all. If I had heard anything about their reasoning, I don't remember. And right now I think I need to come to peace with that somehow. I need to move on. If not for me, then for my son. But what I do know is that it had to do with my father and I hope I never have to see that man again."

"But who is they, Candice? We need to know who kidnapped you. My dad needs that information." Candice stated, pausing briefly between her thoughts. "And how are you going to move on when he's the sheriff?"

"I can't tell you that. I can't tell you who they are either because they threatened to take my child if I say a word about them to anybody. And I can't have that happen. I was already away from my son for I dunno... My mom says three, four weeks? I'm leaving Hollow's Creek. Me, Taylor, and my mom. I don't see any other solution."

Candice heard Valerie loud and clear. It was time for them both to move on in search of new opportunities. They both deserved more than what Hollow's Creek offered and they both seemed to understand that.

EVEN THOUGH THE LOCAL kids were all back in school for the new fall semester, camp always stayed open for the first couple of weeks while the parents arranged their childcare. Summer camp finally closed on the first official day of fall, which had always been the usual in the Hollow Valley. Camp counselors always looked forward to it. They still had plenty of work to do in closing preparations for the year, but there were no more children on the campgrounds. They had the chance to have a good time.

When Candice turned toward Camp Gray, she knew this would be the last time. She knew back in early June when she started the position that this would be her last summer working as a camp counselor. Even though the age limit was twenty four and she wouldn't be turning twenty four until camp opened next season, she knew this was the end for her. She pulled in behind one of the other vehicles parked in front of the administrative building, a sadness washing over her.

Instead of feeling hopeful about the future, she couldn't help feeling bummed about everything that happened over the last few months. Sure, Valerie had been found, but things had changed drastically. Family relationships were changing. And so had her romantic relationships. Things weren't any less complicated with Zak, but Eric was a part of that picture too. Was she involved in a love triangle, she wondered, but there was one thing that was even harder to make peace with.

Becoming a hybrid wolf had changed her life in ways she was still learning and exploring. She found new freedom she had never known before. One that she had longed for and that alone made her heart sing. At the very same time, the newfound presence of the supernatural in her life just made things more complicated for the rest of her entire life. Family life, friendships, and even romantic relationships. How could she just tell someone that she was a hybrid?

She had plenty of research to do to figure out what she had become that she couldn't imagine telling anybody her secret. Not even Valerie let alone her parents. She knew dating Zak or Eric was an easy choice if she chose to stay and they would be able to teach her the ways of living like a werewolf while somehow maintaining some kind of normalcy in Hollow's Creek. She wasn't even sure what her new normal even looked like yet.

For a moment, she also wondered if it would even be safe to stay in the valley considering the story Zak told her about his mother. Would she be run out of town by the pack if she revealed herself as a hybrid looking for some help? None of that sounded like living life.

She parked and shut off the car engine. She pulled the visor down and examined her reflection. She thought she looked great. Even the pink bubblegum lip gloss she wore was shiny and glittery. She had no real reason to be sad for anybody even herself because she had the whole wide world ahead of her. The possibilities were endless. And she didn't need to depend on anybody else for a lifetime.

Candice slipped out of the car and pocketed her keys, heading inside the admin building. Almost all the other counselors and Susan stood waiting at the front of the building when she stepped through the front door. A few of the girls were crying in their little group of friends, but most of the others were talking and laughing as they reminisced over the wonderful memories they made over the summer.

"Don't be shy, Candice. Join the group. After all, this is your very last day here, you know." Susan said with a huge smile on her face, stretching out her arm to guide her toward the front of the room while everyone clapped. She couldn't help, but smile. It was her turn to be honored as the most senior camp counselor. She wouldn't have to go through final inspections either.

The greatest thing about the end of summer camp though was their vacation day. They could do whatever the hell they wanted for the whole day without having to worry about a kid screaming or fighting or being a general pain in the ass. The only ones screaming were her peers as the surface of the cool lake called out to them. She didn't wait long to tug on the old rope and swing right in.

She couldn't believe that she forgot all about the first day of fall because it was an annual tradition. They were the only kids on the property—big kids that is. They had three whole days to clean before final inspections and the Gray family took over the property once again, which she always thought odd, but since her werewolf transformation, that was one thing that made more sense now.

At the end of a full day of being out in the sun and swimming in the lake, Candice went home exhausted and sunburnt. She was redder than a lobster and knew she would be hurting for the next several days. She just hoped she had enough aloe vera to soothe the pain since she didn't think she would be leaving her bed much.

When she came through the front door, she went straight to her room, changed out of her jean shorts and her usual crimson polo into something more comfortable and flowy. A purple summer dress her mother got her years ago. She loved it only because of the color which was rare considering she hated dresses.

Thankfully nobody was home and she could finally be alone for some time. She locked her door, shut the curtains, and hopped onto her bed, leaving her phone on silent. Burying her face into her pillows, she let every bit of her frustration and anxiety go. Warm tears spilled down her cheeks and soon she drifted off to sleep.

There was a loud buzzing sound. She lifted her head, surely marked by the folds of the sheets and pillows from sleeping hard. Annoyance furrowed at her brow. She had a hard time peeling open her swollen, tired eyes. They felt like they had been roughly abused with sandpaper. Whoever was calling be damned.

She laid there, blinking that emotional hangover away while her phone continued to buzz. Finally, she reached over to find she had missed a call, but didn't bother to see who had called. She turned over on to her other side and stared at the curtains. She stared out the bedroom window, just staring into space as she gave herself the time to wake up slowly.

Eventually, she rose out of bed and opened the curtains, squinting when the late afternoon sun sinking in the horizon blasted her in the face. The trees along the highway swayed in the wind. The branches of another nearby tree scraped against the roof.

Somehow a nap helped her finally accept the truth of her new world. She had focused too much of her time and energy on other people and almost none on herself. That alone was doing her no favors. Everyone had been right. She was only delaying what she wanted with her life while everyone else was moving on with theirs.

She was living on past dreams and goals. She knew she was wrong to keep putting herself through so much stress for other people. She needed to do something for herself and not worry about anybody or anything else.

Stepping away from the window, she crawled back on to her bed and grabbed her book, opening it at where she had last placed the bookmark. She was nearly halfway through and with a glance at the clock, she thought maybe she would be able to finish before her parents got home from work for the evening.

She was nearly done with the book when there was a knock. She grumbled and spoke in a groggy voice. "Who is it?"

"It's mom. Can I come in?"

"Yeah, mom. Come on in." She croaked and cleared her throat, sitting up in bed. The door creaked open and her mother stepped into the room still wearing her work clothes. A sheen of sweat made her forehead shiny. With a gentle smile, she crossed the room and sat on the bed, turning to face Candice. She put her hand on the bed and frowned. "Everything ok? Your brothers said you haven't left your room since you got home. You're burning up."

"Yes, I'm ok, mom. I just had a lot of sun today. It was the last day of camp and I just needed some alone time. A lot of stuff has been going on lately. With everything. And everyone."

"Do you need anything? Aloe vera? Cold water? Or maybe talk about anything?"

"I'm not really sure I want to talk right now, but I'm ok." She shrugged, lowering her eyes. She grabbed one of her pillows and hugged it close, slumping down on the bed. Her mom placed her hand on her leg and Candice glanced up at her. She smiled.

"And that's totally fine, Candy. You know this. But if something comes up and you need to talk about it, your dad and I are always here to listen."

Candice just nodded and smiled back. Finally, her mom leaned in and kissed her forehead, rising. "Well, I'll be in downstairs. I was going to have a quick run on my treadmill, but your dad is planning to pick up dinner. If you want anything, just send him a text."

"Thanks, mom."

"Always, baby girl. And please don't stay in bed all evening."

"I won't." She said, watching her mom exit the room.

After rising out of bed, Candice changed into her robe and went down the hall to take a nice cool shower. The water not only cooled her burning skin, but somehow managed to calm every part of her, including the one random thought that creeped into her mind and wouldn't leave her be. Who had actually turned her into a hybrid? Was Eric right about Zak?

Normally, she preferred the feeling of steaming hot water pelting her skin especially since she came home from the hospital after her attack. She knew something in her was changing long before she learned what. Today the cool water was necessary.

When she made it out of the shower and dressed, she grabbed her phone and noticed that Zak had been the one to call her earlier. Except he didn't leave a voice mail. Nor did he send a text. She told herself she didn't care what he wanted, anyway. If it was important, he would've left a damn message instead of just hanging up. She had a pretty clear idea about what he wanted and she didn't give a flying fuck. She cleared the notification and opened her texts to send her dad a text for a dinner request.

Her younger brothers were sitting parked in front of the big screen television and playing video games in the living room when she made her way downstairs. She didn't say a word, but with her nearly finished romance book under her arm, she parked herself on the couch to join them. With a grumble in her stomach, she hoped they wouldn't be waiting long for their dad to arrive with dinner from Troy's Tavern.

"Boys! Let's turn off the video games for now and come eat dinner!" Her dad said the moment he stepped through the front door. They must've been hungry too because he could hardly get the words out of his mouth before Kevin and Cody shut down their PlayStation and ran toward the kitchen. Even Candice stayed out of their way.

After dinner, Candice headed back up to her bedroom and slapped on some makeup to go with her flowy dress. She checked her phone again to find another missed call from Zak, which she cleared before dropping her phone into the black abyss that was her favorite black pleather purse. He could wait.

She went back downstairs in a quick rush, grabbing Chopin's attention for only a moment, and called out. "I'll be back later." To which they yelled back a unanimous "okay!". Luckily, there were no objections on her way out the door, heading to her car.

She started up the engine and sat there, listening, wondering just where she should go to treat herself. She didn't wanna go out to the Hollow Canyon strip mall in case someone recognized her and tried to impose on her alone time. The valley was too small for that.

She pulled out her phone and opened the web browser, watching the blue loading bar progress slowly across the screen before she tossed it into the passenger seat. She shifted into gear and pulled out of the driveway, heading north up the highway. At the end of the county road, where it intersected with the major highway, she headed north and drove out to Craven Hill.

CHAPTER THIRTY

The Rio Linda mall was much larger than Hollow Canyon. There was even a movie theater, which is where she decided to park. She couldn't remember the last movie she had been to since it had been so long. She walked up to the ticket booth and looked at the show time listings. She was drawn to one—another romantic comedy about a British spinster on the search for love only to find herself.

She hesitated when the ticket clerk called for the next person in line. Most of those who bought tickets before her were families and couples. She was the only one who had been there alone. "One ticket for the next showing of Pink and Red. Yes, just one."

Candice smiled brightly and confidently, taking her ticket. She went inside, heading straight for the concession stand. She bought herself a small popcorn, soda, and a box of her favorite chocolate peanut butter candy pieces before heading toward the theater where her movie would be showing, which was nearly all the way at the end of the long hallway.

After the movie, she walked through the lobby and refilled

her coke, feeling content from the movie she watched. Watching a movie alone at the theater wasn't so bad, she thought. In fact, it was kind of nice being able to actually watch the movie instead of being asked a million questions during the movie by her mother. Her brothers weren't so quiet themselves either.

She took a drink from her large soda and walked out into the mall. She walked slowly along, passing several shops while sipping at her coke without a care in the world. She was still thinking about her solo experience and the movie that made her feel less alone when it came to boys even if the main character was much older. She even though about her favorite scene toward the end of the movie where the main character, Bunny, kissed the man she had been crushing on for many years. Butterflies had twittered in her stomach.

In fact, Candice was feeling better in general. That is until she met the gaze of a familiar pair of emerald green eyes. Zak was coming out of one of the nearby shops and she was right in view. Unfortunately, the mall wasn't crowded on a Wednesday evening. She mumbled under her breath. "Fuck..."

She tried to dodge him, lowering her eyes in hopes he wouldn't notice her, but he must've because he called her name. She stopped dead in her tracks and turned to face him with a smile on her face. "Hey, Zak. I didn't expect to see you here."

"Neither did I. I mean about you. You've been ignoring my calls..."

"Sometimes a girl needs some space, Zak. And it's not like we're dating or anything." She grumbled under her breath, but he must've heard her because he rose a brow. He took her arm and led her away from the front of the nearby shops.

She struggled to take her arm back, but soon realized she

wasn't really strong enough to break his hold and accepted his direction. Even as two hybrids, he was stronger than her. Eventually though, she snatched her arm away.

"What's your issue?" He growled at her in a low voice, those gemstone eyes of his darting back and forth while he scanned her face.

"What the hell is that supposed to mean?"

"What? Ace, I'm not speaking in tongues."

"I asked you to stop calling me Ace."

"Fine. I'm sorry, but what's going on? Did I do something wrong here that I don't even know about? I'd appreciate it if you filled me in. I'm a werewolf. Not a fucking mind reader, Candice." Zak snarled.

"I don't know, Zak. There's been a lot going on lately. I've had a lot on mind and I've had to deal with a lot of this shit alone, no thanks to you."

"Well, maybe if you picked up the fucking phone we could talk, Candice." Zak glanced away and took a step back, shaking his head with a look of disbelief on his face. When he stepped in close again, his eyes were closed when he spoke. "Is this why you've been ignoring me? Or is it because we fucked?"

"You have a girlfriend, Zak! You confessed your undying love to me and told me how you couldn't imagine life without me, but you haven't even tried to come see me. You've only called and haven't left any messages. What the hell else am I supposed to think?"

"Visiting someone works both ways, Ace." He snarled. A flicker of anger flashed in his eyes, but it was such a brief moment it could've been a trick of the overhead lighting. She just rose her brow and stared at him for a very long moment before she finally spoke.

"Go fuck yourself!" She said, turning away, except he didn't let her escape. He grabbed her by the wrist, preventing her from leaving. His strength made her wonder if the whole hybrid love story was just made up to get in her pants, but what did she really have to prove about her thoughts?

"What the hell is your problem? You know I've always cared about you. I'm not here to hurt you, Candice. I want to be with you."

"Oh really? Then why can't you just look at me while you're saying that."

"Candice, I care about you. I wouldn't do anything to hurt you ever again." Zak turned toward her and closed the gap between them. He spoke in such a low voice, she knew he didn't want anybody else to hear their conversation.

"You don't, huh? Well, I don't think I even believe you when you say that! Ever since you arrived in town, there's been nothing but problems! Murder! Lies! Cheating!"

"If you don't like it, then maybe you should go talk to Eric. I'm sure he'd love to have you all to himself." He growled deep in his chest. She had to close her eyes, finding that his jealousy was starting to turn her on and she didn't need that. Not now.

"You and Eric sure like to fuck with me. I don't want either one of you assholes because neither of you can tell me the truth about what's actually going on around here. You both blame each other for what happened to me, but neither one of you can own up to it. I'm tired, Zak. I'm done with this shit." She turned, trying to slip out of his grasp, but he stepped in closer. She could feel his warm breath tickle against her skin.

"Candice. Wait." He spoke in a soft, soothing voice, no doubt subduing his anger. She eyed him carefully and waited for him to explain.

"He probably treats you that way—lies to you—because of the bad blood between us. And I know he's always liked you. He would do anything not to see me happy."

"What are you talking about? What does that have to do with any of this hybrid shit, Zak?" Candice said through gritted teeth. Finally, he closed the gap between them and pinned her up against the wall, whispering in her ear. "We can't talk about this hybrid shit in public, Candice. You never know who is listening. Everyone talks."

"Shit. I'm sorry. This is all new to me, you know. Nobody has taught me anything about this new world." She growled back at him. He put a finger to his lips and her eyes lowered to them for only a moment before she stared into his eyes. "There's a reason Eric and I don't get along well anymore. There's a reason for the bad blood between us. And I'm sure that's why he blames me for you becoming a werewolf."

She watched Zak who stood there silent for a very long moment. However, she could see the thoughts spinning through his head. After what felt like an eternity, she parted her lips to respond since he didn't seem likely to continue. Except Zak cut her off.

"It all started long ago, back when I first moved out here to the Valley." He started. "I'm no longer part of the pack here. I haven't been part of the Hollow pack for a very long time so I don't know much about what they've become now. But what I know from my previous experiences and conversations, most of the time, they don't accept hybrids among them. Back then they never knew I was a hybrid. Quinn never found out either."

"Then why are you staying in Hollow's Creek? If they don't accept hybrids, how are you still here? You said your mother was run off and killed for being a hybrid, but here we both are." Candice asked, watching Zak as he shook his head and lowered his eyes. She watched him, her heart racing in anticipation. "Tell me, Zak."

"A few years ago. Back when you, me, and Eric were still in high school, there were murders a lot like there have been around lately. Except these murder victims weren't only men. Some women were killed and even a few werewolves. Mister Gray was also murdered. Allan Gray's father. That's how he inherited that mansion on the other side of town.

"They never really could confirm who was behind the murders. They had solid alibis, but I always knew who it was, and to keep him safe, I left town. I left town to keep the peace. And I didn't want to be part of a pack filled with lies and deception. A pack where the pack master was a murderer."

"Allan Gray murdered his own father?" Candice frowned watching him, but he shook his head. She gasped and covered her mouth. "Was it—"

"Yes, Eric. Eric was the one who killed his grandfather. And I didn't want him to get banished. The Hollow pack is his blood family and when a pure blood wolf gets abjured from their pack, they don't survive long."

"Wait. Do you mean you took the blame for their murders so Eric wouldn't be banished from Hollow's Creek and the pack for their deaths?" Candice lifted her wide eyes in his direction, waiting for him to continue.

"Yes. And I was the only one who knew. Eric's dad didn't even know. Lieutenant Jones, who was still a deputy back then, she was the one to cover it all up to prevent the pack's secret from being exposed. She's still an ally of the pack and she's been the one to cover up all these murders again. Because Lieutenant Jones thinks it's Eric behind these murders again."

"And what's the point in telling me all of this? Who else would be attacking and killing people? What does it all have to do with me being a hybrid now?"

"My point is that Eric has his own skeletons hiding in the closet. Just because he claims to be the better guy between the two of us, doesn't mean that he is the better guy. You think I lied to you? Well, he's keeping things from you too. For all I know he's the one who turned you into a werewolf too." Zak shrugged.

"You telling me these things doesn't make you my savior, Zak. Nor does it excuse you from the bad shit you've done to me either." She said, staring up into his eyes with a burning gaze of anger.

"I know that, but I mean what I said when I said I care about you. You need to be careful out there at night. You can't be taking those late night runs the way you do. Someone could grab you and hurt you. Again." He growled under his breath, his gaze sharp and pointed.

"And you really think you're gonna stop me from doing what I want, Zak?" She smiled. Her eyes turned yellow and flashed for a moment before returning to their natural brown. The ghost of a smirk curled at the corner of his lips. She stepped forward, pushing him out of the way. "I don't trust either one of you."

CHAPTER
THIRTY ONE

Candice's fingers moved easily across the fretboard of her old black guitar, lost in the moment. Nothing could've easily broken her concentration until she was interrupted by a strange sound coming from outside.

An energy from outdoors floated in through the open window. She lowered her hand from the neck of the guitar and listened to the night. The neighborhood dogs started howling. A moment later, sirens wailed off in the distance, growing louder with each second.

She focused on the screech of the siren with a tilt of her head, trying to pinpoint which direction the siren was coming from, but she struggled. The siren grew louder. The neighborhood dogs became louder.

Candice set her guitar down into the old leather case. She rose from her seat and went to the window to look outside. The moon was nearly full, only days away, but there was enough moonlight to see through the shadows.

Suddenly, that silver white wolf dashed across the yard and toward the mountains. The animal's fur glowed under the moonlight. She wondered if it had been sneaking around her neighborhood or spying on her after her last encounter. She needed to confront the wolf. Candice grabbed her cell phone, ran through the quiet house, and out the front door. She glanced up at the sky and took a deep breath.

Something felt different.

"What's going on out here?" Candice's mom came out to the porch. The next door neighbor's dogs were going crazy. Candice glanced over her shoulder, but remained silent. She then took off running into the street and toward the sound of the sirens in the distance, hoping she would find that wolf.

She ran hard, passing neighbor Frank who sat out on his lawn chair like many other nights. He had a beer in one hand and a cigarette in the other. The radio was playing an old song of Elvis' that Candice heard many times when visiting her grandparents as a young girl.

"Where you headed off to now, girl? There're a couple of wolves out on the loose!"

"I know." She muttered still running. Her heart was pounding hard, but her focus kept her moving forward. "I can smell them on the air."

She ran to the farthest end of the street and out on to the main road. When she glanced up at the mountains, the silver wolf was running up the side and disappeared around the corner. Candice knew where she needed to go.

People were screaming her name. Probably her mother and two younger brothers, but she didn't care. She needed to find that wolf. She ran across the street, following the silver wolf. The volume of the sirens pierced her ears, but she wasn't going to let that stop her from finding that wolf. Not this time.

The ambulance and a fire truck had arrived at the end of the road, where the pavement turned into a dead end at the bottom of the hill. There must've been another dead body and wondered if it was because of that wolf. She didn't understand how, but she was able to hone in on that animal's scent, following it right up into the forest. She eventually lost sight of the wolf in the darkest shadows.

She stopped at the entrance of the forest and pulled out her cell phone, trying to catch her breath. She took several steps into the forest. Old leaves crunched beneath her feet, following the worn path. Her eyes wide and alert, she scanned her surroundings. There was nothing to see except for the trees and the dark shadows surrounding her. She suddenly caught that strange, but familiar scent of wildlife beckoning to her from all directions.

A branch snapped. Candice froze. She turned on her cell phone flashlight and spun around until she came face to face with the white wolf. The wolf was much larger than she expected, but it was beautiful even in the darkness. Silvery specks glittered, almost glowing under the dim light of the moon.

The animal's long fangs, exposed with lips curled into a snarling growl, appeared immaculate under the glow of the electronic blue light from her phone. Candice stood her ground though. Maybe it was the inner werewolf energy that made her feel more confident because she wasn't at all afraid.

"You can't hurt me. You can't harm me any further than you have already, bitch." Anger rose. Heat pumped through her veins, carrying a strange feeling with it. Static electricity prickled at her skin. She had no idea what was going to happen. As far as she knew, hybrids weren't able to shift without the light of the full moon, but she was left curious about the white wolf's abilities.

Candice had the strongest urge telling her to shift, but she had no idea how. She now realized that there was a lot more to being a werewolf than what little she learned from Zak. For a baby werewolf, she now wished she knew more. She was staring down danger without knowing a thing about how to tap into her dual nature.

The wolf barked and howled. She tried to back up, slowly, hoping to get enough space from the animal for a running start. When a branch snapped under her sneaker, the wolf lunged ahead, snapping at her arm. She screamed and dropped her phone to the forest floor, but damage had already been done.

The warmth of blood dripped along the side of her arm. The wolf pinned her down, and she did her best to protect her arm. She kicked the wolf away, and she was able to fling the wolf off and into the nearest tree. Candice rose from the ground and took off running with a renewed strength she didn't know she possessed. Yet, the one chasing her was still stronger.

The wolf launched after her. The animal pounced and knocked her back to the forest floor. The wolf gnashed its teeth and lunged forward, aiming for Candice's neck. Candice threw up her arms and closed her eyes, waiting for the inevitable. She waited for the impact of the animal's teeth to rip at her once more, but the wolf was knocked off of her with a yelp.

When she uncovered her eyes, the wolf was laying across the ground. Several men were carrying a large dog crate toward the injured animal. A couple of them she recognized from the last time she had been caught alone out in the wilderness. These men were Rayers she quickly realized. A powerful wave of energy washed through her and she bellowed at the men. "Leave the wolf alone!"

The men turned their gazes towards Candice. Huge grins curled over their lips, but she didn't understand why at first. Whatever had happened during that moment of powerful energy had caused her to shift into her wolf form. There was no pain like the last time her body shifted into its unnatural form.

"Well, well. What do we have here?"

"It smells like a hybrid. Two birds with one stone, boys! What more could we ask for?" Sheriff Loveland suddenly appeared and stood over her, holding a rifle across his chest. He hit her on the shoulder. Upon impact, she cried out in pain. Suddenly, she felt dizzy and started falling into nothingness. He leaned down. His lips and teeth curled into a malicious grin, the smell of his tobacco kept her from drifting too quickly.

"Stay down, whelp. You just need to wait your turn. We won't be forgetting an abomination like you. The world will be a much better place with one less hybrid around. We don't want you magical creatures polluting our human blood lines any more than you already have.

"And maybe you can tell me who gave you that scar on your neck while we have some time." He cackled, backing away from her. Within moments, she finally let the darkness claim her.

When Candice woke, an old kennel smell filled her nose. Dog pee, wet fur, dog kibble, and a hint of industrial soap. Her eyes shot open, and she sat up from the concrete floor. She scanned the area and wondered if she was at the pound, but the room was much too dark. She wasn't sure where she was.

There were other dogs around, she could smell them in the darkness. They weren't in the same kennel. A wall separated her from the others. When her eyes finally adjusted, she scanned her surroundings. She was in a large dog kennel. There was enough room for maybe one or two other people, but she was alone.

She glanced across the room, squinting through the darkness. Across from her, there was another kennel with a human lying face down on the concrete.

CHAPTER THIRTY TWO

ey! Are you alive? Are you awake? Who are you? Where are we?" Candice whispered loudly, hoping someone would hear her. She slipped her fingers through the links of the cage and shook.

"Hey! New girl! Keep it quiet over there. Someone from upstairs could hear you so cut it out before you get us all killed!"

Candice heard a loud voice whisper from somewhere further down the aisle. She glanced around, wondering where that other person was. All she could see were dogs, some smaller while others were larger. Examining her surroundings, she found a few boxes to climb on top of where she was able to see more kennels.

On the opposite side of the room, there were more individuals who looked human. They outnumbered the dogs, so why had they all been thrown into the kennels like she was one of them? Was this how the sheriff treated werewolves?

"Hey. Over there! Where are we?"

"We never saw how we got here."

"We have no fucking clue where we could be!" Another one spoke louder than a whisper. Someone told the loud person to shut up from their corner, but Candice couldn't see just where they spoke from. It was difficult to see even with her new dual natured senses, but she saw enough.

There were plenty of people just standing around in their cages and others were sitting curled up on floors and cots. Many of them just stared into space. How long had any of them been here, she wondered.

"Y'all need to shut the fuck up before the sheriff or one of his henchmen come down here to do it for us. You know what happens when they come down here."

"I don't!"

"Well, if you keep making noise you may find out sooner rather than later. Now be quiet already!" The girl whispered loudly on the other end of the room. Candice climbed down from the top of the box and found a clean, dry spot on the concrete floor to sit.

After what she saw in the other cages, she was thankful to have her own space, but wondered why she was separated from the rest of the crowd. And she wondered the same about the other girl. Hopefully she would find out soon. All they had now was time and there didn't seem to be anything else to do besides wait.

Candice couldn't tell how long passed before the silence of the large basement finally broke once again. The dogs started barking and one of them even howled, but she couldn't tell what was going on. It was still hard to see across the room, but she heard a door creak open. She laid still on the cool pavement, listening to a heavy set of keys jingle and clang.

"What are we supposed to do with all these people?" A voice said, just above a whisper. Candice lay as still as she could, just listening. The two men spoke with unrecognizable accents. Old accents that she couldn't place.

"Why didn't you pay attention, Herb? Mister L says we feed them whatever scraps we don't eat, but if there's nothing at all, we can give them some dog food. We're supposed to feed them whenever we feed the dogs."

"And that's now, you say?"

"Yes. Just grab that big bucket there in the corner and follow me this way."

The sound of kibble shifting slipped through the room. The dogs barked loud with excitement. Someone scooped kibble and dropped it to the bottom of stainless steel bowls. Over and over. Several times over.

"Why are there so many in these two cages, but only one in these two?"

"Mister L said these two are special for some reason, I really don't know why. I never thought of asking neither, but I think one of them is supposed to be his daughter or his girlfriend or something. We give them two the best of the scraps."

Candice rose and listened to the two men argue about what they were to do while down in the basement. She didn't move more though. She waited for the two men in their raggedy outfits to pass by with the large bucket of kibble and scraps from dinner. The way they argued, she thought maybe she could trick them and escape.

Everyone around her were eating their dinner and Candice glanced at the pile of fried chicken and biscuits sitting on a tray, but she wasn't really hungry. Something about being thrown into a basement made her lose her appetite. Still, she sat and waited. The unseen door creaked open again and slammed shut.

There was plenty of scraping and swallowing noises as everyone in the room devoured their meals no matter what they were given. Some sounded much more aggressive than she expected a dog to be. Or were those noises from the werewolf humans? She really couldn't tell. She slipped across the floor and sat near the chain-link fence of the cage. She spoke in a loud, whisper, hoping to grab the other human's attention.

There was no way Valerie had been captured and thrown back into a cage. Not after Candice's dad had found and rescued her only a few weeks ago, but she gave it a shot and called out Valerie's name, hoping the sheriff's goons were stupid and wrong.

"Would you stop fucking yelling over there! They're going to hear you and everyone is going to be in trouble!" Someone whispered loudly across the dark basement. Candice frowned and sat on the cold concrete floor, contorting her legs into a pretzel beneath her.

The naked individual across the aisle woke and slowly sat up, rubbing the sleep from her eyes. She had light brown hair, not blonde like Valerie. Bruises and scratches shadowed her face. When she finally came to, she crossed her arms over her chest and crotch, searching the cage for something to cover herself. A pile of clothes had been placed on the cot in the corner.

"Where am I? What's happened?"

"I'm not sure where we are. Or what happened to you."

"I was running through the forest and the next thing I know; I'm laying fucking naked in the middle of a cage. I knew I shouldn't have come back to this shit hole." She grumbled, sitting on the edge of the cot, dressing in the baggy pile of clothes left for her.

"I was running through the forest. And they captured me too. Somehow, they knew I was a hybrid though." Candice spoke softly. The girl glanced across the aisle toward her and stepped up to the side of the cage.

"I knew it was you following me out in the forest. I could smell you out there. I wanted to fucking kill you for what you did to me." She snarled and growled, low and deep, turning away from Candice.

"What? What did I do?"

"Zak came back here for you. He said he was tired of my shit and he left Denver. He left me in our apartment with no fucking answers. And then I get a call from good old Eric, telling me my boyfriend is running around Hollow's Creek with his favorite human again. I had to see it for myself." Her lips curled into a snarl and her eyes started to glow in the darkness. "He was right. I can smell him on you. But I smell Eric on you too. What a fucking slut you are. I guess that's why they call you everybody's favorite Candy."

"Fuck you, Quinn."

"Nah, thanks, sweetheart. I don't swing that way." A disgusted, yet sarcastic look appeared on her face when she glanced in Candice's direction.

"You're the whole reason Zak left town in the first place. You're the one he left to be with because he thought he had to keep up appearances for the pack. Because you werewolves don't like hybrids I've heard. So, he decided to mate with a fucking pure blood. He doesn't really love you, Quinn."

"Maybe not, but I don't care. Love isn't real, sweetie. Get over it. I'm going to be the one to have his babies, whether you like it or not." Quinn laughed and the sound of her voice pierced through Candice's freshly torn open scars, still bleeding from her last conversation with Zak. A few others yelled across the room and shook their cages.

"Guess what, Quinn...so could I!"

"Hey. Shut up! Stop your fucking bickering and keep it down." One person yelled.

"We don't want to hear it!" And another.

"Don't talk about the supernatural over there! They will come down here and beat us if you keep talking like that! We've been doing just fine and then you two arrived."

"Shut up, Cherry. If these two have some beef over a guy, let the sheriff take them out of here and do away with them. Have them fight it out like all the others. Good riddance." Said another woman almost growling with disapproval.

"What? Why are you giving up so easily? We need to get out of here. All of us! We need the sheriff to pay for what he's doing." Candice said. A few others in the back corner of the basement started laughing. Even Quinn laughed. Candice turned her back toward the dumb bitch.

"Get out of here? What a great idea! We hadn't thought of that before!" That same voice was a growl. Several others hooked their fingers through the holes of the chain-link fence and shook it slightly to emphasize her words. Voices from the other side of the room told her to shut up. She yelled back for them to shut up.

"Darling, you have no idea what you've got yourself caught up in. And you have no idea what this sheriff of ours has been up to. Just wait. Keep making noise and you'll find out for yourself." The one who yelled at Cherry earlier said.

"What are you still doing up here anyway, Quinn? I thought you hated living in the small town." Candice spoke in a soft voice, sitting on the cold concrete floor. Her eyes had finally adjusted much better to the darkness because now she could see Quinn in clear detail. She laid across the floor with her feet against the side of the cage, almost casual.

"What am I doing here? Why should I tell you anything, home wrecker?" Quinn growled back, still staring up at the ceiling of the cage. Candice sat back down and frowned.

"Home wrecker?"

"You know exactly what you did. Zak came here for you."

"That's not what I heard, Q—"

"Are you really going to sit there and tell me you believe everything Zak says to you? Even I know better. Actually, I think you should know by now why he left town the first time." Quinn finally lowered her gaze and stared in Candice's direction, leaving her speechless while she waited for Quinn to continue. "Zak is a good liar. And a cheat, you know."

"Yeah, I remember…"

"He two timed us both back in high school because he's too fucked up to know what he really wants, you know. I wonder if that's a hybrid thing, but what do I know? One moment he wants to be a wolf. And the next, he just wants to be human."

"You knew he was a hybrid?"

"Well, duh! I've known for a while. Why do you think he left Hollow's Creek? Our pack doesn't exactly accept hybrids. And I was dumb enough to leave the pack with him because I thought leaving this bumfuck town would change things.

"For a while I thought that he would want to find a pack accepting of hybrids. Start a family together. But I was wrong. I guess that's why he turned you into a wolf. I can smell him all over you." Quinn shifted, grabbing a hold of the cage bars, pulling herself back up.

"You're not the first person to say that." Candice lowered her eyes and Quinn crossed over to the cot in the far corner of her cage. She turned her back on Quinn before she continued speaking.

"Then it must be true, don't you think? Don't worry though, Candy. I'm just as stupid. You asked why I came back to Hollow's Creek? Well, he's the reason and I couldn't deal with that. With being all alone in Denver."

"But why if you know he's a liar?"

"Because I wanted to prove that he was lying to me again. Only I ended up in deeper shit than some love triangle. I ended up caught by the fucking sheriff and his goons. You see, they don't like supernaturals around here. It's different here than Denver or any of the bigger cities, I hear." Quinn paused and crossed her cage, crouching down on the floor. She spoke in a quiet voice.

"They caught me near a crime scene. The first crime scene, but they didn't believe I wasn't involved. Said they wouldn't make my life miserable if I agreed to work for them. Help them catch hybrids—unnatural beings as they called them. They had a few hybrids killed. All those murders you've heard about on the news? Most of them were hybrids or children of hybrids kidnapped and murdered. They forced me to shift after injecting me with something. Adrenaline maybe?" She said. Listening to what Quinn said made her wonder because she had been under the impression that a pureblood could shift whenever they wanted. Unless there was more to her story than she was revealing.

"How long have you been their captive, Quinn?"

"Weeks. Months even. And we're never getting out of here either." Candice slipped to the floor and leaned against the side of the cage. "The sheriff and his men won't ever let that happen."

CHAPTER THIRTY THREE

Candice couldn't tell how many days passed, locked up in the cage. The sheriff's people showed up at least two or three times a day with a bucket of food. Some dog kibble for all humans and dogs and even a few scraps of burger, chicken, or other meat came on occasion, but it was almost never enough.

Hunger became a horrible pain in her stomach at first, but soon she grew used to it. Some nights she was too tired and hungry to sleep. Other nights she had enough to keep her stomach full enough to sleep, which seemed to be the only relief from the constant hunger and thoughts that came along. She couldn't stop thinking about what Quinn said though.

And we're never getting out of here. They won't ever let that happen.

Those words wriggled deep into her mind and poisoned her thoughts. There was no way Candice would accept that fate for herself or anybody else in that basement—even Quinn who she still felt bitter toward. They would be found and go home.

She wasn't sure how long had passed, but she knew her dad or the force would be looking for her by now. For a while, all she could think about was what Valerie had been through, which brought tears to her eyes. She had never imagined anything like this. After all, Valerie wasn't a hybrid or supernatural. Now it was her turn to experience being held hostage. However, the more she listened to the others hiding in the dark with her, the sooner she started to lose hope for escaping.

A few more nights must've passed. She wasn't sure how long, really. It was always hard to tell these things in the dark. A couple of goons came down some time after dinner, which she knew wasn't the normal routine. However, sitting there listening to everyone's chatter and the fear in their voices, she realized this was normal. The dogs in the cages even cried and yelped, screaming for release from this hidden prison. It hadn't been the first time she heard anybody down in the basement frightened.

"Who's it gone be tonight? Shall we pick a dog? Or maybe one of you wolves here? Or maybe one of these muddy hybrid creatures?" The goon spoke, the keys rattling in his hands. The light he carried bounced and disappeared to the farthest corners of the cavernous room. Candice rose from her cot and climbed the pile of boxes and crates to observe.

"What's happening?" Quinn whispered from her corner. Candice barely popped her head over the top, trying to see what was happening. She shook her head, watching quietly and whispered. "I don't really know... I can't see very well."

The light from the goon's lantern gave enough light for her to see people dodging to get away. He wasn't only short, but he was slow. These werewolves moved much quicker than him, but eventually he grabbed one by the neck and slipped on a strange metallic collar.

Another one of the sheriff's goons appeared from the shadows of the collapsible stairs, carrying another strange metallic collar and chain in his hands. This man was larger than the other and must have handled many large creatures. Candice saw many ghostly scars illuminated on his face.

Shortie struggled to drag one of the human females out of her cage until a third man stepped out of the shadows and jabbed her with a needle, causing her to go limp. When she woke moments later, something strange happened. They had injected her with something from that needle.

The girl woke frightened, thrashing, and fighting the men who had her in their grip. The surrounding air began to shimmer like the surface of a bubble. There was a vibration of energy in the air that even Candice could feel. The strong vibrations influenced her to shift, crying out in pain. Many others must've felt it too because several of those in their cages shifted into a variety of different colored wolves of different sizes.

When Candice woke sometime later, she was lying on the cage floor naked, but she didn't move. She listened to what was going on around her before she finally found the strength to rise. It sounded like the girl the goons took hadn't come back home that night. She heard some people in one of the other cages crying softly.

This was what the sheriff was doing? Dog fighting with hybrids and werewolves?

Several more days passed.

Nobody spoke about what happened, but she still had the strong feeling these forced shifts led to dog fights that had been going on for a while. And she wondered if they were related to the murders. While lying there, she remembered back to when her dad was recently called out to stop a few dog fights and a fighting ring recently, but that's all she remembered hearing. Her dad generally only gave the least bit of information needed to keep his family safe and never the whole story.

The silence in the air was palpable for many days following that painful shift with the group. She wondered how she could've even shifted without the presence of the full moon in the sky, not that there was any way to tell in that dark pit.

They needed to get out of the basement somehow, but it seemed impossible with whatever drug those men had. There were times she could still see that large needle at the forefront of her mind. Sometimes it was hard not to see it with every blink of her eyes. She knew she wasn't the only one who thought of it though. Could they really have only been using adrenaline like Quinn mentioned? Or was there some other toxic drug involved? There was no way for her to know that—at least not yet.

Candice lied on her cot and stared at the ceiling. Even though her eyes had long since adjusted to the darkness, there was nothing to see. But there was even less to do while waiting for something to happen. Waiting for food. Waiting for the sheriff's goons to appear and wind the whole crowd of shifters and canines up. A few others seemed to pass their time crying, except nobody drew attention to any of it.

She soon realized that she wasn't the only one feeling afraid. Several others woke in the middle of the night screaming. She had an idea on how to escape during a regular meal time, but what about escaping the needle if they picked her out of the group one night? She was determined to figure it out somehow, someway. Otherwise, it would be a matter of life and death not only for herself, but the rest of those huddled in the darkness. Even Quinn.

Despite the deep bitterness she felt toward her, she couldn't be angry with what Quinn had said about Zak being a liar and a cheat. She knew both accusations were true, but she never knew just how true until Quinn revealed her side of the story.

Knowing the truth didn't seem to ease the pain though.

Candice continued to stare up at the ceiling when suddenly that familiar creak of the trap door broke the silence. The bright light from upstairs spilled into the basement and several individuals stirred. A few canines barked, and she realized it was meal time before the goon even spoke aloud. "Who's hungry tonight?"

Sure enough, without even turning her attention toward him, she heard that scooping sound. Moments later, kibble dropped into a stainless steel bowl. And another. And another. The man continued to shuffle across the concrete floor of the basement, but she didn't move.

"Are you ladies hungry? I've got tacos with some beans and rice for you tonight. Santa Fe style, if you like." said one of the men. She hardly lifted her eyes in his direction. Tonight, it was shortie, which would work well in her favor.

A cage door slammed shut nearby followed by another. He was getting closer. Still, she didn't move or shift on her cot. She had to lie still and appear dead for her escape plan to work. She needed the shortie to fall for her ruse.

"Did you hear me, puppy?" Shortie said. His keys rattled, and he unlocked the door to her cage, stepping in with a food tray. The smell of the spicy foods—tacos, rice, and beans— made her stomach growl, but she didn't care. She wanted her freedom even more than the food. It was hard to focus though as the hunger perked up at the tantalizing scents.

Candice didn't say a word, but she listened, keeping her hands where they rested on her stomach. Dogs and people alike were sitting down to eat their meals. She could hear the kibble tinkle in many stainless steel bowls.

He set the tray down on the table near the door and left the cage door swinging open. He then stepped over to Candice, still holding the rattling keys in his hands.

"Are you alright? You're the only one who hasn't said a thing tonight. Even the skinny little werewolf bitch who works for us said something. But not you."

A sudden burst of noise and utter chaos filled the room. There was barking, shouting, and general chaos that grabbed shortie's attention before he could reach her. He waddled away and slipped out the open cage door to calm the noise.

"Alright, alright! What is going on out here? Everyone needs to settle down now!" He shouted with little quiet in response. He cleared his throat and spoke louder. "Everyone needs to settle down before I go and get me whip out!"

Candice rose from the cot. While the rest of the crowd continued to make absolute chaos and noise, she carefully slipped out of the open cage door. She crouched down and without a glance over her shoulder, she hurried away in search of the nearest possible vent to make her escape. She knew this was her only chance to find help.

When shortie finally got the rest of the crowd to settle down to a quiet lull and turned to check on Candice, it was already too late. He dropped down to his knees and wailed aloud. "Oh shit! Now look what you all made me do! This one escaped! And the boss is gonna be mad at me!"

A few moments later, he howled in grief in unison with the wolves.

Somehow, Candice managed to slip into the darkest corner and waited listening to shortie waddle around and wail while looking for her. She giggled silently until it was safe to pry open the nearby heating duct, pulling the cover closed behind her.

She crawled quietly, slowly through the tunnels until she heard shortie howling across the basement again. Startled, she glanced over her shoulder, but quickly brushed it off as all that noise grew fainter with each inch she crawled. She shook her head and continued.

There were plenty of odd and dusty smells that tickled at her nose the further she crawled through the network of old heating ducts. She sneezed once, holding it in to keep the noise from alerting shortie. A few times she came across a four-way intersection and stopped to listen for something that would lead her down the right path to an escape. Old cobwebs brushed against her frizzy, unkempt hair.

After some time, Candice had no idea where she was. She was ready to give up with the vague feeling that she was going around in circles. She wasn't sure how long she had been crawling, but she figured she should have found the light at the end by now. With every new turn she took, she was feeling more hopeless about ever escaping from wherever in the hell she was trapped.

She took one final turn to yet another dark tunnel. A wave of hopelessness washed over her and she sat back on her heels. The warmth of tears filled her eyes, and she lifted her hands to her face and cried. Suddenly there was a loud creaking sound somewhere among the maze of tunnels. She dropped her hands to her lap and listened.

A pair of boots approached from somewhere below. Getting back down to her hands and knees, she followed the growing sound. The faint whispers of people talking drifted toward her and that's when she saw the dim light around the corner. There were lights at the end of the tunnel. She continued with caution until those voices became much clearer.

"Did you find her? The deputy's daughter?" A deep, gruff voice spoke and Candice stopped to listen. She sat on her heels and waited, listening.

"No. There was no sign of her anywhere out there, J—"

"Do not say my name out loud! She could be anywhere and she could hear you! You need to find her! We can't let her get out and warn her goddamn father! It's bad enough that the sheriff is working with us, but we don't need them snooping around trying to find her with all those dogs and unpure creatures down there."

"But, sir! It wasn't my fa—"

"I said what I said! Find the girl at once! Or I'll have that mangy bitch mutt kill you too! Now go! I don't want to hear anymore goddamn excuses from you tonight!" He growled. There was a brief scuffle below and then silence.

She sat and waited for something more, but the silence hung heavy in the air. She hadn't even heard those boots. Before long, she noticed her foot was starting to fall asleep. She shifted, but immediately regretted it.

The floor of the tunnel shifted and started to crack. She gasped. The tunnel started to collapse. She screamed with absolutely no regard for her own safety. She knew she was going to be caught before she even landed.

That same gruff voice yelled out, but she was too focused on what was happening. It sounded like he spoke in another unfamiliar language. She threw her arms over her head while the weight of the tunnels fell over her.

She laid there, waiting for the rubble to settle. When she lowered her arms, she looked up into the face of a strange man. She assumed he was the man with the boots because he was much taller than shortie. He had a narrow nose and blazing bright blue eyes. A crooked grin curled over his lips and he lifted his foot.

"Well, well, well. I was right, wasn't I? A little snoop was spying on us. And we can't have you escaping neither. Nighty, night, little red."

He kicked her in the face.

Everything went dark.

When Candice awoke, she was staring up into the dark of the old familiar ceiling of her personal cage. Lying there for the moment, she couldn't remember the last time she saw anything other than the darkness of the cage that had become her home. She was starting to believe Quinn's words.

And we're never getting out of here. They won't ever let that happen.

CHAPTER THIRTY FOUR

The days felt like weeks, but there was no way to truly tell since they were surrounded by the darkness every waking moment. Did the goons come down every week or was it every few days? Eventually, she lost track of how often they came downstairs.

One night the unexpected happened. Normally, the goons went after the loudest bunch of people and dogs across the basement, but not tonight. Tonight, she would learn just how special she was to the sheriff.

Sometime after dinner, she was half asleep with a belly full of beans and rice. Almost content despite her dire circumstances. She blinked and rubbed the sleep from her eyes to find one of the larger men had appeared and opened the door to her cage. She wondered where shortie was since she hadn't seen him in some time. Not even at dinner.

A second man appeared behind the other who had entered her cage. They tried to drag her from the cage, but Candice kicked and thrashed against them. Fully awake, she noticed there were two other large men who had brought out Quinn, who growled on the ground beside her. She wasn't sure what exactly was happening, but she was sure they had finally been chosen for the backyard dog fights.

What better way to get out one's anger and frustration than fight the very woman who she had always thought took her true love—except she had the sinking feeling Quinn was much stronger than she. Then she saw the large silver needle from the corner of her eye coming toward her. She screamed, barely aware of what was going on. Barely hearing the words coming out of Quinn's mouth.

"I'm going to kill you for what you have done to me, you bitch! I fucking hate you!" Quinn's dark eyes were blazing yellow and filled with venom. She thrashed and squirmed. Candice kicked harder and faster, trying to keep the needle away.

Candice screamed when another large man came down the stairs to help hold her down. The needle came closer and for a moment, her life flashed before her eyes. After everything she witnessed over the past few weeks, she knew that this was the end. There would be no waking up from her dual natured side because she would be dead by morning. All at the hands of Quinn.

The needle barely pierced her skin when she was dropped to the ground. There was more screaming and shouting. Something wet and sticky splashed across her face. When she touched her cheek, she brought her fingers down to see blood on her hands. She heard the thrashing and gnashing of another animal, but she didn't think it was Quinn.

A few of the men had been thrown to the floor and others had been tossed across the basement into a bleeding mess of bodies. A large black wolf had attacked the men, saving her and Quinn. The large wolf tore at one of the men's flesh and ripped off his arm in one bite. The beast growled low and took a step toward the two women.

"He says for us to get out of here, Candice. We need to get out of here now." Quinn glanced over at her and rose to her feet, taking off up the stairs, but Candice couldn't leave. Not yet when there were many others waiting to be saved.

"How do you know what he's saying?" Candice screeched, staring at the black wolf, hunkering close by. She couldn't take her eyes off the animal. There was something strangely familiar about the animal, but she couldn't pinpoint what. "What about the others?"

"Don't worry about that now! Just get your ass out of here before the others come. Don't be stupid!" Quinn yelled, already lost to Candice somewhere in the darkness. She rushed across the room and yanked cage doors open, letting out at least half a dozen humans and dogs from captivity.

The werewolf roared at Candice again and she just stood there, feeling their hot breath against her face, nearly shaking her down to the bone. She couldn't move. Not one inch. One of the taller men freed from the cage turned toward her.

"Thank you for saving us, but you need to get out of here too! You need to save yourself before the sheriff or John show up. They will track us all down and put us all back in those cages. Save yourself!"

She knew he was right, but before she could move, she put out a hand to touch the werewolf, growling. He made no move to attack her, which only solidified the familiar feeling in the pit of her stomach. The wolf relaxed when she touched the wet, bloodied nose. The wolf growled again only louder, pulling her into the present moment.

Bloody spit dripped from their fangs and every inch of fur stood on end. She lifted her eyes, looking past the matted fur to meet a pair of pale green eyes that appeared almost yellow.

Something deep inside her knew the man beneath the monster and her first thoughts sprung to Zak, but another part of her secretly hoped it was Eric.

Candice turned and went up the stairs. The rest of the group was already far ahead. She could only see the silhouette of the last few stragglers. They all must've had a super human speed. Suddenly, the energy of the room changed. She felt an electricity in the air. She collapsed to her knees and covered her ears, screaming until the sensation faded.

"Hurry up! Follow me!" Quinn shouted from somewhere in the darkness, breaking the trance Candice found herself under. She rose to her feet and ran, turning down a dark corridor, following the familiar scent of people ahead.

Candice couldn't see where the hell she was going, but she could hear her heart pounding. Others around her were panting as they ran down the corridors to escape the basement. Had they actually been underground?

"Are you sure you know where we're going?"

"Just follow me! Turn to the left corner." Quinn shouted back. Her voice echoed from further down the hall, but she was close enough to see her silhouette. Maybe that was just her baby supernatural senses kicking in while following the group through the darkness.

"Where are we going, Quinn?"

"Shut up and follow!" Quinn barked. Her voice sounded much farther away. A heavy vibration filled the air again and Candice covered her ears with her arms. She closed her eyes and screamed when the vibrations continued without pause.

The vibrations suddenly came to a stop and Candice opened her eyes, waiting for something to happen. When it finally seemed safe, she uncovered her ears and turned in the direction where everyone else had been running earlier. That's when someone from behind called out.

"Get that red head! She's the one!"

"And where do you think you're going? Everyone else is too far ahead of you. You will be captured! If not by me or one of my men, surely after the sheriff or one of his other men. And he has many men out there waiting for creatures like you."

"My father will find me!" Candice yelled.

A deep bellowing laugh filled the room, echoing off the walls. Candice couldn't help lifting her hands to her ears at the sound of his piercing voice. She fell to her knees, feeling helpless as that laugh reverberated through the room.

The laughing finally came to a stop and a muddy light flickered on. When she lifted her head, she was surrounded by strange, unknown men in black hooded capes and they were all much larger than her. Each of them held a candle in their hands, but there were too many shadows to see their faces.

Several of the candles flickered to life as a breeze slipped through the large cavernous room. Candice glanced around. She was no longer in the corridors to escape. She was in a large room with many stalagmites of different sizes carved into the cathedral ceiling. She was nowhere near escaping this hell. A sense of dread washed over her. "Where am I?"

CHAPTER THIRTY FIVE

You're in my kingdom now, puppy." A voice echoed through the room. She whipped her head around, trying to find the source. She knew his voice from when she had been captured earlier, but she wasn't able to see his face. Suddenly, an older man appeared before her. His dark hair was streaked with salt and pepper. His face wrinkled and scarred from many years of fighting.

She paused when she saw the faded Nordic wolf tattoo on his neck. Her father had warned her before about trusting men with that very tattoo. It was made famous by the Gray heir many, many years ago—except she couldn't remember his name. He and his people were very dangerous men, but there was something different about this man. Maybe it was his posture that made him appear so commanding, but she knew he was not one to fuck with.

"I know who you are… you're one of those Rayers…" She whispered.

"You know who we are, do you?" He laughed, his voice echoing off the walls. Only this time, she couldn't lift her hands to her ears. When she tried to move, her hands were shackled behind her back. How she didn't realize that before was a mystery. It must've been all those vibrations in the air made to confuse her. "My dear, you don't know the half of who we are! Or of what we can even do.

"And your stupid father won't find you here. Nobody knows about this place because we are far in the depths of the woods. Nobody ever comes out here because of the vampires and werewolves and demons. The monsters like you. People don't want to be sticking their noses out here in someone else's business. That someone being like me!"

"You're wrong! My father is always searching and arresting men like you! The supernatural deserve to live a life like the rest of us."

"Oh no, dear, not like the rest of us! They deserve to suffer after what they did to my family. I watched my baby sister and my parents get ripped to pieces by these monsters. And come to find out, my own best friend was the werewolf who did it. Family friends for years betrayed us! And I cannot have that kind of filth roaming around free to breed in this world of ours!" He said, starting to pace the room with a crooked grin gracing his lips.

"And what would you do if you found out that humans are being turned against their will? Without your consent and knowledge? You just go around killing people who find themselves in bed with a werewolf? Who gave you the authority to tell us what we can and cannot do with our bodies?"

"I'm not quite sure what you mean, little red. Are you accusing me of being the one out there killing all these creatures they are talking about on the news?" He laughed aloud, pulling a cigarette out of one of his pockets. He struck a match and lit the end, taking a long drag. He stepped forward and blew the smoke in her face. "I'm waiting."

"Someone has been going around killing people. Women and men. And the sheriff keeps blaming animals for these murders. Some have even said it is a werewolf murdering people. Or is it multiple werewolves going after these people so you capture them and have them brought to your basement?"

"These people you are referring to are the scum of this earth! These people are hybrids. Not pure blood anything. None of these people are innocent like you think. Hybrids aren't innocent. Not even you." He started, taking another drag from his cigarette, pausing as he looked into the air. "Not all of these hybrids die. That's a lie that the news made up. There's so much more to all of this than you even know about, little red."

"So, you admit that you're involved in these murders? That you're kidnapping or killing these werewolves who have attacked the very same humans who have been caught up in werewolf business? You're letting the werewolves kill these people so you don't have to be involved with their murders, but you are."

"Aren't you a smart one?" The older man took a deep hit off his cigarette, flicking ash off in her direction. Smoke trickled past his nostrils and floated into her face. She coughed violently. "Maybe that is exactly how it goes. And what do you think you're going to do about that? You're just a young girl. Nobody would listen to you in this town. Not over me. Sweetheart, I am John Gray the second, and everyone listens to me."

"Y-y-you're—John Gray would be hundreds of years old and there's no way he'd still even be alive. I don't fucking believe you!"

"Tsk. Tsk. A shame how you young women speak now. Eff this, eff that. Not very lady like language, you know. But yes, I am hundreds of years old. I am no longer human, really. Not anymore."

"So you're just hunting your own kind? What kind of monster does that?" She snarled back at him. With a growl, he lunged across the room and crouched down to his haunches, staring into her eyes. His dark eyes sparkled with a malice she'd never seen in another's eyes before. He spoke in a very soft voice. Hardly more than a whisper.

"Why would you want someone to live a miserable life as a werewolf? Or even as a hybrid? Especially as a poor hybrid. At least a pureblood is able to join a pack, but a hybrid? No. They are shunned from their own pack and treated like a fucking leper by humans. Hybrids are freaks, baby. And believe me, nobody wants to live that life."

John Gray the second rose from the ground. His gaze still narrowed in Candice's direction. She mirrored his narrowed gaze. Except he appeared sad and remorseful. Like he actually knew what it meant to live like a hybrid. Could he have been a hybrid himself, but she would never find out now. She knew this was her end.

Just then a large dark brown werewolf appeared out of nowhere. This wolf was different from one of those who had tried to save her earlier. The wolf lunged through the air and pounced on John, shredding his back into ribbons. Blood splattered everywhere and Candice looked away. The man screamed for mercy and another strange vibration filled the air causing her to feel lightheaded.

The black werewolf joined in the cave in a blur of movement. Candice's vision went blurry and she could barely see what was happening, swaying on her knees. She could hardly focus, but she saw the scene. Another wolf suddenly appeared in the pile, but he looked a lot less wolfy than the other two. That must've been John. A few loud screams later, the cave finally went silent.

When Candice finally opened her eyes, all she could see was the grisly remains of the hybrid wolf laying across the cavern floor. Dark pools of blood spotted the ground, reflecting some of the torch light. Other body parts littered the area. Some with tattoos and others just hairy. Her stomach churned, and she turned to relieve herself.

She slammed her eyes shut and started whispering a few words of encouragement to herself as her heart pounded anxiously. The adrenaline had finally worn off, and she felt sick even queasy. The changes in the energy. All the blood and excitement. But she knew freedom was just outside the mouth of the cave.

When she lifted her head again, she saw the two dark haired wolves sitting nearby. Their muzzles shiny with blood, but within moments, there were vibrations in the air once again and the wolves transformed into two naked men standing over the bodily gore. Both of them splattered with blood. Their faces covered with a deep red that made her dizzy and sway. Somehow, she steadied herself and focused her gaze on something other than the grisly remains of the showdown.

She soon recognized the men. Zak and Eric had arrived to save her from the grasp of the notorious immortal hunter. She glanced over at them standing there, naked, and splattered with blood. Some patches were dried black. Her eyes fell over their muscular bodies and her cheeks turned red. Although, she had seen Zak naked at least half a dozen times, Eric wasn't in bad shape himself either. She started stammering and turned around, but the words she meant to speak never found their way past her lips.

"Sorry, Candice." Eric grumbled, but all she could do was nod in response. She closed her eyes, trying to clear her mind of the naughty thoughts that had started to surface, but she still couldn't resist. All she could think about was their toned, naked bodies covered in blood.

She had to remind herself that a man had just been killed. He was the very man who had his goons kidnap her and many others and kept them in the dark basement in the middle of nowhere. He had even tried to force everyone in the basement to shift not long ago. But she was still alive. She had survived.

Her heart raced when their naked behinds trudged past on their way out the cavern. She glanced back when she noticed a couple of old tattoos that Eric had hidden and the one on his shoulder looked much like the same wolf tattoo that Zak had on his chest. She wondered if it was a pack tattoo, but she supposed she would never find out.

"Wait... can one of you..." She said tugging at her chains. Eric turned and in one quick movement, he ripped the chains apart. He cleared his throat and turned to head out of the cave. When they finally disappeared, leaving her alone in the quiet of the cavern, she closed her eyes once again. She took in several deep breaths to clear her mind. Tears fell down her cheeks as she kneeled there reflecting over what had happened not just tonight, but over the last several weeks.

Above everything, she was alive.

CHAPTER THIRTY SIX

When Candice finally found the strength to rid of the chains around her wrists and exit the cavern, she found a whole crime scene waiting for her. There were police cars and even an ambulance truck or two. There were even more people just waiting behind the yellow crime scene tape stretched across the trees.

Police lights flashed through the darkness of the forest. Several county deputies stood by the crime scene tape to keep the crowd of people away from the entrance of the cave. Candice glanced around, searching for Quinn, Zak, or even Eric only to find many unfamiliar faces being tended by the nearby EMTs. From the looks of many of them, they really needed the medical attention. She knew she probably needed some herself, but not nearly as bad as the rest of them.

She had been privileged during her time in captivity because she was a deputy's daughter. Candice walked across the clearing near the edge of the woods and glanced up at the sky with a chill rolling down her spine. The darkness consumed every bit she could see. The waning full moon peeked through the cloudy night. She frowned, wondering how Zak could've shifted inside the cave without the light of the moon. Something wasn't adding up, but what more could she expect from him?

She knew there was more to being a hybrid than she knew, including the heightened senses she had recently honed in the darkness. Her hearing and sense of smell were much stronger than they used to be. She could smell the scent of smoke nearby, but when she glanced around, there were no signs of a bonfire anywhere.

She returned her attention to the small crowd of people. She didn't know most of them, but she assumed they were the werewolves and hybrids who had been held captive for so long. She knew her dad had to be around, but she didn't see him anywhere. She wanted to see him and her mom again. Even those two little shits she called her brothers. She just wanted to be with her family again. Her attention was suddenly pulled in another direction when she heard the sheriff yell aloud.

"Don't you know who I am? I'm your sheriff! You will pay for this!"

"Yeah, yeah. Save it for court, sheriff. I'm sure the county will love to hear all about your excuses as to why you've been hiding a dog fighting ring on your property. And why you had so many hostages in the basement." Said one of the two deputies who looked like they were her dad's age. She didn't recognize either one of them and figured they were in a different department from him.

A wicked grin curled over her lips watching them guide the handcuffed sheriff into the back of their vehicle. The sheriff was finally getting his just desserts for all the pain and misguided law he had been imposing on people when he was no better himself. She let out a breath, less than a snort, and shook her head.

She lifted her gaze again and noticed both Zak and Eric over by the nearest ambulance. They were being thoroughly examined by a couple of EMTs with their rubber gloves and cotton gauze. Eric yelled out when the shorter of the two EMTs pressed a fresh cotton ball to a bad scrape on his cheek. She waved him off with an obscene name and continued cleaning him.

Suddenly, someone called out her name. Candice whipped her head around and under the flashing lights of the emergency vehicles, her mom's bright red hair appeared beyond the line of deputies. Beside her was her dad dressed in an old pair of sweats and a tshirt. Had he been involved with her case?

A smile beamed across her face and she ran toward them. Even her brothers were there. They all wrapped themselves around her in a huge hug. Her mom started crying.

"Candice! My little Candy! I've been so worried about you! I thought we lost you!"

"I'm alive. I'm here now."

"I know, Candy. I know and I am so grateful. You were gone so long."

"Too long. We thought mom was going to have a nervous breakdown." Kevin said, stepping away with a crooked grin on his face. Their mom glanced over at him without taking her arms from Candice. Candice knew that look on her face. She was ready to smack him. She even lifted her had. He laughed and backed further away from the group hug, already primed to run off.

"I'm just glad to have my Candy girl back. My family is whole again! My heart is whole again! I love my family."

"Me too, mom."

"Candice!" Another familiar voice called out to her and it wasn't Zak or Eric. And it wasn't Valerie either. She paused and slipped out of the family hug, turning toward the tall, lean brunette woman. She stood under the canopy of trees nearby. Quinn was dressed in an old t-shirt with Hollow Canyon Fire Department printed across the front.

"I'll be right back, mom." Candice said. She stepped away and approached Quinn with caution. The two of them weren't necessarily on the best of terms and she had the strange feeling in her gut that Quinn had led her toward the wolf hunter on purpose. She wasn't sure she would ever know the answer to that though. "Yes...?"

"I just wanted to tell you that I'm not angry with you. I can't blame you for Zak's behavior. I'm more upset at myself for fucking believing things would change. I knew Zak would run off to fuck around with you again. I truly thought things had changed when he found out I was pregnant, but they didn't."

"I'm sorry. I had no i—" Candice's heart sank into her stomach, feeling a familiar pain that reminded her of when she found out Zak had cheated on her. Except now that pain didn't hurt the same now. She felt worse knowing now that she wasn't the only one who had been hurt.

"Don't be sorry. I'm not proud of what I did, but I—did what I needed to do about that situation." Quinn lowered her eyes. Candice could feel the pain of that decision radiating from her. "I'm better off. We both are. And I don't want to see you in that situation either. Zak's not worth all that pain. Believe me, girl. You're too good for him."

"So are you, Quinn." Candice smiled. A smile widened across Quinn's lips and she muttered a word of gratitude under her breath. She held her head a little higher though. In fact, both girls did. The energy between them had changed in a way that Candice never expected.

"Thanks, Candice. I have to leave New Mexico. Even Colorado for that matter. Find something else out there because I can't keep holding on to this small town. Or the puppies in this pack. If you want to come along with me, I'd be down to have some company. Even if it's only for a little while." Quinn smiled.

"Where are you heading?"

"I'm not too sure yet. New York City, maybe? LA? I'll figure it out when I finally get out of here." Quinn shrugged. "But give it some thought, Candice. I need to take care of a few things before I leave Hollow's Creek. I'll stop by your place though and let you know when since I can't really give you my number... I kinda lost my phone somewhere..." Quinn glanced over her shoulder and toward the forest.

"Thanks, Quinn. I'll see you soon?"

"Yeah. Soon." Quinn turned and with a smile, walked away. Candice cleared her throat and was about to speak, to ask her if there was anything she needed after everything she had been through. Instead, she stood there and watched her disappear into the night, deciding it wasn't the right time. She watched Quinn slip under the canopy of massive evergreens and shift under their safety.

When the silver wolf disappeared, Candice turned and went back to her family. She already knew what she wanted to do. It was time to do something for herself and the little friendly gesture from Quinn was all she needed to make up her mind.

CHAPTER
THIRTY SEVEN

The news didn't break about the Silver Coin hostages until after Thanksgiving only a week after Candice, Quinn, and the others escaped the basement. None of them had known they were held hostage there until after the news broke out on the local news channels. At least that's when she learned the story the local authorities were telling the public. She was sure the truth was being covered by the authorities.

"Owners of the old boarding house property have been arrested in conjunction with the finding of Deputy Olson's daughter and many other individuals malnourished and neglected in the basement. Local authorities have seized the building, which has left other local small business owners in financial jeopardy including the owners of the Silver Coin and the local music amphitheater."

Her mother reached over and clicked off the television. Candice frowned and grumbled at her mother. She just shook her head in response, her mouth still full of frosted flake cereal with strawberry milk. She finally swallowed and wiped her mouth with the back of her hand. "You don't need to listen to that. You're getting out of here now, Candy."

"What really did happen, dad?" Candice glanced over at him who was slurping the last of his chocolate flavored milk from his bowl. He didn't hear her the first time though and continued slurping. She elbowed him and asked again when he finally put the bowl down.

"You know I hate talking about cases. I wasn't even supposed to be involved in this case, Candy." He said. "Personal interests they said and made me take a paid leave of absence for the last month and a half."

"I just don't understand how Zak and Eric found us out there so easily." She said, taking another spoonful of her half crunchy frosted flakes. Her dad just stared at her and blinked with a blank expression on his face.

"Did you forget what my job is? Remember I found Valerie out there and that turned into my case, but all the bureaucratic bullshit prevented anybody from acting on it any sooner." He said. Candice frowned, trying to understand what he meant.

"What bureaucratic bullshit, dad?" She said. Her mom just lowered her bowl and glared at her but she stayed quiet, like she was waiting to hear the story herself. He sighed, not wanting to reveal his information, but he continued.

"Well, the sheriff owning the property was a huge obstacle. He didn't know we had been building a case against him for dog fighting out there. Then the Rayers started getting involved in the local politics. Then the whole Valerie thing happened, so I had a lot of work cut out for me at the station. Then when you went missing, I was forced to take leave, and I told Zak to wait until the right time.

"Eric and his father, what's his name? Allan. He got involved too and well; he had the money for the resources we needed to get a warrant to search the property. That's when Zak and Eric finally showed up to save you and the others."

"But we don't need to talk about that. This is our last night together as a family. Our last holiday weekend as a family under this roof so we need to enjoy it while we can. What does everyone say to a movie?" Her dad asked, rising from his spot on the sofa to start collecting their empty cereal bowls.

"What should we watch tonight?" Her mom asked, clicking the television back on and surfing the channels for something to watch. The boys groaned asking for a movie from their collection instead. "Then go pick one."

The boys raced over to the movie racks in the corner to find something. Candice on the other hand rose from her seat and glanced at her mom. "Mom, I'm tired. I love the attention and all, but I have a long day of driving ahead of me tomorrow."

Her mom had done all she could to be with her daughter every moment of the day when Candice finally made it back home over a week ago. She had made her favorite foods and even let her pick several movies that they had watched together as a family. Candice needed some space for a little while.

Without any objection, her mom rose to wrap her in a tight hug before wishing her a good night. Moments later, the boys were heading back over to the coffee table with a couple of DVDs in their hands. She stepped out of the living room and headed upstairs to her room.

The next morning, after a hot cup of coffee, she grabbed her hoodie and grabbed a large box from her bedroom and took it outside. She set the box down in the driveway and stood there for a moment, admiring the evergreens and the colors of the changing leaves of the late fall.

A chilly breeze slipped through the air, carrying a few yellowed leaves down to the ground. Candice shrugged her shoulders, hoping that somehow her hoodie would wrap in closer to her body. Suddenly, she heard the front door slam and her mother call out to her.

"Are you sure about this whole trip to Hollywood thing? There's plenty for you to do here in Hollow's Creek. And you have your family and friends here. Maybe we can even do some stuff together too."

"Yes, mom. I'm totally sure because there isn't enough for me to do here. I can't stay right now. I need to get away from here. Figure out a few things on my own. I need to figure out who I am and what I want to do with this crazy life."

"I'm proud of you, Candy. Not staying here because of some boy."

"They're a big reason I'm leaving, mom." Candice said, lowering her gaze for only a brief moment. When she lifted her head again, her mom was frowning deeply. And she knew why. She and Candice already had this conversation many times over the last week.

"I'm sorry, mom. Like I said...I'm not ready to talk about some of this stuff right now because I don't really know how to explain any of it. I don't even really understand any of it myself, but when I do, you'll be the first to know. I'll be back, I promise. Even if it's just to visit, mom." Candice reached over to open the truck parked in the driveway and her mom brought the box over. She then turned to head back in when her mom set the box down for another hug.

"Alright. I believe you."

"Will you please let me go now?" Candice grumbled against her mom's ear. Candice stepped away from her mother and stepped toward the house when another moving van pulled up by the sidewalk. Valerie stuck her head out the window and waved, calling out to her. She crossed the yard to meet her once she had parked and shut off the engine, jumping down to give her friend a proper goodbye.

"Don't forget to call me! Tell me what Hollywood is like,

Candy!"

"Are you kidding? I'm gonna have you come visit me when I'm famous!" Candice squeezed Valerie tight. She noticed Taylor sitting in his car seat with his grandmother driving Valerie's old SUV. Even the little golden puppy popped its head out the window and barked. Except he wasn't very small any longer.

She waved to them with a smile.

"Be safe out there!" Doreen yelled out her window and Candice stepped over to give her a final hug through the window. Doreen kissed her cheek and whispered in her ear. "Thank you for everything. Thank you for bringing my girl home to me."

Candice gave one last squeeze and pulled away, glancing over at Quinn who appeared from the backseat of a taxi, giving the driver a few bills before stepping out of the vehicle. A crooked grin appeared on her face the moment they looked at each other.

She never would've pictured herself leaving on a cross-country road trip with Quinn of all people, but she was ready. She wasn't sure what was going to happen since Ramona and Tommie decided to leave when they hadn't heard from her in weeks. She wondered how they would feel if they knew she had been kidnapped. "Are you ready to go now?"

"Yes. I'm ready now." Candice blew a few more kisses to Valerie before crossing the yard to finish packing the last few boxes of must keeps inside the truck. Thankfully, neither one of them really had much they wanted to take besides clothes, records, books, and few other odds and ends. Once the final box was stacked, she shut the truck. Her hands were shaking. For the first time in weeks, she realized the reality of what was happening.

She was finally leaving Hollow's Creek. She and Quinn were

leaving for Hollywood together after years of bitterness toward each other, which had somehow vanished after one long overdue apology. Candice wanted to find her musical muse once again. She wanted to experience life and the world outside of the small town of Hollow's Creek.

She climbed into the truck and stuffed her cell phone into the side pocket, reaching down to start the engine. Moments later, Quinn jumped into the cab beside her, placing her water bottle in one of the cup holders. "Are you ready, Quinny?"

"Please don't call me that, Candy." She laughed, pulling out her cellphone to drop it into the side pocket. Candice just smiled and locked the truck, rolling her window down. Her family was still yelling out at them when suddenly a little red sports car pulled down the road.

Candice froze when the car parked a few houses down. She reached down and put her hand on the gear selector when Zak stepped out of the vehicle, leaning against the side. She watched him for a very long moment and he smiled. She smiled back, waiting for a wave of uncertainty to reappear with his sudden presence, but it never did. She shook her head and Zak nodded. He already knew. Quinn put her hand on Candice's thigh and she started to pull away from the curb.

"Let's go, Candy. We don't have time for him."

Candice will return...

THANK YOU FOR READING

Thank you for reading! Books take time to write as well as read.Our time is short and valuable and I appreciate you taking the time out of your busy schedule to spend time with my story. Ifit's not too much to ask, I'd love to hear your thoughts in areview, which also helps other readers discover my books.

You can leave a review where you purchased or even onsocial media. My books can also be found on StoryGraph. Andtell your bookish friends looking for something new to read. However you decide to share, I'd be forever grateful!

~ H.M. Colugo

ABOUT THE AUTHOR

Colugo lives in New Mexico with her husband and their threecats. With a background in English, technical writing, training,and troubleshooting, and a certi!cation in copy editing, sheweaves together the supernatural and women empowermentinto her character driven stories where many of her charactersand stories come to life in the world of Hollow's Creek.

When she isn't playing the role of creator, she enjoys roadtrips, gaming, gardening and taming her wild felines. To ! ndout more about her work and sign up for her mailing list, please visit darkmusestudio.com/hmcolugo.